nebula #13

NEBULA WINNERS THIRTEEN

Nebula Winners Thirteen

EDITED BY SAMUEL R. DELANY

HARPER & ROW, PUBLISHERS

NEW YORK

Cambridge
Hagerstown
Philadelphia
San Francisco

1817

London
Mexico City
São Paulo
Sydney

Grateful acknowledgment is made for permission to reprint:

"Jeffty Is Five" by Harlan Ellison. Copyright © 1977 by Harlan Ellison. Reprinted by arrangement with, and permission of, the Author and the Author's agent, Robert P. Mills, Ltd., New York. All rights reserved.

"Air Raid" by John Varley. First appeared in *Isaac Asimov's Science Fiction Magazine*. Copyright © 1977 by Davis Publications, Inc. Reprinted by permission of the author and the author's agents, Kirby McCauley, Ltd.

"The Screwfly Solution" by Raccoona Sheldon. First appeared in *Analog Science Fiction/Science Fact*. Copyright ©1977 by Alice B. Sheldon. Reprinted by permission of the author and the author's agent, Robert P. Mills, Ltd.

"Particle Theory" by Edward Bryant. First appeared in *Analog Science Fiction/Science Fact*. Copyright © 1977 by the Condé Nast Publications, Inc. Reprinted by permission of the author.

"Stardance" by Spider and Jeanne Robinson. First appeared in *Analog Science Fiction/Science Fact*. Copyright © 1977 by Condé Nast Publications, Inc. Reprinted by permission of the author and the author's agents, Robert P. Mills, Ltd.

"Aztecs" by Vonda N. McIntyre. Copyright © 1977 by Vonda N. McIntyre. From *2076: The American Tricentennial*, edited by Edward Bryant. Published by Pyramid Books.

FIRST EDITION

Library of Congress Cataloging in Publication Data
Main entry under title:

Nebula winners thirteen.

1. Science fiction, American. I. Delany, Samuel R.
PZ1.N2573 1980 [PS648.S3]   813'.0876   66-20974
ISBN (U.S.A. and Canada) 0-06-013786-X
(except U.S.A. and Canada) 0-06-337-009-3

80 81 82 83 10 9 8 7 6 5 4 3 2 1

In memoriam
  Leigh Brackett
  Edmund Hamilton
  Francis J. McComas
  Ward Moore
  Ray Palmer
  Tom Reamey
  Eric Frank Russell

Contents

Introduction

Weight?

Approximately twelve pounds.

The base is black, surmounted by rectilinear faces of clear lucite. Within rises a quartz crystal below a mica galaxy, frozen in wait for light. The Nebula Awards of the Science Fiction Writers of America are lovely, comparatively costly as such trophies go, and are freighted now with a baker's dozen years of tradition.

The awards are voted on by the active membership of the Science Fiction Writers of America, founded in 1964 under President Damon Knight. The editorship of the awards volume is assigned by the current president—this year, Andrew J. Offutt. Other than the generally acknowledged assumption that the volume will contain the winning stories in the short story, novelette, and novella categories, the general arrangement of the annual volume is left pretty much to the editor's discretion. (The winning novel—this year, Frederik Pohl's *Gateway*—is of course too long to include.) Some editors in the past have filled out the rest of the volume with stories they personally felt were highly worthy but which, for one reason or another, had been overlooked during nominations. Others have invited scholars to write essays on SF, or have commissioned summaries of the science fiction production for the entire year.

My own approach will be very conservative—following Gordon

R. Dickson's precedent in last year's *Nebula Winners Twelve.* I shall present the winning stories. They are indicated by an ornament next to the title and a footnote citing the award in its category. The other stories are my favorites among the two or three runners-up in each area. All the stories in this volume, then, were on the final ballot.

This introduction will go on to talk a bit about the various tales. Then you will find the stories themselves, each headed by a brief personal note from your editor. At the end of the volume is a list of past winners, compiled with the help of Donald Franson's and Howard DeVore's *A History of the Hugo, Nebula, and International Fantasy Awards* (available from Misfit Press, 4705 Weddel Street, Dearborn, Michigan 48125), a book produced with love and accuracy and whose cover, incidentally, is printed by hand.

Harlan Ellison's winning short story, "Jeffty Is Five," is a fantasy about nostalgia. But through its precision of observation it becomes something different from a simple yowl for "the good old days." It is not a request to retreat; it is a demand to preserve. This is one of Mr. Ellison's finest-written stories, and if by some fluke this is the first time you have read this inventive and energetic writer, you are in for a happy surprise, not only from this superb tale, but from just how many more tales there are making up his finest written work.

Following Ellison's gentle and poignant fantasy, "Air Raid," by John Varley, is a single screech, all twisted metal and shattering glass. To achieve, and maintain, such a pitch in a story of this length is quite a tour de force. Science fiction has had its share of meteoric careers (which never look anywhere near as meteoric to the meteor in question as they do to the rest of us), notably Roger Zelazny's in the early 1960s, and Ursula Le Guin's in the early 1970s. John Varley is the most recent of these SF shooting stars. The job that a meteor has to do is not simply write good stories. Writing good stories is hard enough, but the several hundred-odd writers in the SFWA can usually manage to produce, among them, at least two or three volumes full each year. What a meteor has to do is write stories that make readers who have begun to tire a little of SF, the bad and the good, suddenly *want* to read more science fiction; a meteor must write stories that make writers who have begun to wonder if, really, movie scripts wouldn't in the long run be more challenging, *want* to write more science fiction. Varley, who has only recently emerged on the upper side of thirty, has written a number of such stories—a whole book of them, in fact. It's called *The Persistence of Vision.* "Air Raid" is the second story in that book.

What makes Raccoona Sheldon's "The Screwfly Solution" an extraordinarily effective horror tale is that, though a "biological explanation" for the mass-murders the story depicts is set up from the beginning and is eventually revealed, the suspicion must linger with the reader that perhaps the explanation is, after all, sociological. Sigmund Freud, in his late and brief book *Beyond the Pleasure Principle,* in one of his speculative sections, suggests the notion of a "death instinct," which *he* saw as diametrically opposed to the pleasure principle—which, till then, Freud had seen as contouring all human behavior. What is so uncanny about Sheldon's tale (and "the uncanny" was another subject Freud wrote on with concerted insight; his major insight was that for something to seem uncanny much of it must be *very* familiar) is that Sheldon, at least for the duration of her story, sees the two of them as nowhere near all *that* opposed.

Edward Bryant's haunting "Particle Theory" puts me in mind of a number of early J. G. Ballard tales of the ilk of "Voices of Time" and "Terminal Beach." Yet if one actually returns to the Ballard texts to locate the comparisons, one is far more aware of the differences than the similarities—specifically in terms of the greater rhetorical risks Bryant, twenty years later, is willing to take. Also, whatever affective congruences we might locate for the sake of a historical contrast, Bryant is using his story to make a

personal statement that readers of his other stories in his collec-
tions *Cinnebar* and *Among the Dead* will recognize as very much
his own.

The psychologist Havelock Ellis is only one of many thinkers to
consider the dance the ultimate human art form. The video cameraman who narrates Spider and Jeanne Robinson's novella
"Stardance" reminds me of a conversation I once had with a
filmmaker who had once wanted to be the best filmer of dance in
the world ". . . until I realized something. To film a dance, you
don't simply film the dancer's motions. You must film the whole
space the dancer's motion controls. Sometimes that's as little as the
three or four cubic inches between the dancer's fingers. That can
be filmed. But sometimes it's a whole hundred and eighty degrees
of the vision of a spectator seated a hundred yards away from the
performer. You can't film that." As you finish this story, consider
how much space Shara's final performance for the aliens must fill.
Science fiction boasts at least one notable terpsichorean meditation: Charles L. Harness's *The Rose.* (Along with Bester's *The Stars
My Destination,* Harness's *The Rose* was one of the critical texts
for the writers of the middle 1960s who clustered around Michael
Moorcock's British-based magazine, *New Worlds.*) The Robinsons
have collaborated on a novella that bids fair to join it. Despite the
opulence of the settings, the suggestions of an incredibly harsh
world just off stage keep reappearing to remind the reader what
all this opulence is a reaction against. It is those suggestions that
lend a considered intelligence to this flaringly romantic narrative.

When I've taught science fiction in universities, one of the
things I've found to help those students who have trouble with the
texts is to remind them to pay particularly close attention not only
to the relations between the characters but to the world itself, the
landscape, the surroundings in which the characters move—particularly from a sociological point of view. One sentence in Vonda
McIntyre's "Aztecs" states directly what the rest of the tale drama-
tizes about the future earth under whose oceans her story largely

takes place. I quote it here: "But the economic structure of her world was based on service, not production, and she had always taken the results for granted." "Aztecs" is a story of a transition, a rite of passage, but a rite manifested by no ritual; rather it is a revelation of a thoroughly human experience. There is a famous science fiction story, first published in 1954, written in a clumsy diction with mawkish characters, that nevertheless remains an immensely powerful statement about the working universe: Tom Godwin's "The Cold Equations." The equations that govern McIntyre's story are only slightly less chilly, and the verbal surface of her tale is far more highly wrought. "Aztecs" is a story that centers our attention on something that is more or less evident in every story in this volume—and in doing so suggests a general observation about much science fiction in the latter half of the 1970s. I've mentioned the distinction between character and landscape implicit in science fiction. In a very real way, in every one of the tales here, the alteration in the "landscape" has gone so far as to include a significant alteration in the body of one or more of the main characters. In "The Screwfly Solution," "Particle Theory," and "Stardance," the alterations are comparatively gradual, or at least revealed at the end as the kicker. In "Jeffty Is Five," "Air Raid," and "Aztecs," they are there from the beginning of the story. ("Air Raid," "The Screwfly Solution," and "Particle Theory" all in a sense deal with one kind of plague or another.) In the first years of this decade, I noted the swing in SF from interest in physics and cosmology (which had dominated in the 1950s and the 1960s) toward biology. And even though the two novellas that conclude this volume take place against a comparatively conventional—if vividly wrought—"space opera" background, the subtexts that modulate the actions and drive the characters to their final decisions are biological changes in the human organism.

All human beings take in and process, through the concert of the senses, tremendous amounts of information about their world. By comparison, the information human beings put out—even an Einstein or a Tolstoy, not to mention you and me—is minuscule.

Art, science, and criticism all begin with an urge to put out more, and more accurate (and more appropriate), information in response to what comes in than, in the ordinary course of things, we are likely to.

It has been my contention for some time that people who read science fiction with any regularity are experiencing more (and more varied orders of) information than is usually talked of—even by people who try to criticize science fiction sympathetically. To locate this information, the questions we must ask (and not of single SF texts but of whole ranges and varieties of SF stories) are: In the various worlds and universes that SF writers construct, what social processes are seen as variables and what processes are seen as invariant? For principle X to be variable, what other processes, Y and/or Z, must *stay* invariant? Similarly: By keeping principle P invariant, what principles, Q and/or R, are allowed free play? Similar questions have to be asked about the behavior and psychology of characters in the tales. And, of course, the particular question this year's SF brings to the fore: Just how variable is the boundary itself between character and landscape? For the rushing river into which Radu falls in his dream (in McIntyre's "Aztecs") is, of course, Laenea's pulseless bloodstream itself; and Bryant's tale will leave us mulling on the relation between the death of a star by nova and the death of a cancer cell, both brought on by the same superabundance of mazons.

This year we have an exciting volume of stories, which leaves us with a host of exciting questions—not least of which is: What will next year's science fiction look like?

SAMUEL R. DELANY

New York, N. Y.

NEBULA WINNERS THIRTEEN

HARLAN ELLISON

❧ *Jeffty Is Five*

Harlan Ellison is a sensitive, generous, and highly thinking man—qualities we usually associate with quiet, retiring types. Harlan also happens
to be loud, witty, raunchy, and eloquent. In fourteen years he's won a
handful of these awards and may well deserve two or three of those he
didn't win. Harlan's presence in the SF field is rather like a (usually)
friendly earthquake. But even earthquakes, apparently, have their moments of quiet recall.

❧ Nebula Award of the Science Fiction Writers of America for Best Short Story,
1977.

When I was five years old, there was a little kid I played with: Jeffty. His real name was Jeff Kinzer, and everyone who played with him called him Jeffty. We were five years old together, and we had good times playing together.

When I was five, a Clark Bar was as fat around as the gripping end of a Louisville Slugger, and pretty nearly six inches long, and they used real chocolate to coat it, and it crunched very nicely when you bit into the center, and the paper it came wrapped in smelled fresh and good when you peeled off one end to hold the bar so it wouldn't melt onto your fingers. Today, a Clark Bar is as thin as a credit card, they use something artificial and awful-tasting instead of pure chocolate, the thing is soft and soggy, it costs fifteen or twenty cents instead of a decent, correct nickel, and they wrap it so you think it's the same size it was twenty years ago, only it isn't; it's slim and ugly and nasty tasting and not worth a penny, much less fifteen or twenty cents.

When I was that age, five years old, I was sent away to my Aunt Patricia's home in Buffalo, New York, for two years. My father was going through "bad times" and Aunt Patricia was very beautiful, and had married a stockbroker. They took care of me for two years. When I was seven, I came back home and went to find Jeffty, so we could play together.

4

I was seven. Jeffty was still five. I didn't notice any difference. I didn't know: I was only seven.

When I was seven years old, I used to lie on my stomach in front of our Atwater Kent radio and listen to swell stuff. I had tied the ground wire to the radiator, and I would lie there with my coloring books and my Crayolas (when there were only sixteen colors in the big box), and listen to the NBC red network: Jack Benny on the Jell-O Program, Amos 'n' Andy, Edgar Bergen and Charlie McCarthy on the Chase and Sanborn Program, One Man's Family, First Nighter; the NBC blue network: Easy Aces, the Jergens Program with Walter Winchell, Information Please, Death Valley Days; and best of all, the Mutual network with The Green Hornet, The Lone Ranger, The Shadow and Quiet Please. Today, I turn on my car radio and go from one end of the dial to the other and all I get is 100 strings orchestras, banal housewives and insipid truckers discussing their kinky sex lives with arrogant talk show hosts, country and western drivel and rock music so loud it hurts my ears.

When I was ten, my grandfather died of old age and I was "a troublesome kid," and they sent me off to military school, so I could be "taken in hand."

I came back when I was fourteen. Jeffty was still five.

When I was fourteen years old, I used to go to the movies on Saturday afternoons and a matinee was ten cents and they used real butter on the popcorn and I could always be sure of seeing a western like Lash LaRue, or Wild Bill Elliott as Red Ryder with Bobby Blake as Little Beaver, or Roy Rogers, or Johnny Mack Brown; a scary picture like *House of Horrors* with Rondo Hatton as the Strangler, or *The Cat People,* or *The Mummy,* or *I Married a Witch* with Fredric March and Veronica Lake; plus an episode of a great serial like The Shadow with Victor Jory, or Dick Tracy or Flash Gordon; and three cartoons; a James Fitzpatrick Travel-Talk; Movietone News; a singalong and, if I stayed on till evening, Bingo or Keeno; and free dishes. Today, I go to movies and see

Clint Eastwood blowing people's heads apart like ripe can-
taloupes.

At eighteen, I went to college. Jeffty was still five. I came back
during the summers, to work at my Uncle Joe's jewelry store. Jeffty
hadn't changed. Now I knew there was something different about
him, something wrong, something weird. Jeffty was still five years
old, not a day older.

At twenty-two, I came home for keeps. To open a Sony television franchise in town, the first one. I saw Jeffty from time to time.
He was five.

Things are better in a lot of ways. People don't die from
some of the old diseases any more. Cars go faster and get you
there more quickly on better roads. Shirts are softer and silkier.
We have paperback books even though they cost as much as a
good hardcover used to. When I'm running short in the bank I
can live off credit cards till things even out. But I still think
we've lost a lot of good stuff. Did you know you can't buy lino-
leum any more, only vinyl floor covering? There's no such
thing as oilcloth any more; you'll never again smell that special,
sweet smell from your grandmother's kitchen. Furniture isn't
made to last thirty years or longer, because they took a survey
and found that young homemakers like to throw their furniture
out and bring in all new, color-coded, borax every seven years.
Records don't feel right; they're not thick and solid like the old
ones, they're thin and you can bend them . . . that doesn't
seem right to me. Restaurants don't serve cream in pitchers
any more, just that artificial glop in little plastic tubs, and one
is never enough to get coffee the right color. You can make a
dent in a car fender with only a sneaker. Everywhere you go,
all the towns look the same with Burger Kings and McDonald's
and 7-Elevens and Taco Bells and motels and shopping centers.
Things may be better, but why do I keep thinking about the
past?

What I mean by five years old is not that Jeffty was retarded. I don't think that's what it was. Smart as a whip for five years old; very bright, quick, cute, a funny kid.

But he was three feet tall, small for his age, and perfectly formed: no big head, no strange jaw, none of that. A nice, normal-looking five-year-old kid. Except that he was the same age as I was: twenty-two.

When he spoke it was with the squeaking, soprano voice of a five-year-old; when he walked it was with the little hops and shuffles of a five-year-old; when he talked to you it was about the concerns of a five-year-old . . . comic books, playing soldier, using a clothes pin to attach a stiff piece of cardboard to the front fork of his bike so the sound it made when the spokes hit was like a motorboat, asking questions like *why does that thing do that like that,* how high is up, how old is old, why is grass green, what's an elephant look like? At twenty-two, he was five.

Jeffty's parents were a sad pair. Because I was still a friend of Jeffty's, still let him hang around with me in the store, sometimes took him to the county fair or to the miniature golf or the movies, I wound up spending time with *them.* Not that I much cared for them, because they were so awfully depressing. But then, I suppose one couldn't expect much more from the poor devils. They had an alien thing in their home, a child who had grown no older than five in twenty-two years, who provided the treasure of that special childlike state indefinitely, but who also denied them the joys of watching the child grow into a normal adult.

Five is a wonderful time of life for a little kid . . . or it *can* be, if the child is relatively free of the monstrous beastliness other children indulge in. It is a time when the eyes are wide open and the patterns are not yet set; a time when one has not yet been hammered into accepting everything as immutable and hopeless; a time when the hands can not do enough, the mind can not learn enough, the world is infinite and colorful and filled with mysteries.

Five is a special time before they take the questing, unquenchable, quixotic soul of the young dreamer and thrust it into dreary school-room boxes. A time before they take the trembling hands that want to hold everything, touch everything, figure everything out, and make them lie still on desktops. A time before people begin saying "act your age" and "grow up" or "you're behaving like a baby." It is a time when a child who acts adolescent is still cute and responsive and everyone's pet. A time of delight, of wonder, of innocence.

Jeffty had been stuck in that time, just five, just so.

But for his parents it was an ongoing nightmare from which no one—not social workers, not priests, not child psychologists, not teachers, not friends, not medical wizards, not psychiatrists, no one—could slap or shake them awake. For seventeen years their sorrow had grown through stages of parental dotage to concern, from concern to worry, from worry to fear, from fear to confusion, from confusion to anger, from anger to dislike, from dislike to naked hatred, and finally, from deepest loathing and revulsion to a stolid, depressive acceptance.

John Kinzer was a shift foreman at the Balder Tool & Die plant. He was a thirty-year man. To everyone but the man living it, his was a spectacularly uneventful life. In no way was he remarkable . . . save that he had fathered a twenty-two-year-old five-year-old.

John Kinzer was a small man; soft, with no sharp angles; with pale eyes that never seemed to hold mine for longer than a few seconds. He continually shifted in his chair during conversations, and seemed to see things in the upper corners of the room, things no one else could see . . . or wanted to see. I suppose the word that best suited him was *haunted*. What his life had become . . . well, *haunted* suited him.

Leona Kinzer tried valiantly to compensate. No matter what hour of the day I visited, she always tried to foist food on me. And when Jeffty was in the house she was always at *him* about eating: "Honey, would you like an orange? A nice orange? Or a tangerine?

I have tangerines. I could peel a tangerine for you." But there was clearly such fear in her, fear of her own child, that the offers of sustenance always had a faintly ominous tone.

Leona Kinzer had been a tall woman, but the years had bent her. She seemed always to be seeking some area of wallpapered wall or storage niche into which she could fade, adopt some chintz or rose-patterned protective coloration and hide forever in plain sight of the child's big brown eyes, pass her a hundred times a day and never realize she was there, holding her breath, invisible. She always had an apron tied around her waist, and her hands were red from cleaning. As if by maintaining the environment immaculately she could pay off her imagined sin: having given birth to this strange creature.

Neither of them watched television very much. The house was usually dead silent, not even the sibilant whispering of water in the pipes, the creaking of timbers settling, the humming of the refrigerator. Awfully silent, as if time itself had taken a detour around that house.

As for Jeffty, he was inoffensive. He lived in that atmosphere of gentle dread and dulled loathing, and if he understood it, he never remarked in any way. He played, as a child plays, and seemed happy. But he must have sensed, in the way of a five-year-old, just how alien he was in their presence.

Alien. No, that wasn't right. He was *too* human, if anything. But out of phase, out of synch with the world around him, and resonating to a different vibration than his parents, God knows. Nor would other children play with him. As they grew past him, they found him at first childish, then uninteresting, then simply frightening as their perceptions of aging became clear and they could see he was not affected by time as they were. Even the little ones, his own age, who might wander into the neighborhood, quickly came to shy away from him like a dog in the street when a car backfires.

Thus, I remained his only friend. A friend of many years. Five years. Twenty-two years. I liked him; more than I can say. And never knew exactly why. But I did, without reserve.

But because we spent time together, I found I was also—polite society—spending time with John and Leona Kinzer. Dinner, Saturday afternoons sometimes, an hour or so when I'd bring Jeffty back from a movie. They were grateful: slavishly so. It relieved them of the embarrassing chore of going out with him, of having to pretend before the world that they were loving parents with a perfectly normal, happy, attractive child. And their gratitude extended to hosting me. Hideous, every moment of their depression, hideous.

I felt sorry for the poor devils, but I despised them for their inability to love Jeffty, who was eminently lovable.

I never let on, of course, even during the evenings in their company that were awkward beyond belief.

We would sit there in the darkening living room—*always* dark or darkening, as if kept in shadow to hold back what the light might reveal to the world outside through the bright eyes of the house—we would sit and silently stare at one another. They never knew what to say to me.

"So how are things down at the plant?" I'd say to John Kinzer.

He would shrug. Neither conversation nor life suited him with any ease or grace. "Fine, just fine," he would say, finally.

And we would sit in silence again.

"Would you like a nice piece of coffee cake?" Leona would say. "I made it fresh just this morning." Or deep dish green apple pie. Or milk and tollhouse cookies. Or a brown betty pudding.

"No, no, thank you, Mrs. Kinzer; Jeffty and I grabbed a couple of cheeseburgers on the way home." And again, silence.

Then, when the stillness and the awkwardness became too much even for them (and who knew how long that total silence reigned when they were alone, with that thing they never talked about any more, hanging between them), Leona Kinzer would say, "I think he's asleep."

John Kinzer would say, "I don't hear the radio playing."

Just so, it would go on like that, until I could politely find excuse to bolt away on some flimsy pretext. Yes, that was the way it would go on, every time, just the same . . . except once.

"I don't know what to do any more," Leona said. She began crying. "There's no change, not one day of peace."

Her husband managed to drag himself out of the old easy chair and went to her. He bent and tried to soothe her, but it was clear from the graceless way in which he touched her graying hair that the ability to be compassionate had been stunned in him. "Shhh, Leona, it's all right. Shhh." But she continued crying. Her hands scraped gently at the antimacassars on the arms of the chair.

Then she said, "Sometimes I wish he had been stillborn."

John looked up into the corners of the room. For the nameless shadows that were always watching him? Was it God he was seeking in those spaces? "You don't mean that," he said to her, softly, pathetically, urging her with body tension and trembling in his voice to recant before God took notice of the terrible thought. But she meant it; she meant it very much.

I managed to get away quickly that evening. They didn't want witnesses to their shame. I was glad to go.

And for a week I stayed away. From them, from Jeffty, from their street, even from that end of town.

I had my own life. The store, accounts, suppliers' conferences, poker with friends, pretty women I took to well-lit restaurants, my own parents, putting anti-freeze in the car, complaining to the laundry about too much starch in the collars and cuffs, working out at the gym, taxes, catching Jan or David (whichever one it was) stealing from the cash register. I had my own life.

But not even *that* evening could keep me from Jeffty. He called me at the store and asked me to take him to the rodeo. We chummed it up as best a twenty-two-year-old with other interests *could* . . . with a five-year-old. I never dwelled on what bound us together; I always thought it was simply the years. That, and affection for a kid who could have been the little brother I never had. (Except I *remembered* when we had played together, when we had both been the same age; I *remembered* that period, and Jeffty was still the same.)

And then, one Saturday afternoon, I came to take him to a double feature, and things I should have noticed so many times before, I first began to notice only that afternoon.

I came walking up to the Kinzer house, expecting Jeffty to be sitting on the front porch steps, or in the porch glider, waiting for me. But he was nowhere in sight.

Going inside, into that darkness and silence, in the midst of May sunshine, was unthinkable. I stood on the front walk for a few moments, then cupped my hands around my mouth and yelled, "Jeffty? Hey, Jeffty, come on out, let's go. We'll be late."

His voice came faintly, as if from under the ground.

"Here I am, Donny."

I could hear him, but I couldn't see him. It was Jeffty, no question about it: as Donald H. Horton, President and Sole Owner of The Horton TV & Sound Center, no one but Jeffty called me Donny. He had never called me anything else.

(Actually, it isn't a lie. I *am*, as far as the public is concerned, Sole Owner of the Center. The partnership with my Aunt Patricia is only to repay the loan she made me, to supplement the money I came into when I was twenty-one, left to me when I was ten by my grandfather. It wasn't a very big loan, only eighteen thousand, but I asked her to be a silent partner, because of when she had taken care of me as a child.)

"Where are you, Jeffty?"

"Under the porch in my secret place."

I walked around the side of the porch, and stooped down and pulled away the wicker grating. Back in there, on the pressed dirt, Jeffty had built himself a secret place. He had comics in orange crates, he had a little table and some pillows, it was lit by big fat candles, and we used to hide there when we were both . . . five.

"What'cha up to?" I asked, crawling in and pulling the grate closed behind me. It was cool under the porch, and the dirt smelled comfortable, the candles smelled clubby and familiar. Any kid would feel at home in such a secret place: there's never been a kid who didn't spend the happiest, most productive, most deliciously mysterious times of his life in such a secret place.

"Playin'," he said. He was holding something golden and round. It filled the palm of his little hand.

"You forget we were going to the movies?"

"Nope. I was just waitin' for you here."

"Your mom and dad home?"

"Momma."

I understood why he was waiting under the porch. I didn't push it any further. "What've you got there?"

"Captain Midnight Secret Decoder Badge," he said, showing it to me on his flattened palm.

I realized I was looking at it without comprehending what it was for a long time. Then it dawned on me what a miracle Jeffty had in his hand. A miracle that simply could *not* exist.

"Jeffty," I said softly, with wonder in my voice, "where'd you get that?"

"Came in the mail today. I sent away for it."

"It must have cost a lot of money."

"Not so much. Ten cents an' two inner wax seals from two jars of Ovaltine."

"May I see it?" My voice was trembling, and so was the hand I extended. He gave it to me and I held the miracle in the palm of my hand. It was *wonderful*.

You remember. *Captain Midnight* went on the radio nation-wide in 1940. It was sponsored by Ovaltine. And every year they issued a Secret Squadron Decoder Badge. And every day at the end of the program, they would give you a clue to the next day's installment in a code that only kids with the official badge could decipher. They stopped making those wonderful Decoder Badges in 1949. I remember the one I had in 1945: it was beautiful. It had a magnifying glass in the center of the code dial. *Captain Midnight* went off the air in 1950, and though I understand it was a short-lived television series in the mid-Fifties, and though they issued Decoder Badges in 1955 and 1956, as far as the *real* badges were concerned, they never made one after 1949.

The Captain Midnight Code-O-Graph I held in my hand, the one Jeffty said he had gotten in the mail for ten cents *(ten cents!!!)* and two Ovaltine labels, was brand new, shiny gold metal, not a dent or a spot of rust on it like the old ones you can find at exorbitant prices in collectible shoppes from time to time . . . it was a *new* Decoder. And the date on it was *this* year.

But *Captain Midnight* no longer existed. Nothing like it existed on the radio. I'd listened to the one or two weak imitations of old-time radio the networks were currently airing, and the stories were dull, the sound effects bland, the whole feel of it wrong, out of date, cornball. Yet I held a *new* Code-O-Graph.

"Jeffty, tell me about this," I said.

"Tell you what, Donny? It's my new Capt'n Midnight Secret Decoder Badge. I use it to figger out what's gonna happen tomorrow."

"Tomorrow how?"

"On the program."

"*What* program?!"

He stared at me as if I was being purposely stupid. "On Capt'n *Mid*night! Boy!" I was being dumb.

I still couldn't get it straight. It was right there, right out in the open, and I still didn't know what was happening. "You mean one of those records they made of the old-time radio programs? Is that what you mean, Jeffty?"

"What records?" he asked. He didn't know what *I* meant.

We stared at each other, there under the porch. And then I said, very slowly, almost afraid of the answer, "Jeffty, how do you hear *Captain Midnight?*"

"Every day. On the radio. On my radio. Every day at five-thirty."

News. Music, dumb music, and news. That's what was on the radio every day at 5:30. Not *Captain Midnight.* The Secret Squadron hadn't been on the air in twenty years.

"Can we hear it tonight?" I asked.

"Boy!" he said. I was being dumb. I knew it from the way he said it; but I didn't know *why.* Then it dawned on me: this was Saturday. *Captain Midnight* was on Monday through Friday. Not on Saturday or Sunday.

"We goin' to the movies?"

He had to repeat himself twice. My mind was somewhere else. Nothing definite. No conclusions. No wild assumptions leapt to. Just off somewhere trying to figure it out, and concluding—as *you* would have concluded, as *any*one would have concluded rather than accepting the truth, the impossible and wonderful truth—just finally concluding there was a simple explanation I didn't yet perceive. Something mundane and dull, like the passage of time that steals all good, old things from us, packratting trinkets and plastic in exchange. And all in the name of Progress.

"We goin' to the movies, Donny?"

"You bet your boots we are, kiddo," I said. And I smiled. And I handed him the Code-O-Graph. And he put it in his side pants pocket. And we crawled out from under the porch. And we went

to the movies. And neither of us said anything about *Captain
Midnight* all the rest of that day. And there wasn't a ten-minute
stretch, all the rest of that day, that I didn't think about it.

It was inventory all that next week. I didn't see Jeffty till late
Thursday. I confess I left the store in the hands of Jan and David,
told them I had some errands to run, and left early. At 4:00. I got
to the Kinzers' right around 4:45. Leona answered the door, looking exhausted and distant. "Is Jeffty around?" She said he was
upstairs in his room . . .

 . . . listening to the radio.

I climbed the stairs two at a time.

All right, I had finally made that impossible, illogical leap. Had
the stretch of belief involved anyone but Jeffty, adult or child, I
would have reasoned out more explicable answers. But it *was*
Jeffty, clearly another kind of vessel of life, and what he might
experience should not be expected to fit into the ordered scheme.

I admit it: I *wanted* to hear what I heard.

Even with the door closed, I recognized the program:

"There he goes, Tennessee! Get him!"

There was the heavy report of a rifle shot and the keening whine
of the slug ricocheting, and then the same voice yelled trium-
phantly, *"Got him! D-e-a-a-a-a-d center!"*

He was listening to the American Broadcasting Company,
790 kilocycles, and he was hearing *Tennessee Jed,* one of my
most favorite programs from the Forties, a western adventure I
had not heard in twenty years, because it had not existed for
twenty years.

I sat down on the top step of the stairs, there in the upstairs hall
of the Kinzer home, and I listened to the show. It wasn't a rerun
of an old program, because there were occasional references in
the body of the drama to current cultural and technological developments, and phrases that had not existed in common usage in the

Forties: aerosol spray cans, laserasing of tattoos, Tanzania, the word "uptight."

I could not ignore the fact. Jeffty was listening to a *new* segment of *Tennessee Jed.*

I ran downstairs and out the front door to my car. Leona must have been in the kitchen. I turned the key and punched on the radio and spun the dial to 790 kilocycles. The ABC station. Rock music.

I sat there for a few moments, than ran the dial slowly from one end to the other. Music, news, talk shows. No *Tennessee Jed.* And it was a Blaupunkt, the best radio I could get. I wasn't missing some perimeter station. It simply was not there!

After a few moments I turned off the radio and the ignition and went back upstairs quietly. I sat down on the top step and listened to the entire program. It was *wonderful.*

Exciting, imaginative, filled with everything I remembered as being most innovative about radio drama. But it was modern. It wasn't an antique, re-broadcast to assuage the need of that dwindling listenership who longed for the old days. It was a new show, with all the old voices, but still young and bright. Even the commercials were for currently available products, but they weren't as loud or as insulting as the screamer ads one heard on radio these days.

And when *Tennessee Jed* went off at 5:00, I heard Jeffty spin the dial on his radio till I heard the familiar voice of the announcer Glenn Riggs proclaim, *"Presenting Hop Harrigan! America's ace of the airwaves!"* There was the sound of an airplane in flight. It was a prop plane, *not* a jet! Not the sound kids today have grown up with, but the sound *I* grew up with, the *real* sound of an airplane, the growling, revving, throaty sound of the kind of airplanes G-8 and His Battle Aces flew, the kind Captain Midnight flew, the kind Hop Harrigan flew. And then I heard Hop say, *"CX-4 calling control tower. CX-4 calling control tower. Standing by!"* A pause, then, *"Okay, this is Hop Harrigan . . . coming in!"*

And Jeffty, who had the same problem all of us kids had had in the Forties with programming that pitted equal favorites against one another on different stations, having paid his respects to Hop Harrigan and Tank Tinker, spun the dial and went back to ABC, where I heard the stroke of a gong, the wild cacophony of nonsense Chinese chatter, and the announcer yelled, *"T-e-e-e-rry and the Pirates!"*

I sat there on the top step and listened to Terry and Connie and Flip Corkin and, so help me God, Agnes Moorehead as The Dragon Lady, all of them in a new adventure that took place in a Red China that had not existed in the days of Milton Caniff's 1937 version of the Orient, with river pirates and Chiang Kai-shek and warlords and the naive Imperialism of American gunboat diplomacy.

Sat, and listened to the whole show, and sat even longer to hear *Superman* and part of *Jack Armstrong, the All-American Boy* and part of *Captain Midnight,* and John Kinzer came home and neither he nor Leona came upstairs to find out what had happened to me, or where Jeffty was, and sat longer, and found I had started crying, and could not stop, just sat there with tears running down my face, into the corners of my mouth, sitting and crying until Jeffty heard me and opened his door and saw me and came out and looked at me in childish confusion as I heard the station break for the Mutual Network and they began the theme music of *Tom Mix,* "When It's Round-up Time in Texas and the Bloom Is on the Sage," and Jeffty touched my shoulder and smiled at me, with his mouth and his big brown eyes, and said, "Hi, Donny. Wanna come in an' listen to the radio with me?"

Hume denied the existence of an absolute space, in which each thing has its place; Borges denies the existence of one single time, in which all events are linked.

Jeffty received radio programs from a place that could not, in logic, in the natural scheme of the space-time universe as conceived by Einstein, exist. But that wasn't all he received. He got mail order premiums that no one was manufacturing. He read comic books that had been defunct for three decades. He saw movies with actors who had been dead for twenty years. He was the receiving terminal for endless joys and pleasures of the past that the world had dropped along the way. On its headlong suicidal flight toward New Tomorrows, the world had razed its treasurehouse of simple happinesses, had poured concrete over its playgrounds, had abandoned its elfin stragglers, and all of it was being impossibly, miraculously shunted back into the present through Jeffty. Revivified, updated, the traditions maintained but contemporaneous. Jeffty was the unbidding Aladdin whose very nature formed the magic lampness of his reality.

And he took me into his world with him.

Because he trusted me.

We had breakfast of Quaker Puffed Wheat Sparkies and warm Ovaltine we drank out of *this* year's Little Orphan Annie Shake-Up Mugs. We went to the movies and while everyone else was seeing a comedy starring Goldie Hawn and Ryan O'Neal, Jeffty and I were enjoying Humphrey Bogart as the professional thief Parker in John Huston's brilliant adaptation of the Donald Westlake novel *Slayground.* The second feature was Spencer Tracy, Carole Lombard and Laird Cregar in the Val Lewton–produced film of *Leinengen Versus the Ants.*

Twice a month we went down to the newsstand and bought the current pulp issues of *The Shadow, Doc Savage* and *Startling Stories.* Jeffty and I sat together and I read to him from the magazines. He particularly liked the new short novel by Henry Kuttner, "The Dreams of Achilles," and the new Stanley G. Weinbaum series of short stories set in the subatomic particle universe of Redurna. In September we enjoyed the first installment of the new Robert E. Howard Conan novel, ISLE OF THE BLACK ONES, in *Weird Tales;* and in August we were only mildly disappointed by Edgar Rice Burroughs' fourth novella in the Jupiter series featuring John Carter of Barsoom—"Corsairs of Jupiter." But the editor of *Argosy All-Story Weekly* promised there would be two more stories in the series, and it was such an unexpected revelation for Jeffty and me that it dimmed our disappointment at the lessened quality of the current story.

We read comics together, and Jeffty and I both decided—separately, before we came together to discuss it—that our favorite characters were Doll Man, Airboy and The Heap. We also adored the George Carlson strips in *Jingle Jangle Comics,* particularly the Pie-Face Prince of Old Pretzleburg stories, which we read together and laughed over, even though I had to explain some of the esoteric puns to Jeffty, who was too young to have that kind of subtle wit.

How to explain it? I can't. I had enough physics in college to make some offhand guesses, but I'm more likely wrong than right. The laws of the conservation of energy occasionally break. These are laws that physicists call "weakly violated." Perhaps Jeffty was a catalyst for the weak violation of conservation laws we're only now beginning to realize exist. I tried doing some reading in the area—muon decay of the "forbidden" kind: gamma decay that doesn't include the muon neutrino among its products—but nothing I encountered, not even the latest readings from the Swiss Institute for Nuclear Research near Zurich gave me an insight. I was thrown back on a vague acceptance of the philosophy that the real name for "science" is *magic.*

No explanations, but enormous good times.

The happiest time of my life.

I had the "real" world, the world of my store and my friends and my family, the world of profit&loss, of taxes and evenings with young women who talked about going shopping or the United Nations, of the rising cost of coffee and microwave ovens. And I had Jeffty's world, in which I existed only when I was with him.

The things of the past he knew as fresh and new, I could experience only when in his company. And the membrane between the two worlds grew ever thinner, more luminous and transparent. I had the best of both worlds. And knew, somehow, that I could carry nothing from one to the other.

Forgetting that, for just a moment, betraying Jeffty by forgetting, brought an end to it all.

Enjoying myself so much, I grew careless and failed to consider how fragile the relationship between Jeffty's world and my world really was. There is a reason why the present begrudges the existence of the past. I never really understood. Nowhere in the beast books, where survival is shown in battles between claw and fang, tentacle and poison sac, is there recognition of the ferocity the present always brings to bear on the past. Nowhere is there a detailed statement of how the present lies in wait for What-Was, waiting for it to become Now-This-Moment so it can shred it with its merciless jaws.

Who could know such a thing . . . at any age . . . and certainly not at my age . . . who could understand such a thing?

I'm trying to exculpate myself. I can't. It was my fault.

It was another Saturday afternoon.

"What's playing today?" I asked him, in the car, on the way downtown.

He looked up at me from the other side of the front seat and smiled one of his best smiles. "Ken Maynard in *Bullwhip Justice* an' *The Demolished Man.*" He kept smiling, as if he'd really put one over on me. I looked at him with disbelief.

"You're *kid*ding!" I said, delighted. "Bester's THE DEMOLISHED MAN?" He nodded his head, delighted at my being delighted. He knew it was one of my favorite books. "Oh, that's super!"

"Super *duper,*" he said.

"Who's in it?"

"Franchot Tone, Evelyn Keyes, Lionel Barrymore and Elisha Cook, Jr." He was much more knowledgeable about movie actors than I'd ever been. He could name the character actors in any movie he'd ever seen. Even the crowd scenes.

"And cartoons?" I asked.

"Three of 'em: a *Little Lulu,* a *Donald Duck* and a *Bugs Bunny.* An' a *Pete Smith Specialty* an' a Lew Lehr *Monkeys is da* C-r-r-r-aziest *Peoples.*"

"Oh boy!" I said. I was grinning from ear to ear. And then I looked down and saw the pad of purchase order forms on the seat. I'd forgotten to drop it off at the store.

"Gotta stop by the Center," I said. "Gotta drop off something. It'll only take a minute."

"Okay," Jeffty said. "But we won't be late, will we?"

"Not on your tintype, kiddo," I said.

When I pulled into the parking lot behind the Center, he decided to come in with me and we'd walk over to the theater. It's not a large town. There are only two movie houses, the Utopia and the Lyric. We were going to the Utopia and it was only three blocks from the Center.

I walked into the store with the pad of forms, and it was bedlam. David and Jan were handling two customers each, and there were people standing around waiting to be helped. Jan turned a look on me and her face was a horror-mask of pleading. David was running from the stockroom to the showroom and all he could murmur as he whipped past was "Help!" and then he was gone.

"Jeffty," I said, crouching down, "listen, give me a few minutes. Jan and David are in trouble with all these people. We won't be late, I promise. Just let me get rid of a couple of these customers." He looked nervous, but nodded okay.

I motioned to a chair and said, "Just sit down for a while and I'll be right with you."

He went to the chair, good as you please, though he knew what was happening, and he sat down.

I started taking care of people who wanted color television sets. This was the first really substantial batch of units we'd gotten in —color television was only now becoming reasonably priced and this was Sony's first promotion—and it was bonanza time for me. I could see paying off the loan and being out in front for the first time with the Center. It was business.

In my world, good business comes first.

Jeffty sat there and stared at the wall. Let me tell you about the wall.

Stanchion and bracket designs had been rigged from the floor to within two feet of the ceiling. Television sets had been stacked artfully on the wall. Thirty-three television sets. All playing at the same time. Black and white, color, little ones, big ones, all going at the same time.

Jeffty sat and watched thirty-three television sets, on a Saturday afternoon. We can pick up a total of thirteen channels including the UHF educational stations. Golf was on one channel; baseball was on a second; celebrity bowling was on a third; the fourth channel was a religious seminar; a teen-age dance show was on the fifth; the sixth was a rerun of a situation comedy; the seventh was a rerun of a police show; eighth was a nature program showing a man flycasting endlessly; ninth was news and conversation; tenth was a stock car race; eleventh was a man doing logarithms on a blackboard; twelfth was a woman in a leotard doing sitting-up exercises; and on the thirteenth channel was a badly animated cartoon show in Spanish. All but six of the shows were repeated on three sets. Jeffty sat and watched that wall of television on a Saturday afternoon while I sold as fast and as hard as I could, to pay back my Aunt Patricia and stay in touch with my world. It was business.

I should have known better. I should have understood about the present and the way it kills the past. But I was selling with both hands. And when I finally glanced over at Jeffty, half an hour later, he looked like another child.

He was sweating. That terrible fever sweat when you have stomach flu. He was pale, as pasty and pale as a worm, and his little hands were gripping the arms of the chair so tightly I could see his knuckles in bold relief. I dashed over to him, excusing myself from the middle-aged couple looking at the new 21" Mediterranean model.

"Jeffty!"

He looked at me, but his eyes didn't track. He was in absolute terror. I pulled him out of the chair and started toward the front door with him, but the customers I'd deserted yelled at me, "Hey!" The middle-aged man said, "You wanna sell me this thing or don't you?"

I looked from him to Jeffty and back again. Jeffty was like a zombie. He had come where I'd pulled him. His legs were rubbery and his feet dragged. The past, being eaten by the present, the sound of something in pain.

I clawed some money out of my pants pocket and jammed it into Jeffty's hand. "Kiddo . . . listen to me . . . get out of here right now!" He still couldn't focus properly. *"Jeffty,"* I said as tightly as I could, *"listen* to me!" The middle-aged customer and his wife were walking toward us. "Listen, kiddo, get out of here right this minute. Walk over to the Utopia and buy the tickets. I'll be right behind you." The middle-aged man and his wife were almost on us. I shoved Jeffty through the door and watched him stumble away in the wrong direction, then stop as if gathering his wits, turn and go back past the front of the Center and in the direction of the Utopia. "Yes sir," I said, straightening up and facing them, "yes, ma'am, that is one terrific set with some sen*sa*tional features! If you'll just step back here with me . . . ."

There was a terrible sound of something hurting, but I couldn't tell from which channel, or from which set, it was coming.

Most of it I learned later, from the girl in the ticket booth, and from some people I knew who came to me to tell me what had happened. By the time I got to the Utopia, nearly twenty minutes later, Jeffty was already beaten to a pulp and had been taken to the Manager's office.

"Did you see a very little boy, about five years old, with big brown eyes and straight brown hair . . . he was waiting for me?"

"Oh, I think that's the little boy those kids beat up?"

"What!?! *Where is he?*"

"They took him to the Manager's office. No one knew who he was or where to find his parents—"

A young girl wearing an usher's uniform was kneeling down beside the couch, placing a wet paper towel on his face.

I took the towel away from her and ordered her out of the office. She looked insulted and snorted something rude, but she left. I sat on the edge of the couch and tried to swab away the blood from the lacerations without opening the wounds where the blood had caked. Both his eyes were swollen shut. His mouth was ripped badly. His hair was matted with dried blood.

He had been standing in line behind two kids in their teens. They started selling tickets at 12:30 and the show started at 1:00. The doors weren't opened till 12:45. He had been waiting, and the kids in front of him had had a portable radio. They were listening to the ball game. Jeffty had wanted to hear some program, God knows what it might have been, *Grand Central Station, Let's Pretend, Land of the Lost,* God only knows which one it might have been.

He had asked if he could borrow their radio to hear the program for a minute, and it had been a commercial break or something, and the kids had given him the radio, probably out of some malicious kind of courtesy that would permit them to take offense and rag the little boy. He had changed the station . . . and they'd been unable to get it to go back to the ball game. It was locked into the past, on a station that was broadcasting a program that didn't exist for anyone but Jeffty.

They had beaten him badly . . . as everyone watched.

And then they had run away.

I had left him alone, left him to fight off the present without sufficient weaponry. I had betrayed him for the sale of a 21″ Mediterranean console television, and now his face was pulped meat. He moaned something inaudible and sobbed softly.

"Shhh, it's okay, kiddo, it's Donny. I'm here. I'll get you home, it'll be okay."

I should have taken him straight to the hospital. I don't know why I didn't. I should have. I should have done that.

When I carried him through the door, John and Leona Kinzer just stared at me. They didn't move to take him from my arms. One of his hands was hanging down. He was conscious, but just barely. They stared, there in the semi-darkness of a Saturday afternoon in the present. I looked at them. "A couple of kids beat him up at the theater." I raised him a few inches in my arms and extended him. They stared at me, at both of us, with nothing in their eyes, without movement. "Jesus Christ," I shouted, "he's been beaten! He's your son! Don't you even want to touch him? What the hell kind of people are you?!"

Then Leona moved toward me very slowly. She stood in front of us for a few seconds, and there was a leaden stoicism in her face that was terrible to see. It said, *I have been in this place before, many times, and I cannot bear to be in it again; but I am here now.*

So I gave him to her. God help me, I gave him over to her.

And she took him upstairs to bathe away his blood and his pain.

John Kinzer and I stood in our separate places in the dim living room of the their home, and we stared at each other. He had nothing to say to me.

I shoved past him and fell into a chair. I was shaking.

I heard the bath water running upstairs.

After what seemed a very long time Leona came downstairs, wiping her hands on her apron. She sat down on the sofa and after a moment John sat down beside her. I heard the sound of rock music from upstairs.

"Would you like a piece of nice pound cake?" Leona said.

I didn't answer. I was listening to the sound of the music. Rock music. On the radio. There was a table lamp on the end table beside the sofa. It cast a dim and futile light in the shadowed living room. *Rock music from the present, on a radio upstairs?* I started to say something, and then *knew* . . . Oh, God . . . *no!*

I jumped up just as the sound of hideous crackling blotted out the music, and the table lamp dimmed and dimmed and flickered. I screamed something, I don't know what it was, and ran for the stairs.

Jeffty's parents did not move. They sat there with their hands folded, in that place they had been for so many years.

I fell twice rushing up the stairs.

There isn't much on television that can hold my interest. I bought an old cathedral-shaped Philco radio in a second-hand store, and I replaced all the burnt-out parts with the original tubes from old radios I could cannibalize that still worked. I don't use transistors or printed circuits. They wouldn't work. I've sat in front of that set for hours sometimes, running the dial back and forth as slowly as you can imagine, so slowly it doesn't look as if it's moving at all sometimes.

But I can't find *Captain Midnight* or *The Land of the Lost* or *The Shadow* or *Quiet Please.*

So she did love him, still, a little bit, even after all those years. I can't hate them: they only wanted to live in the present world again. That isn't such a terrible thing.

It's a good world, all things considered. It's much better than it used to be, in a lot of ways. People don't die from the old diseases any more. They die from new ones, but that's Progress, isn't it?

Isn't it?

Tell me.

Somebody please tell me.

JOHN VARLEY

Air Raid

John Varley—Herb to his friends—is a tall, quiet man from Oregon. His stories have dominated the various annual "best SF" anthologies for a small handful of years now. That's because he can write stories like blue (or green, or golden—he's a writer who can take his pick!) blazes.

﷯

﷯

I was jerked awake by the silent alarm vibrating my skull. It won't shut down until you sit up, so I did. All around me in the darkened bunkroom the Snatch Team members were sleeping singly and in pairs. I yawned, scratched my ribs, and patted Gene's hairy flank. He turned over. So much for a romantic send-off.

Rubbing sleep from my eyes, I reached to the floor for my leg, strapped it on, and plugged it in. Then I was running down the rows of bunks toward Ops.

The situation board glowed in the gloom. Sun-Belt Airlines Flight 128, Miami to New York, September 15, 1979. We'd been looking for that one for three years. I should have been happy, but who can afford it when you wake up?

Liza Boston muttered past me on the way to Prep. I muttered back and followed. The lights came on around the mirrors, and I groped my way to one of them. Behind us, three more people staggered in. I sat down, plugged in, and at last I could lean back and close my eyes.

They didn't stay closed for long. Rush! I sat up straight as the sludge I use for blood was replaced with supercharged go-juice. I looked around me and got a series of idiot grins. There was Liza, and Pinky and Dave. Against the far wall Cristabel was already turning slowly in front of the airbrush, getting a Caucasian paint job. It looked like a good team.

I opened the drawer and started preliminary work on my face. It's a bigger job every time. Transfusion or no, I looked like death. The right ear was completely gone now. I could no longer close my lips; the gums were permanently bared. A week earlier, a finger had fallen off in my sleep. And what's it to you, bugger?

While I worked, one of the screens around the mirror glowed. A smiling young woman, blonde, high brow, round face. Close enough. The crawl line read *Mary Katrina Sondergard, born Trenton, New Jersey, age in 1979: 25.* Baby, this is your lucky day.

The computer melted the skin away from her face to show me the bone structure, rotated it, gave me cross sections. I studied the similarities with my own skull, noted the differences. Not bad, and better than some I'd been given.

I assembled a set of dentures that included the slight gap in the upper incisors. Putty filled out my cheeks. Contact lenses fell from the dispenser and I popped them in. Nose plugs widened my nostrils. No need for ears; they'd be covered by the wig. I pulled a blank plastiflesh mask over my face and had to pause while it melted in. It took only a minute to mold it to perfection. I smiled at myself. How nice to have lips.

The delivery slot clunked and dropped a blonde wig and a pink outfit into my lap. The wig was hot from the styler. I put it on, then the pantyhose.

"Mandy? Did you get the profile on Sondergard?" I didn't look up; I recognized the voice.

"Roger."

"We've located her near the airport. We can slip you in before take-off, so you'll be the joker."

I groaned and looked up at the face on the screen. Elfreda Baltimore-Louisville, Director of Operational Teams: lifeless face and tiny slits for eyes. What can you do when all the muscles are dead?

"Okay." You take what you get.

She switched off, and I spent the next two minutes trying to get dressed while keeping my eyes on the screens. I memorized names and faces of crew members plus the few facts known about them. Then I hurried out and caught up with the others. Elapsed time from first alarm: twelve minutes and seven seconds. We'd better get moving.

"Goddam Sun-Belt," Cristabel groused, hitching at her bra.

"At least they got rid of the high heels," Dave pointed out. A year earlier we would have been teetering down the aisles on three-inch platforms. We all wore short pink shifts with blue and white diagonal stripes across the front, and carried matching shoulder bags. I fussed trying to get the ridiculous pillbox cap pinned on.

We jogged into the dark Operations Control Room and lined up at the gate. Things were out of our hands now. Until the gate was ready, we could only wait.

I was first, a few feet away from the portal. I turned away from it; it gives me vertigo. I focused instead on the gnomes sitting at their consoles, bathed in yellow lights from their screens. None of them looked back at me. They don't like us much. I don't like them, either. Withered, emaciated, all of them. Our fat legs and butts and breasts are a reproach to them, a reminder that Snatchers eat five times their ration to stay presentable for the masquerade. Meantime we continue to rot. One day I'll be sitting at a console. One day I'll be *built in* to a console, with all my guts on the outside and nothing left of my body but stink. The hell with them.

I buried my gun under a clutter of tissues and lipsticks in my purse. Elfreda was looking at me.

"Where is she?" I asked.

"Motel room. She was alone from ten P.M. to noon on flight day."

Departure time was 1:15. She had cut it close and would be in a hurry. Good.

"Can you catch her in the bathroom? Best of all, in the tub?"

"We're working on it." She sketched a smile with a fingertip drawn over lifeless lips. She knew how I liked to operate, but she was telling me I'd take what I got. It never hurts to ask. People are at their most defenseless stretched out and up to their necks in water.

"Go!" Elfreda shouted. I stepped through, and things started to go wrong.

I was facing the wrong way, stepping *out* of the bathroom door and facing the bedroom. I turned and spotted Mary Katrina Sondergard through the haze of the gate. There was no way I could reach her without stepping back through. I couldn't even shoot without hitting someone on the other side.

Sondergard was at the mirror, the worst possible place. Few people recognize themselves quickly, but she'd been looking right at herself. She saw me and her eyes widened. I stepped to the side, out of her sight.

"What the hell is . . . hey? Who the hell—" I noted the voice, which can be the trickiest thing to get right.

I figured she'd be more curious than afraid. My guess was right. She came out of the bathroom, passing through the gate as if it wasn't there, which it wasn't, since it only has one side. She had a towel wrapped around her.

"Jesus Christ! What are you doing in my—" Words fail you at a time like that. She knew she ought to say something, but what? *Excuse me, haven't I seen you in the mirror?*

I put on my best stew smile and held out my hand.

"Pardon the intrusion. I can explain everything. You see, I'm—" I hit her on the side of the head and she staggered and went down hard. Her towel fell to the floor. "—working my way through college." She started to get up, so I caught her under the chin with my artificial knee. She stayed down.

"Standard fuggin' *oil!*" I hissed, rubbing my injured knuckles. But there was no time. I knelt beside her, checked her pulse. She'd be okay, but I think I loosened some front teeth. I paused a moment. Lord, to look like that with no makeup, no prosthetics! She nearly broke my heart.

I grabbed her under the knees and wrestled her to the gate. She was a sack of limp noodles. Somebody reached through, grabbed her feet, and pulled. *So long, love! How would you like to go on a long voyage?*

I sat on her rented bed to get my breath. There were car keys and cigarettes in her purse, genuine tobacco, worth its weight in blood. I lit six of them, figuring I had five minutes of my very own. The room filled with sweet smoke. They don't make 'em like that anymore.

The Hertz sedan was in the motel parking lot. I got in and headed for the airport. I breathed deeply of the air, rich in hydrocarbons. I could see for hundreds of yards into the distance. The perspective nearly made me dizzy, but I live for those moments. There's no way to explain what it's like in the pre-meck world. The sun was a fierce yellow ball through the haze.

The other stews were boarding. Some of them knew Sondergard so I didn't say much, pleading a hangover. That went over well, with a lot of knowing laughs and sly remarks. Evidently it wasn't out of character. We boarded the 707 and got ready for the goats to arrive.

It looked good. The four commandos on the other side were identical twins for the women I was working with. There was nothing to do but be a stewardess until departure time. I hoped there would be no more glitches. Inverting a gate for a joker run into a motel room was one thing, but in a 707 at twenty thousand feet . . .

The plane was nearly full when the woman Pinky would impersonate sealed the forward door. We taxied to the end of the runway, then we were airborne. I started taking orders for drinks in first.

The goats were the usual lot, for 1979. Fat and sassy, all of them, and as unaware of living in a paradise as a fish is of the sea. *What would you think, ladies and gents, of a trip to the future? No? I can't say I'm surprised. What if I told you this plane is going to—*

My alarm beeped as we reached cruising altitude. I consulted the indicator under my Lady Bulova and glanced at one of the restroom doors. I felt a vibration pass through the plane. *Damn it, not so soon.*

The gate was in there. I came out quickly, and motioned for Diana Gleason—Dave's pigeon—to come to the front.

"Take a look at this," I said, with a disgusted look. She started to enter the restroom, stopped when she saw the green glow. I planted a boot on her fanny and shoved. Perfect. Dave would have a chance to hear her voice before popping in. Though she'd be doing little but screaming when she got a look around. . . .

Dave came through the gate, adjusting his silly little hat. Diana must have struggled.

"Be disgusted," I whispered.

"What a mess," he said as he came out of the restroom. It was a fair imitation of Diana's tone, though he'd missed the accent. It wouldn't matter much longer.

"What is it?" It was one of the stews from tourist. We stepped aside so she could get a look, and Dave shoved her through. Pinky popped out very quickly.

"We're minus on minutes," Pinky said. "We lost five on the other side."

"Five?" Dave-Diana squeaked. I felt the same way. We had a hundred and three passengers to process.

"Yeah. They lost contact after you pushed my pigeon through. It took that long to realign."

You get used to that. Time runs at different rates on each side of the gate, though it's always sequential, past to future. Once we'd started the Snatch with me entering Sondergard's room, there was no way to go back any earlier on either side. Here, in 1979, we had a rigid ninety-four minutes to get everything done. On the other side, the gate could never be maintained longer than three hours.

"When you left, how long was it since the alarm went in?"

"Twenty-eight minutes."

It didn't sound good. It would take at least two hours just customizing the wimps. Assuming there was no more slippage on 79-time, we might just make it. But there's *always* slippage. I shuddered, thinking about riding it in.

"No time for any more games, then," I said. "Pink, you go back to tourist and call both of the other girls up here. Tell 'em to come one at a time, and tell 'em we've got a problem. You know the bit."

"Biting back the tears. Got you." She hurried aft. In no time the first one showed up. Her friendly Sun-Belt Airlines smile was stamped on her face, but her stomach would be churning. *Oh God, this is it!*

I took her by the elbow and pulled her behind the curtains in front. She was breathing hard.

"Welcome to the twilight zone," I said, and put the gun to her head. She slumped, and I caught her. Pinky and Dave helped me shove her through the gate.

"Fug! The rotting thing's flickering."

Pinky was right. A very ominous sign. But the green glow stabilized as we watched, with who knows how much slippage on the other side. Cristabel ducked through.

"We're plus thirty-three," she said. There was no sense talking about what we were all thinking: things were going badly.

"Back to tourist," I said. "Be brave, smile at everyone, but make it just a little bit too good, got it?"

"Check," Cristabel said.

We processed the other quickly, with no incident. Then there was no time to talk about anything. In eighty-nine minutes Flight 128 was going to be spread all over a mountain whether we were finished or not.

Dave went into the cockpit to keep the flight crew out of our hair. Me and Pinky were supposed to take care of first class, then back up Cristabel and Liza in tourist. We used the standard "coffee, tea, or milk" gambit, relying on our speed and their inertia.

I leaned over the first two seats on the left.

"Are you enjoying your flight?" Pop, pop. Two squeezes on the trigger, close to the heads and out of sight of the rest of the goats.

"Hi, folks. I'm Mandy. Fly me." Pop, Pop.

Halfway to the galley, a few people were watching us curiously. But people don't make a fuss until they have a lot more to go on. One goat in the back row stood up, and I let him have it. By now there were only eight left awake. I abandoned the smile and squeezed off four quick shots. Pinky took care of the rest. We hurried through the curtains, just in time.

There was an uproar building in the back of tourist, with about 60 percent of the goats already processed. Cristabel glanced at me, and I nodded.

"Okay, folks," she bawled. "I want you to be quiet. Calm down and listen up. *You,* fathead, *pipe down* before I cram my foot up your ass sideways."

The shock of hearing her talk like that was enough to buy us a little time, anyway. We had formed a skirmish line across the width of the plane, guns out, steadied on seat backs, aimed at the milling, befuddled group of thirty goats.

The guns are enough to awe all but the most foolhardy. In essence, a standard-issue stunner is just a plastic rod with two grids about six inches apart. There's not enough metal in it to set off a hijack alarm. And to people from the Stone Age to about 2190 it doesn't look any more like a weapon than a ball-point pen. So Equipment Section jazzes them up in a plastic shell to real Buck Rogers blasters, with a dozen knobs and lights that flash and a barrel like the snout of a hog. Hardly anyone ever walks into one.

"We are in great danger, and time is short. You must all do exactly as I tell you, and you will be safe."

You can't give them time to think, you have to rely on your status as the Voice of Authority. The situation is just *not* going to make sense to them, no matter how you explain it.

"Just a minute, I think you owe us—"

An airborne lawyer. I made a snap decision, thumbed the fireworks switch on my gun, and shot him.

The gun made a sound like a flying saucer with hemorrhoids, spit sparks and little jets of flame, and extended a green laser finger to his forehead. He dropped.

All pure kark, of course. But it sure is impressive.

And it's damn risky, too. I had to choose between a panic if the fathead got them to thinking, and a possible panic from the flash of the gun. But when a 20th gets to talking about his "rights" and what he is "owed," things can get out of hand. It's infectious.

It worked. There was a lot of shouting, people ducking behind seats, but no rush. We could have handled it, but we needed some of them conscious if we were ever going to finish the Snatch.

"Get up. Get *up*, you *slugs!*" Cristabel yelled. "He's stunned, nothing worse. But I'll *kill* the next one who gets out of line. Now *get to your feet* and do what I tell you. *Children first! Hurry,* as fast as you can, to the front of the plane. Do what the stewardess tells you. Come on, kids, *move!*"

I ran back into first class just ahead of the kids, turned at the open restroom door, and got on my knees.

They were petrified. There were five of them—crying, some of them, which always chokes me up—looking left and right at dead people in the first class seats, stumbling, near panic.

"Come on, kids," I called to them, giving my special smile. "Your parents will be along in just a minute. Everything's going to be all right, I promise you. Come on."

I got three of them through. The fourth balked. She was determined not to go through that door. She spread her legs and arms and I couldn't push her through. I will *not* hit a child, never. She raked her nails over my face. My wig came off, and she gaped at my bare head. I shoved her through.

Number five was sitting in the aisle, bawling. He was maybe seven. I ran back and picked him up, hugged him and kissed him, and tossed him through. God, I needed a rest, but I was needed in tourist.

"You, you, you, and you. Okay, you too. Help him, will you?" Pinky had a practiced eye for the ones that wouldn't be any use to anyone, even themselves. We herded them toward the front of the plane, then deployed ourselves along the left side where we could cover the workers. It didn't take long to prod them into action. We had them dragging the limp bodies forward as fast as they could go. Me and Cristabel were in tourist, with the others up front.

Adrenaline was being catabolized in my body now; the rush of action left me and I started to feel very tired. There's an unavoidable feeling of sympathy for the poor dumb goats that starts to get me about this stage of the game. Sure, they were better off; sure, they were going to die if we didn't get them off the plane. But when they saw the other side they were going to have a hard time believing it.

The first ones were returning for a second load, stunned at what they'd just seen: dozens of people being put into a cubicle that was crowded when it was empty. One college student looked like he'd been hit in the stomach. He stopped by me and his eyes pleaded.

"Look, I want to *help* you people, just . . . what's going *on?* Is this some new kind of rescue? I mean, are we going to crash—"

I switched my gun to prod and brushed it across his cheek. He gasped and fell back.

"Shut your fuggin' mouth and get moving, or I'll kill you." It would be hours before his jaw was in shape to ask any more stupid questions.

We cleared tourist and moved up. A couple of the work gang were pretty damn pooped by then. Muscles like horses, all of them, but they can hardly run up a flight of stairs. We let some of them go through, including a couple that were at least fifty years old. *Je*-zuz. Fifty! We got down to a core of four men and two women who seemed strong, and worked them until they nearly dropped. But we processed everyone in twenty-five minutes.

The portapak came through as we were stripping off our clothes. Cristabel knocked on the door to the cockpit and Dave came out, already naked. A bad sign.

"I had to cork 'em," he said. "Bleeding captain just *had* to make his grand march through the plane. I tried *every*thing."

Sometimes you have to do it. The plane was on autopilot, as it normally would be at this time. But if any of us did anything detrimental to the craft, changed the fixed course of events in any way, that would be it. All that work for nothing, and Flight 128 inaccessible to us for all Time. I don't know sludge about time theory, but I know the practical angles. We can do things in the past only at times and in places where it won't make any difference. We have to cover our tracks. There's flexibility; once a Snatcher left her gun behind and it went in with the plane. Nobody found it, or if they did, they didn't have the smoggiest idea of what it was, so we were okay.

Flight 128 was mechanical failure. That's the best kind; it means we don't have to keep the pilot unaware of the situation in the cabin right down to ground level. We can cork him and fly the plane, since there's nothing he could have done to save the flight anyway. A pilot-error smash is almost impossible to snatch. We mostly work midairs, bombs, and structural failures. If there's even one survivor, we can't touch it. It would not fit the fabric of space-time, which is immutable (though it can stretch a little), and we'd all just fade away and appear back in the ready room.

My head was hurting. I wanted that portapak very badly.

"Who has the most hours on a 707?" Pinky did, so I sent her to the cabin, along with Dave, who could do the pilot's voice for air traffic control. You have to have a believable record in the flight recorder, too. They trailed two long tubes from the portapak, and the rest of us hooked in up close. We stood there, each of us smoking a fistful of cigarettes, wanting to finish them but hoping there wouldn't be time. The gate had vanished as soon as we tossed our clothes and the flight crew through.

But we didn't worry long. There's other nice things about Snatching, but nothing to compare with the rush of plugging into a portapak. The wake-up transfusion is nothing but fresh blood, rich in oxygen and sugars. What we were getting now was an insane brew of concentrated adrenaline, supersaturated hemoglobin, methedrine, white lightning, TNT, and Kickapoo joyjuice. It was like a firecracker in your heart; a boot in the box that rattled your sox.

"I'm growing hair on my chest," Cristabel said solemnly. Everyone giggled.

"Would someone hand me my eyeballs?"

"The blue ones, or the red ones?"

"I think my ass just fell off."

We'd heard them all before, but we howled anyway. We were strong, *strong,* and for one golden moment we had no worries. Everything was hilarious. I could have torn sheet metal with my eyelashes.

But you get hyper on that mix. When the gate didn't show, and didn't show, and *didn't sweetjeez show* we all started milling. This bird wasn't going to fly all that much longer.

Then it did show, and we turned on. The first of the wimps came through, dressed in the clothes taken from a passenger it had been picked to resemble.

"Two thirty-five elapsed upside time," Cristabel announced.

"Je-zuz."

It is a deadening routine. You grab the harness around the wimp's shoulders and drag it along the aisle, after consulting the seat number painted on its forehead. The paint would last three minutes. You set it, strap it in, break open the harness and carry it back to toss through the gate as you grab the next one. You have to take it for granted they've done the work right on the other side: fillings in the teeth, fingerprints, the right match in height and weight and hair color. Most of those things don't matter much, especially on Flight 128 which was a crash-and-burn. There would be bits and pieces, and burned to a crisp at that. But you can't take chances. Those rescue workers are pretty thorough on the parts they *do* find; the dental work and fingerprints especially are important.

I hate wimps. I really hate 'em. Every time I grab the harness of one of them, if it's a child, I wonder if it's Alice. *Are you my kid, you vegetable, you slug, you slimy worm?* I joined the Snatchers right after the brain bugs ate the life out of my baby's head. I couldn't stand to think she was the last generation, that the last humans there would ever be would live with nothing in their heads, medically dead by standards that prevailed even in 1979, with computers working their muscles to keep them in tone. You grow up, reach puberty still fertile—one in a thousand—rush to get pregnant in your first heat. Then you find out your mom or pop passed on a chronic disease bound right into the genes, and none of your kids will be immune. I *knew* about the paraleprosy; I grew up with my toes rotting away. But this was too much. What do you do?

Only one in ten of the wimps had a customized face. It takes time and a lot of skill to build a new face that will stand up to a doctor's autopsy. The rest came premutilated. We've got millions of them; it's not hard to find a good match in the body. Most of them would stay breathing, too dumb to stop, until they went in with the plane.

The plane jerked, hard. I glanced at my watch. Five minutes to impact. We should have time. I was on my last wimp. I could hear Dave frantically calling the ground. A bomb came through the gate, and I tossed it into the cockpit. Pinky turned on the pressure sensor on the bomb and came running out, followed by Dave. Liza was already through. I grabbed the limp dolls in stewardess costume and tossed them to the floor. The engine fell off and a piece of it came through the cabin. We started to depressurize. The bomb blew away part of the cockpit (the ground crash crew would read it—we hoped—that part of the engine came through and killed the crew: no more words from the pilot on the flight recorder) and we turned, slowly, left and down. I was lifted toward the hole in the side of the plane, but I managed to hold on to a seat. Cristabel wasn't so lucky. She was blown backwards.

We started to rise slightly, losing speed. Suddenly it was uphill from where Cristabel was lying in the aisle. Blood oozed from her temple. I glanced back; everyone was gone, and three pink-suited wimps were piled on the floor. The plane began to stall, to nose down, and my feet left the floor.

"Come on, Bel!" I screamed. That gate was only three feet away from me, but I began pulling myself along to where she floated. The plane bumped, and she hit the floor. Incredibly, it seemed to wake her up. She started to swim toward me, and I grabbed her hand as the floor came up to slam us again. We crawled as the plane went through its final death agony, and we came to the door. The gate was gone.

There wasn't anything to say. We were going in. It's hard enough to keep the gate in place on a plane that's moving in a straight line. When a bird gets to corkscrewing and coming apart, the math is fearsome. So I've been told.

I embraced Cristabel and held her bloodied head. She was groggy, but managed to smile and shrug. You take what you get. I hurried into the restroom and got both of us down on the floor. Back to the forward bulkhead, Cristabel between my legs, back to front. Just like in training. We pressed our feet against the other wall. I hugged her tightly and cried on her shoulder.

And it was there. A green glow to my left. I threw myself toward it, dragging Cristabel, keeping low as two wimps were thrown headfirst through the gate above our heads. Hands grabbed and pulled us through. I clawed my way a good five yards along the floor. You can leave a leg on the other side and I didn't have one to spare.

I sat up as they were carrying Cristabel to Medical. I patted her arm as she went by on the stretcher, but she was passed out. I wouldn't have minded passing out myself.

For a while, you can't believe it all really happened. Sometimes it turns out it *didn't* happen. You come back and find out all the goats in the holding pen have softly and suddenly vanished away because the continuum won't tolerate the changes and paradoxes you've put into it. The people you've worked so hard to rescue are spread like tomato surprise all over some goddam hillside in Carolina and all you've got left is a bunch of ruined wimps and an exhausted Snatch Team. But not this time. I could see the goats milling around in the holding pen, naked and more bewildered than ever. And just starting to be *really* afraid.

Elfreda touched me as I passed her. She nodded, which meant well-done in her limited repertoire of gestures. I shrugged, wondering if I cared, but the surplus adrenaline was still in my veins and I found myself grinning at her. I nodded back.

Gene was standing by the holding pen. I went to him, hugged him. I felt the juices start to flow. *Damn it, let's squander a little ration and have us a good time.*

Someone was beating on the sterile glass wall of the pen. She shouted, mouthing angry words at us. *Why? What have you done to us?* It was Mary Sondergard. She implored her bald, one-legged twin to make her understand. She thought she had problems. God, was she pretty. I hated her guts.

Gene pulled me away from the wall. My hands hurt, and I'd broken off all my fake nails without scratching the glass. She was sitting on the floor now, sobbing. I heard the voice of the briefing officer on the outside speaker.

". . . Centauri Three is hospitable, with an Earthlike climate. By that, I mean *your* Earth, not what it has become. You'll see more of that later. The trip will take five years, shiptime. Upon landfall, you will be entitled to one horse, a plow, three axes, two hundred kilos of seed grain . . ."

I leaned against Gene's shoulder. At their lowest ebb, this very moment, they were so much better than us. I had maybe ten years, half of that as a basket case. They are our best, our very brightest hope. Everything is up to them.

". . . that no one will be forced to go. We wish to point out again, not for the last time, that you would all be dead without our intervention. There are things you should know, however. You cannot breathe our air. If you remain on Earth, you can never leave this building. We are not like you. We are the result of a genetic winnowing, a mutation process. We are the survivors, but our enemies have evolved along with us. They are winning. You, however, are immune to the diseases that afflict us . . ."

I winced and turned away.

". . . the other hand, if you emigrate you will be given a chance at a new life. It won't be easy, but as Americans you should be proud of your pioneer heritage. Your ancestors survived, and so will you. It can be a rewarding experience, and I urge you . . ."

Sure. Gene and I looked at each other and laughed. *Listen to this, folks. Five percent of you will suffer nervous breakdowns in the next few days, and never leave. About the same number will commit suicide, here and on the way. When you get there, sixty to seventy percent will die in the first three years. You will die in childbirth, be eaten by animals, bury two out of three of your babies, starve slowly when the rains don't come. If you live, it will be to break your back behind a plow, sun-up to dusk. New Earth is Heaven, folks!*

God, how I wish I could go with them.

RACCOONA SHELDON

✿ *The Screwfly Solution*

Raccoona Sheldon is one of the pen names (James Tiptree, Jr., is another) of a retired psychologist who has decided to take a hard look at
what goes on in the world and make some distressing speculations.*

✿Nebula Award of the Science Fiction Writers of America for Best Novelette,
1977.

۞

The young man sitting at 2° N, 75° W sent a casually venomous glance up at the nonfunctional shoofly *ventilador* and went on reading his letter. He was sweating heavily, stripped to his shorts in the hotbox of what passed for a hotel room in Cuyapán.

How do other wives do it? I stay busy-busy with the Ann Arbor grant review programs and the seminar, saying brightly "Oh yes, Alan is in Colombia setting up a biological pest control program, isn't it wonderful?" But inside I imagine you surrounded by nineteen-year-old raven-haired cooing beauties, every one panting with social dedication and filthy rich. And forty inches of bosom busting out of her delicate lingerie. I even figured it in centimeters, that's 101.6 centimeters of busting. Oh, darling, darling, do what you want only come home safe.

Alan grinned fondly, briefly imagining the only body he longed for. His girl, his magic Anne. Then he got up to open the window another cautious notch. A long pale mournful face looked in—a goat. The room opened on the goatpen, the stench was vile. Air, anyway. He picked up the letter.

Everything is just about as you left it, except that the Peedsville horror seems to be getting worse. They're calling it the Sons of Adam cult now. Why can't they do something, even if it is a religion? The Red Cross has set up a refugee camp in Ashton, Georgia. Imagine, refugees in the U.S.A. I heard two little girls were carried out all slashed up. Oh, Alan.

Which reminds me, Barney came over with a wad of clippings he wants me to send you. I'm putting them in a separate envelope; I know what happens to very fat letters in foreign POs. He says, in case you don't get them, what do the following have in common? Peedsville, São Paulo, Phoenix, San Diego, Shanghai, New Delhi, Tripoli, Brisbane, Johannesburg and Lubbock, Texas. He says the hint is, remember where the Intertropical Convergence Zone is now. That makes no sense to me, maybe it will to your superior ecological brain. All I could see about the clippings was that they were fairly horrible accounts of murders or massacres of women. The worst was the New Delhi one, about "rafts of female corpses" in the river. The funniest(!) was the Texas Army officer who shot his wife, three daughters and his aunt, because God told him to clean the place up.

Barney's such an old dear, he's coming over Sunday to help me take off the downspout and see what's blocking it. He's dancing on air right now; since you left, his spruce budworm-moth antipheromone program finally paid off. You know he tested over 2,000 compounds? Well, it seems that good old 2,-097 really works. When I asked him what it does he just giggled, you know how shy he is with women. Anyway, it seems that a one-shot spray program will save the forests without harming a single other thing. Birds and people can eat it all day, he says.

Well sweetheart, that's all the news except Amy goes back to Chicago to school Sunday. The place will be a tomb, I'll miss

*her frightfully in spite of her being at the stage where I'm her
worst enemy. The sullen sexy subteens, Angie says. Amy sends
love to her Daddy. I send you my whole heart, all that words
can't say.*

Your Anne

Alan put the letter safely in his note file and glanced over the
rest of the thin packet of mail, refusing to let himself dream of
home and Anne. Barney's "fat envelope" wasn't there. He threw
himself on the rumpled bed, yanking off the lightcord a minute
before the town generator went off for the night. In the darkness
the list of places Barney had mentioned spread themselves around
a misty globe that turned, troublingly, briefly in his mind. Something . . .

But then the memory of the hideously parasitized children he
had worked with at the clinic that day took possession of his
thoughts. He set himself to considering the data he must collect.
Look for the vulnerable link in the behavioral chain—how often
Barney—Dr. Barnhard Braithwaite—had pounded it into his skull.
Where was it, where? In the morning he would start work on
bigger canefly cages. . . .

At that moment, five thousand miles north, Anne was writing:

*Oh, darling, darling, your first three letters are here, they all
came together. I knew you were writing. Forget what I said about
swarthy heiresses, that was all a joke. My darling I know, I know
. . . us. Those dreadful canefly larvae, those poor little kids. If you
weren't my husband I'd think you were a saint or something. (I
do anyway.)*

I have your letters pinned up all over the house, makes it a lot less lonely. No real news here except things feel kind of quiet and spooky. Barney and I got the downspout out, it was full of a big rotted hoard of squirrel nuts. They must have been dropping them down the top. I'll put a wire over it. (Don't worry, I'll use a ladder this time.)

Barney's in an odd, grim mood. He's taking this Sons of Adam thing very seriously, it seems he's going to be on the investigation committee if that ever gets off the ground. The weird part is that nobody seems to be doing anything, as if it's just too big. Selina Peters has been printing some acid comments, like When one man kills his wife you call it murder, but when enough do it we call it a lifestyle. I think it's spreading, but nobody knows because the media have been asked to downplay it. Barney says it's being viewed as a form of contagious hysteria. He insisted I send you this ghastly interview. It's not going to be published, of course. The quietness is worse, though, it's like something terrible was going on just out of sight. After reading Barney's thing I called up Pauline in San Diego to make sure she was all right. She sounded funny, as if she wasn't saying everything . . . my own sister. Just after she said things were great she suddenly asked if she could come and stay here awhile next month. I said come right away, but she wants to sell her house first. I wish she'd hurry.

Oh, the diesel car is okay now, it just needed its filter changed. I had to go out to Springfield to get one, but Eddie installed it for only $2.50. He's going to bankrupt his garage.

In case you didn't guess, those places of Barney's are all about latitude 30° N or S—the horse latitudes. When I said not exactly, he said remember the equatorial convergence zone shifts in winter, and to add in Libya, Osaka, and a place I forget—wait, Alice Springs, Australia. What has this to do with anything? I asked. He said, "Nothing—I hope." I leave it to you, great brains like Barney can be weird.

My dearest, here's all of me to all of you. Your letters make life possible. But don't feel you have to, I can tell how tired you must be. Just know we're together, always everywhere.

Your Anne

P.S. I had to open this to put Barney's thing in, it wasn't the secret police. Here it is. All love again. A.

In the goat-infested room where Alan read this, rain was drumming on the roof. He put the letter to his nose to catch the faint perfume once more, and folded it away. Then he pulled out the yellow flimsy Barney had sent and began to read, frowning.

PEEDSVILLE CULT/SONS OF ADAM SPECIAL. Statement by driver Sgt. Willard Mews, Globe Fork, Ark. We hit the roadblock about 80 miles west of Jacksonville. Major John Heinz of Ashton was expecting us, he gave us an escort of two riot vehicles headed by Capt. T. Parr. Major Heinz appeared shocked to see that the NIH medical team included two women doctors. He warned us in the strongest terms of the danger. So Dr. Patsy Putnam (Urbana, Ill.), the psychologist, decided to stay behind at the Army cordon. But Dr. Elaine Fay (Clinton, N.J.) insisted on going with us, saying she was the epi-something (epidemiologist).

We drove behind one of the riot cars at 30 mph for about an hour without seeing anything unusual. There were two big signs saying SONS OF ADAM—LIBERATED ZONE. We passed some small pecan packing plants and a citrus processing plant. The men there looked at us but did not do anything unusual. I didn't see any children or women of course. Just outside Peedsville we stopped at a big barrier made of oil drums in front of a large citrus warehouse. This area is old, sort of a shantytown and trailer park. The new part of town with the shopping center and developments is about a mile further on. A warehouse worker with a shotgun came out and told us to wait for the Mayor. I don't think he saw Dr. Elaine Fay then, she was sitting sort of bent down in back.

Mayor Blount drove up in a police cruiser and our chief, Dr. Premack, explained our mission from the Surgeon General. Dr. Premack was very

careful not to make any remarks insulting to the Mayor's religion. Mayor
Blount agreed to let the party go on into Peedsville to take samples of the
soil and water and so on and talk to the doctor who lives there. The mayor
was about 6′ 2″, weight maybe 230 or 240, tanned, with grayish hair. He
was smiling and chuckling in a friendly manner.

Then he looked inside the car and saw Dr. Elaine Fay and he blew up.
He started yelling we had to all get the hell back. But Dr. Premack talked
to him and cooled him down and finally the Mayor said Dr. Fay should
go into the warehouse office and stay there with the door closed. I had to
stay there too and see she didn't come out, and one of the Mayor's men
would drive the party.

So the medical people and the Mayor and one of the riot vehicles went
on into Peedsville and I took Dr. Fay back into the warehouse office and
sat down. It was real hot and stuffy. Dr. Fay opened a window, but when
I heard her trying to talk to an old man outside I told her she couldn't do
that and closed the window. The old man went away. Then she wanted
to talk to me but I told her I did not feel like conversing. I felt it was real
wrong, her being there.

So then she started looking through the office files and reading papers
there. I told her that was a bad idea, she shouldn't do that. She said the
government expected her to investigate. She showed me a booklet or
magazine they had there, it was called *Man Listens to God* by Reverend
McIllhenny. They had a carton full in the office. I started reading it and
Dr. Fay said she wanted to wash her hands. So I took her back along a kind
of enclosed hallway beside the conveyor to where the toilet was. There
were no doors or windows so I went back. After a while she called out that
there was a cot back there, she was going to lie down. I figured that was
all right because of the no windows, also I was glad to be rid of her
company.

When I got to reading the book it was very intriguing. It was very deep
thinking about how man is now on trial with God and if we fulfill our duty
God will bless us with a real new life on Earth. The signs and portents
show it. It wasn't like, you know, Sunday school stuff. It was deep.

After a while I heard some music and saw the soldiers from the other
riot car were across the street by the gas tanks, sitting in the shade of
some trees and kidding with the workers from the plant. One of them was

playing a guitar, not electric, just plain. It looked so peaceful.

Then Mayor Blount drove up alone in the cruiser and came in. When he saw I was reading the book he smiled at me sort of fatherly, but he looked tense. He asked me where Dr. Fay was and I told him she was lying down in back. He said that was okay. Then he kind of sighed and went back down the hall, closing the door behind him. I sat and listened to the guitar man, trying to hear what he was singing. I felt really hungry, my lunch was in Dr. Premack's car.

After a while the door opened and Mayor Blount came back in. He looked terrible, his clothes were messed up and he had bloody scrape marks on his face. He didn't say anything, he just looked at me hard and fierce, like he might have been disoriented. I saw his zipper was open and there was blood on his clothing and also on his (private parts).

I didn't feel frightened, I felt something important had happened. I tried to get him to sit down. But he motioned me to follow him back down the hall, to where Dr. Fay was. "You must see," he said. He went into the toilet and I went into a kind of little room there, where the cot was. The light was fairly good, reflected off the tin roof from where the walls stopped. I saw Dr. Fay lying on the cot in a peaceful appearance. She was lying straight, her clothing was to some extent different but her legs were together. I was glad to see that. Her blouse was pulled up and I saw there was a cut or incision on her abdomen. The blood was coming out there, or it had been coming out there, like a mouth. It wasn't moving at this time. Also her throat was cut open.

I returned to the office. Mayor Blount was sitting down, looking very tired. He had cleaned himself off. He said, "I did it for you. Do you understand?"

He seemed like my father, I can't say it better than that. I realized he was under a terrible strain, he had taken a lot on himself for me. He went on to explain how Dr. Fay was very dangerous, she was what they call a cripto-female (crypto?), the most dangerous kind. He had exposed her and purified the situation. He was very straightforward, I didn't feel confused at all, I knew he had done what was right.

We discussed the book, how man must purify himself and show God a clean world. He said some people raise the question of how can man reproduce without women but such people miss the point. The point is that as long as man depends on the old filthy animal way God won't help him. When man gets rid of his animal part, which is woman, this is the signal God is waiting for. Then God will reveal the new true clean way, maybe angels will come bringing new souls, or maybe we will live forever, but it is not our place to speculate, only to obey. He said some men here had seen an Angel of the Lord. This was very deep, it seemed like it echoed inside me, I felt it was an inspiration.

Then the medical party drove up and I told Dr. Premack that Dr. Fay had been taken care of and sent away, and I got in the car to drive them out of the Liberated Zone. However four of the six soldiers from the roadblock refused to leave. Capt. Parr tried to argue them out of it but finally agreed they could stay to guard the oil-drum barrier.

I would have liked to stay too, the place was so peaceful, but they need-ed me to drive the car. If I had known there would be all this hassle I never would have done them the favor. I am not crazy and I have not done anything wrong and my lawyer will get me out. That is all I have to say.

In Cuyapán the hot afternoon rain had temporarily ceased. As Alan's fingers let go of Sgt. Willard Mews's wretched document he caught sight of pencil-scrawled words in the margin. Barney's spider hand. He squinted.

"Man's religion and metaphysics are the voices of his glands. Schönweiser, 1878."

Who the devil Schönweiser was Alan didn't know, but he knew what Barney was conveying. This murderous crackpot religion of McWhosis was a symptom, not a cause. Barney believed some-thing was physically affecting the Peedsville men, generating psy-chosis, and a local religious demagogue had sprung up to "explain" it.

Well, maybe. But cause or effect, Alan thought only of one thing: eight hundred miles from Peedsville to Ann Arbor. Anne should be safe. She *had* to be.

He threw himself on the lumpy cot, his mind going back exul-tantly to his work. At the cost of a million bites and cane cuts he was pretty sure he'd found the weak link in the canefly cycle. The male mass-mating behavior, the comparative scarcity of ovulant females. It would be the screwfly solution all over again with the sexes reversed. Concentrate the pheromone, release sterilized females. Luckily the breeding populations were comparatively isolated. In a couple of seasons they ought to have it. Have to let them go on spraying poison meanwhile, of course; damn pity, it was slaughtering everything and getting in the water, and the caneflies had evolved to immunity anyway. But in a couple of seasons, maybe three, they could drop the canefly populations below reproductive viability. No more tormented human bodies with those stinking larvae in the nasal passages and brain. . . . He drifted off for a nap, grinning.

Up north, Anne was biting her lip in shame and pain.

Sweetheart, I shouldn't admit it but your wife is ⱥⱥⱥⱥⱥ a bit jittery. Just female nerves or something, nothing to worry about. Everything is normal up here. It's so eerily normal, nothing in the papers, nothing anywhere except what I hear through Barney and Lillian. But Pauline's phone won't answer out in San Diego; the fifth day some strange man yelled at me and banged the phone down. Maybe she's sold her house—but why wouldn't she call?

Lillian's on some kind of Save-the-Women committee, like we were an endangered species, ha-ha—you know Lillian. It seems the Red Cross has started setting up camps. But she says, after the first rush, only a trickle are coming out of what they call "the affected areas." Not many children, either, even little boys. And they have some air photos around Lubbock showing what look like mass graves. Oh, Alan . . . so far it seems to be mostly spreading west, but something's happening in St. Louis, they're cut off. So many places seem to have just vanished from the news, I had a nightmare that there isn't a woman left alive down there. And nobody's doing anything. They talked about spraying with tran-

*quillizers for a while and then that died out. What could it do?
Somebody at the U.N. has proposed a convention on—you won't
believe this—femicide. It sounds like a deodorant spray.*

*Excuse me, honey, I seem to be a little hysterical. George Searles
came back from Georgia talking about God's Will—Searles the
lifelong atheist. Alan, something crazy is happening.*

*But there aren't any facts. Nothing. The Surgeon General issued
a report on the bodies of the Rahway Rip-Breast Team—I guess I
didn't tell you about that. Anyway, they could find no pathology.
Milton Baines wrote a letter saying in the present state of the art
we can't distinguish the brain of a saint from a psychopathic
killer, so how could they expect to find what they don't know how
to look for?*

*Well, enough of these jitters. It'll be all over by the time you get
back, just history. Everything's fine here, I fixed the car's muffler
again. And Amy's coming home for the vacation, that'll get my
mind off faraway problems.*

*Oh, something amusing to end with—Angie told me what Bar-
ney's enzyme does to the spruce budworm. It seems it blocks the
male from turning around after he connects with the female, so
he mates with her head instead. Like clockwork with a cog missing. There're going to be some pretty puzzled female spruceworms.
Now why couldn't Barney tell me that? He really is such a sweet
shy old dear. He's given me some stuff to put in, as usual. I didn't
read it.*

Now don't worry, my darling, everything's fine.

I love you, I love you so.

Always, all ways your Anne

Two weeks later in Cuyapán when Barney's enclosures slid
out of the envelope, Alan didn't read them either. He stuffed
them into the pocket of his bush jacket with a shaking hand
and started bundling his notes together on the rickety table,

with a scrawled note to Sister Dominique on top. The hell with the canefly, the hell with everything except that tremor in his Anne's firm handwriting. The hell with being five thousand miles away from his woman, his child, while some deadly madness raged. He crammed his meager belongings into his duffel. If he hurried he could catch the bus through to Bogotá and maybe make the Miami flight.

He made it, but in Miami he found the planes north jammed. He failed a quick standby; six hours to wait. Time to call Anne. When the call got through some difficulty he was unprepared for the rush of joy and relief that burst along the wires.

"Thank God—I can't believe it—Oh, Alan, my darling, are you really—I can't believe—"

He found he was repeating too, and all mixed up with the canefly data. They were both laughing hysterically when he finally hung up.

Six hours. He settled in a frayed plastic chair opposite Aerolineas Argentinas, his mind half back at the clinic, half on the throngs moving by him. Something was oddly different here, he perceived presently. Where was the decorative fauna he usually enjoyed in Miami, the parade of young girls in crotch-tight pastel jeans? The flounces, boots, wild hats and hairdos, and startling expanses of newly tanned skin, the brilliant fabrics barely confining the bob of breasts and buttocks? Not here—but wait; looking closely, he glimpsed two young faces hidden under unbecoming parkas, their bodies draped in bulky, nondescript skirts. In fact, all down the long vista he could see the same thing: hooded ponchos, heaped-on clothes, and baggy pants, dull colors. A new style? No, he thought not. It seemed to him their movements suggested furtiveness, timidity. And they moved in groups. He watched a lone girl struggle to catch up with others ahead of her, apparently strangers. They accepted her wordlessly.

They're frightened, he thought. Afraid of attracting notice.

Even that gray-haired matron in a pantsuit, resolutely leading a flock of kids, was glancing around nervously.

And at the Argentine desk opposite he saw another odd thing: two lines had a big sign over them, *Mujeres*. Women. They were crowded with the shapeless forms and very quiet.

The men seemed to be behaving normally; hurrying, lounging, griping, and joking in the lines as they kicked their luggage along. But Alan felt an undercurrent of tension, like an irritant in the air. Outside the line of storefronts behind him a few isolated men seemed to be handing out tracts. An airport attendant spoke to the nearest man; he merely shrugged and moved a few doors down.

To distract himself Alan picked up a *Miami Herald* from the next seat. It was surprisingly thin. The international news occupied him for a while; he had seen none for weeks. It too had a strange, empty quality, even the bad news seemed to have dried up. The African war which had been going on seemed to be over, or went unreported. A trade summit meeting was haggling over grain and steel prices. He found himself at the obituary pages, columns of close-set type dominated by the photo of a defunct ex-senator. Then his eye fell on two announcements at the bottom of the page. One was too flowery for quick comprehension, but the other stated in bold plain type:

THE FORSETTE FUNERAL HOME
REGRETFULLY ANNOUNCES
IT WILL NO LONGER ACCEPT FEMALE
CADAVERS

Slowly he folded the paper, staring at it numbly. On the back was an item headed "Navigational Hazard Warning," in the shipping news. Without really taking it in, he read:

AP/NASSAU: The excursion liner *Carib Swallow* reached port under tow today after striking an obstruction in the Gulf Stream off Cape Hatteras. The obstruction was identified as part of a commercial trawler's seine floated by female corpses. This confirms reports from Florida and the Gulf of the use of such seines, some of them over a mile in length. Similar reports coming from the Pacific coast and as far away as Japan indicate a growing hazard to coastwise shipping.

Alan flung the thing into the trash receptacle and sat rubbing his forehead and eyes. Thank God he had followed his impulse to come home. He felt totally disoriented, as though he had landed by error on another planet. Four and a half hours more to wait. . . . At length he recalled the stuff from Barney he had thrust in his pocket, and pulled it out and smoothed it.

The top item was from the *Ann Arbor News.* Dr. Lillian Dash, together with several hundred other members of her organization, had been arrested for demonstrating without a permit in front of the White House. They had started a fire in a garbage can, which was considered particularly heinous. A number of women's groups had participated; the total struck Alan as more like thousands than hundreds. Extraordinary security precautions were being taken despite the fact that the President was out of town at the time.

The next item had to be Barney's acerbic humor.

UP/VATICAN CITY, 19 JUNE. Pope John IV today intimated that he does not plan to comment officially on the so-called Pauline Purification cults advocating the elimination of women as a means of justifying man to God. A spokesman emphasized that the Church takes no position on these cults but repudiates any doctrine involving a "challenge" to or from God to reveal His further plans for man.

Cardinal Fazzoli, spokesman for the European Pauline movement, reaffirmed his view that the Scriptures define woman as merely a temporary companion and instrument of Man. Women, he states, are nowhere defined as human, but merely as a transitional expedient or state. "The time of transition to full humanity is at hand," he concluded.

The next item was a thin-paper Xerox from a recent issue of *Science:*

SUMMARY REPORT OF THE AD HOC
EMERGENCY COMMITTEE ON FEMICIDE

The recent worldwide though localized outbreaks of femicide appear to represent a recurrence of similar outbreaks by groups or sects which are not uncommon in world history in times of psychic stress. In this case the root cause is undoubtedly the speed of social and technological change augmented by population pressure, and the spread and scope are aggravated by instantaneous world communications, thus exposing more susceptible persons. It is not viewed as a medical or epidemiological problem; no physical pathology has been found. Rather it is more akin to the various manias which swept Europe in the seventeenth century, e.g., the Dancing Manias; and like them, should run its course and disappear. The chiliastic cults which have sprung up around the affected areas appear to be unrelated, having in common only the idea that a new means of human reproduction will be revealed as a result of the "purifying" elimination of women.

We recommended that (1) inflammatory and sensational reporting be suspended; (2) refugee centers be set up and maintained for women escapees from the focal areas; (3) containment of affected areas by military cordon be continued and enforced; and (4) after a cooling-down period and the subsidence of the mania, qualified mental health teams and appropriate professional personnel go in to undertake rehabilitation.

SUMMARY OF THE MINORITY
REPORT OF THE AD HOC COMMITTEE

The nine members signing this report agree that there is no evidence for epidemiological contagion of femicide in the strict sense. *However,* the geographical relation of the focal areas of outbreak strongly suggests that they cannot be dismissed as purely psychosocial phenomena. The initial outbreaks have occurred around the globe near the 30th parallel, the area of principal atmospheric downflow of upper winds coming from the Intertropical Convergence Zone. An agent or condition in the upper equatorial atmosphere would thus be expected to reach ground level along the 30th parallel, with certain seasonal variations. One principal variation is that the downflow moves north over the East Asian continent during the late winter months, and those areas south of it (Arabia, Western India, parts of North Africa) have in fact been free of outbreaks until recently, when the downflow zone moved south. A similar downflow occurs in the Southern Hemisphere, and outbreaks have been reported along the 30th parallel running through Pretoria, and Alice Springs, Australia. (Information from Argentina is currently unavailable.)

This geographical correlation cannot be dismissed, and it is therefore urged that an intensified search for a physical cause be instituted. It is also urgently recommended that the rate of spread from known focal points be correlated with wind conditions. A watch for similar outbreaks along the secondary down-welling zones at 60° north and south should be kept.

(signed for the minority)
Barnhard Braithwaite

Alan grinned reminiscently at his old friend's name, which seemed to restore normalcy and stability to the world. It looked as if Barney was onto something, too, despite the prevalence of horses' asses. He frowned, puzzling it out.

Then his face slowly changed as he thought how it would be, going home to Anne. In a few short hours his arms would be around her, the tall, secretly beautiful body that had come to obsess him. Theirs had been a late-blooming love. They'd married, he supposed now, out of friendship, even out of friends' pressure. Everyone said they were made for each other, he big and chunky and blond, she willowy brunette; both shy, highly controlled, cerebral types. For the first few years the friendship had held, but sex hadn't been all that much. Conventional necessity. Politely reassuring each other, privately—he could say it now—disappointing.

But then, when Amy was a toddler, something had happened. A miraculous inner portal of sensuality had slowly opened to them, a liberation into their own secret unsuspected heaven of fully physical bliss . . . Jesus, but it had been a wrench when the Colombia thing had come up. Only their absolute sureness of each other had made him take it. And now, to be about to have her again, trebly desirable from the spice of separation—feeling-see-ing-hearing-smelling-grasping. He shifted in his seat to conceal his body's excitement, half mesmerized by fantasy.

And Amy would be there, too; he grinned at the memory of that prepubescent little body plastered against him. She was going to be a handful, all right. His manhood understood Amy a lot better than her mother did; no cerebral phase for Amy. . . . But Anne, his exquisite shy one, with whom he'd found the way into the almost unendurable transports of the flesh. . . . First the conventional greeting, he thought; the news, the unspoken, savored, mounting excitement behind their eyes; the light touches; then the seeking of their own room, the falling clothes, the caresses, gentle at first—the flesh, the *nakedness*—the delicate teasing, the grasp, the first thrust—

A terrible alarm bell went off in his head. Exploded from his dream, he stared around, then finally down at his hands. *What was he doing with his open clasp knife in his fist?*

Stunned, he felt for the last shreds of his fantasy and realized that the tactile images had not been of caresses, but of a frail neck strangling in his fist, the thrust had been the plunge of a blade seeking vitals. In his arms, legs, phantasms of striking and trampling, bones cracking. And Amy—

Oh, God. Oh, God—

Not sex, bloodlust.

That was what he had been dreaming. The sex was there, but it was driving some engine of death.

Numbly he put the knife away, thinking only over and over, It's got me. It's got me. Whatever it is, it's got me. *I can't go home.*

After an unknown time he got up and made his way to the United counter to turn in his ticket. The line was long. As he waited, his mind cleared a little. What could he do here in Miami? Wouldn't it be better to get back to Ann Arbor and turn himself in to Barney? Barney could help him, if anyone could. Yes, that was best. But first he had to warn Anne.

The connection took even longer this time. When Anne finally answered he found himself blurting unintelligibly, it took a while to make her understand he wasn't talking about a plane delay.

"I tell you, I've caught it. Listen, Anne, for God's sake. If I should come to the house don't let me come near you. I mean it. I mean it. I'm going to the lab, but I might lose control and try to get to you. Is Barney there?"

"Yes, but darling—"

"Listen. Maybe he can fix me, maybe this'll wear off. But I'm not safe, Anne. Anne, I'd kill you, can you understand? Get a—get a weapon. I'll try not to come to the house. But if I do, don't let me get near you. Or Amy. It's a sickness, it's real. Treat me—treat me like a fucking wild animal. Anne, say you understand, say you'll do it."

They were both crying when he hung up.

He went shaking back to sit and wait. After a time his head seemed to clear a little more. *Doctor, try to think.* The first thing he thought of was to take the loathsome knife and throw it down a trash slot. As he did so he realized there was one more piece of Barney's material in his pocket. He uncrumpled it; it seemed to be a clipping from *Nature.*

At the top was Barney's scrawl: *"Only guy making sense. U.K. infected now, Oslo, Copenhagen out of communication. Damfools still won't listen. Stay put."*

COMMUNICATION FROM

PROFESSOR IAN MACINTYRE, GLASGOW UNIV.

A potential difficulty for our species has always been implicit in the close linkage between the behavioural expression of aggression/predation and sexual reproduction in the male. This close linkage involves (a) many neuromuscular pathways which are utilized both in predatory and sexual pursuit: grasping, mounting, etc., and (b) similar states of adrenergic arousal which are activated in both. The same linkage is seen in the males of many other species; in some, the expression of aggression and copulation alternate or even coexist, an all-too-familiar example being the common house cat. Males of many species bite, claw, bruise, tread, or otherwise assault receptive females during the act of intercourse; indeed, in some species the male attack is necessary for female ovulation to occur.

In many if not all species it is the aggressive behaviour which appears first, and then changes to copulatory behaviour when the appropriate signal is presented (e.g., the three-tined stickleback and the European robin). Lacking the inhibiting signal, the male's fighting response continues and the female is attacked or driven off.

It seems therefore appropriate to speculate that the present crisis might be caused by some substance, perhaps at the viral or enzymatic level, which effects a failure of the switching or triggering function in the higher primates. (Note: Zoo gorillas and chimpanzees have recently been observed to attack or destroy their mates; rhesus not.) Such a dysfunction could be expressed by the failure of mating behaviour to modify or supervene over the aggressive/predatory response; i.e., sexual stimulation would produce attack only, the stimulation discharging itself through the destruction of the stimulating object.

In this connection it might be noted that exactly this condition is a commonplace of male functional pathology in those cases where murder occurs as a response to, and apparent completion of, sexual desire.

It should be emphasized that the aggression/copulation linkage discussed here is specific to the male; the female response (e.g., lordotic reflex) being of a different nature.

Alan sat holding the crumpled sheet a long time; the dry, stilted Scottish phrases seemed to help clear his head, despite the sense of brooding tension all around him. Well, if pollution or whatever had produced some substance, it could presumably be countered, filtered, neutralized. Very, very carefully, he let himself consider his life with Anne, his sexuality. Yes; much of their loveplay could be viewed as genitalized, sexually gentled savagery. Play-predation. . . . He turned his mind quickly away. Some writer's phrase occurred to him: "The panic element in all sex." Who? Fritz Leiber? The violation of social distance, maybe; another threatening element. Whatever, it's our weak link, he thought. Our vulnerability. . . . The dreadful feeling of *rightness* he had experienced when he found himself knife in hand, fantasizing violence, came back to him. As though it was the right, the only way. Was that what

Barney's budworms felt when they mated with their females wrong-end-to?

At long length, he became aware of body need and sought a toilet. The place was empty, except for what he took to be a heap of clothes blocking the door of the far stall. Then he saw the red-brown pool in which it lay, and the bluish mounds of bare, thin buttocks. He backed out, not breathing, and fled into the nearest crowd, knowing he was not the first to have done so.

Of course. Any sexual drive. Boys, men, too.

At the next washroom he watched to see men enter and leave normally before he ventured in.

Afterward he returned to sit, waiting, repeating over and over to himself: *Go to the lab. Don't go home. Go straight to the lab.* Three more hours; he sat numbly at 26° N, 81° W, breathing, breathing. . . .

Dear diary. Big scene tonite, Daddy came home!!! Only he acted so funny, he had the taxi wait and just held onto the doorway, he wouldn't touch me or let us come near him. (I mean funny weird, not funny ha-ha.) He said, I have something to tell you, this is getting worse not better. I'm going to sleep in the lab but I want you to get out, Anne, Anne, I can't trust myself any more. First thing in the morning you both get on the plane for Martha's and stay there. So I thought he had to be joking, I mean with the dance next week and Aunt Martha lives in Whitehorse where there's nothing nothing nothing. So I was yelling and Mother was yelling and Daddy was groaning. Go now! And then he started crying. Crying!!! So I realized, wow, this is serious, and I started to go over to him but Mother yanked me back and then I saw she had this big KNIFE!!! And she shoved me in back of her and started crying too Oh Alan, Oh Alan, like she was insane. So I said, Daddy, I'll never leave you, it felt like the perfect thing to say. And it was thrilling, he looked at me real sad and deep like I was a grown-up while Mother was treating me like I was a mere infant as usual.

*But Mother ruined it, raving, Alan the child is mad, darling go.
So he ran out the door yelling, Be gone. Take the car. Get out
before I come back.*

*Oh I forgot to say I was wearing what but my gooby green with
my curltites still on, wouldn't you know of all the shitty luck, how
could I have known such a beautiful scene was ahead we never
know life's cruel whimsy. And mother is dragging out suitcases
yelling Pack your things hurry! So she's going I guess but I am not
repeat not going to spend the fall sitting in Aunt Martha's grain
silo and lose the dance and all my summer credits. And Daddy
was trying to communicate with us, right? I think their relationship is obsolete. So when she goes upstairs I am splitting, I am
going to go over to the lab and see Daddy.*

*Oh P.S. Diane tore my yellow jeans. She promised me I could use
her pink ones. Ha-ha that'll be the day.*

I ripped that page out of Amy's diary when I heard the squad
car coming. I never opened her diary before but when I found
she'd gone I looked. . . . Oh, my darling girl. She went to him, my
little girl, my poor little fool child. Maybe if I'd taken time to
explain, maybe—

Excuse me, Barney. The stuff is wearing off, the shots they gave
me. I didn't feel anything. I mean, I knew somebody's daughter
went to see her father and he killed her. And cut his throat. But
it didn't mean anything.

Alan's note, they gave me that but then they took it away. Why
did they have to do that? His last handwriting, the last words he
wrote before his hand picked up the, before he—

I remember it. *"Sudden and light as that, the bonds gave And
we learned of finalities besides the grave.* The bonds of our humanity have broken, we are finished. I love—"

I'm all right, Barney, really. Who wrote that, Robert Frost? *The
bonds gave.* . . . Oh, he said tell Barney, *"The terrible rightness."*
What does that mean?

You can't answer that, Barney dear. I'm just writing this to stay sane, I'll put it in your hidey-hole. Thank you, thank you, Barney dear. Even as blurry as I was, I knew it was you. All the time you were cutting off my hair and rubbing dirt on my face, I knew it was right because it was you. Barney, I never thought of you as those horrible words you said. You were always Dear Barney.

By the time the stuff wore off I had done everything you said, the gas, the groceries. Now I'm here in your cabin. With those clothes you made me put on I guess I do look like a boy, the gas man called me "Mister."

I still can't really realize, I have to stop myself from rushing back. But you saved my life, I know that. The first trip in I got a paper, I saw where they bombed the Apostle Islands refuge. And it had about those three women stealing the Air Force plane and bombing Dallas, too. Of course they shot them down, over the Gulf. Isn't it strange how we do nothing? Just get killed by ones and twos. Or more, now they've started on the refuges. . . . Like hypnotized rabbits. We're a toothless race.

Do you know I never said "we" meaning women before? "We" was always me and Alan, and Amy of course. Being killed selectively encourages group identification. . . . You see how sane-headed I am.

But I still can't really realize.

My first trip in was for salt and kerosene. I went to that little Red Deer store and got my stuff from the old man in the back, as you told me—you see, I remembered! He called me "Boy," but I think maybe he suspects. He knows I'm staying at your cabin.

Anyway, some men and boys came in the front. They were all so *normal*, laughing and kidding. I just couldn't believe, Barney. In fact I started to go out past them when I heard one of them say, "Heinz saw an angel." An *angel*. So I stopped and listened. They said it was big and sparkly. Coming to see if man is carrying out God's Will, one of them said. And he said, Moosonee is now a liberated zone, and all up by Hudson Bay. I turned and got out the

back, fast. The old man had heard them too. He said to me quietly,
"I'll miss the kids."

Hudson Bay, Barney, that means it's coming from the north too,
doesn't it? That must be about 60°.

But I have to go back once again, to get some fishhooks. I can't
live on bread. Last week I found a deer some poacher had killed,
just the head and legs. I made a stew. It was a doe. Her eyes; I
wonder if mine look like that now.

I went to get the fishhooks today. It was bad, I can't ever go back.
There were some men in front again, but they were different.
Mean and tense. No boys. And there was a new sign out in front.
I couldn't see it; maybe it says Liberated Zone too.

The old man gave me the hooks quick and whispered to me,
"Boy, them woods'll be full of hunters next week." I almost ran
out.

About a mile down the road a blue pickup started to chase me.
I guess he wasn't from around there, I ran the VW into a logging
draw and he roared on by. After a long while I drove out and came
on back, but I left the car about a mile from here and hiked in. It's
surprising how hard it is to pile enough brush to hide a yellow VW.

Barney, I can't stay here. I'm eating perch raw so nobody will
see my smoke, but those hunters will be coming through. I'm
going to move my sleeping bag out to the swamp by that big rock,
I don't think many people go there.

Since the last lines I moved out. It feels safer. Oh, Barney, how
did this *happen?*

Fast, that's how. Six months ago I was Dr. Anne Alstein. Now I'm
a widow and bereaved mother, dirty and hungry, squatting in a
swamp in mortal fear. Funny if I'm the last woman left alive on
Earth. I guess the last one around here, anyway. May be some
holed out in the Himalayas, or sneaking through the wreck of New
York City. How can we last?

We can't.

And I can't survive the winter here, Barney. It gets to 40° below. I'd have to have a fire, they'd see the smoke. Even if I worked my way south, the woods end in a couple hundred miles. I'd be potted like a duck. No. No use. Maybe somebody is trying something somewhere, but it won't reach here in time . . . and what do I have to live for?

No. I'll just make a good end, say up on that rock where I can see the stars. After I go back and leave this for you. I'll wait to see the beautiful color in the trees one last time.

Goodbye, dearest dearest Barney.

I know what I'll scratch for an epitaph.

HERE LIES THE SECOND MEANEST
PRIMATE ON EARTH

I guess nobody will ever read this, unless I get the nerve and energy to take it back to Barney's. Probably I won't. Leave it in a Baggie, I have one here; maybe Barney will come and look. I'm up on the big rock now. The moon is going to rise soon, I'll do it then. Mosquitoes, be patient. You'll have all you want.

The thing I have to write down is that I saw an angel too. This morning. It was big and sparkly, like the man said; like a Christmas tree without the tree. But I knew it was real because the frogs stopped croaking and two bluejays gave alarm calls. That's important; it was *really there.*

I watched it, sitting under my rock. It didn't move much. It sort of bent over and picked up something, leaves or twigs, I couldn't see. Then it did something with them around its middle, like putting them into an invisible sample pocket.

Let me repeat—it was *there.* Barney, if you're reading this, THERE ARE THINGS HERE. And I think they've done whatever it is to us. Made us kill ourselves off.

Why? Well, it's a nice place, if it wasn't for people. How do you get rid of people? Bombs, death rays—all very primitive. Leave a big mess. Destroy everything, craters, radioactivity, ruin the place.

This way there's no muss, no fuss. Just like what we did to the screwfly. Pinpoint the weak link, wait a bit while we do it for them. Only a few bones around; make good fertilizer.

Barney dear, goodbye. I saw it. It was there.

But it wasn't an angel.

I think I saw a real estate agent.

EDWARD BRYANT

Particle Theory

I first met Ed Bryant when he was a young student at an early Clarion SF Writers Workshop where I was an *almost* equally as young teacher. In the dozen years since—while unfortunately I have seen him less than a dozen times—he's produced a series of moving and richly felt tales, among which this is one of my favorites.

꙲

꙲

I see my shadow flung like black iron against the wall. My sundeck
blazes with untimely summer. Eliot was wrong; Frost, right.
Nanoseconds . . .
Death is as relativistic as any other apparent constant. I wonder,
Am I dying?

I thought it was a cliché with no underlying truth.
"Lives *do* flash in a compressed instant before dying eyes,"
said Amanda. She poured me another glass of burgundy the
color of her hair. The fire highlighted both. "A psychologist
named Noyes—" She broke off and smiled at me. "You really
want to hear this?"
"Sure." The fireplace light softened the taut planes of her face.
I saw a flicker of the gentler beauty she had possessed thirty years
before.
"Noyes catalogued testimonial evidence for death's-door
phenomena in the early seventies. He termed it 'life review,' the
second of three clearly definable steps in the process of dying; like
a movie, and not necessarily linear."
I drink, I have a low threshold of intoxication, I ramble. "Why
does it happen? How?" I didn't like the desperation in my voice.

We were suddenly much further apart than the geography of the table separating us; I looked in Amanda's eyes for some memory of Lisa. "Life goes shooting off—or we recede from it—like Earth and an interstellar probe irrevocably severed. Mutual recession at light-speed, and the dark fills in the gap." I held my glass by the stem, rotated it, peered through the distorting bowl.

Pine logs crackled. Amanda turned her head, and her eyes' image shattered in the flames.

The glare, the glare—

When I was thirty I made aggrieved noises because I'd screwed around for the past ten years and not accomplished nearly as much as I should. Lisa only laughed, which sent me into a transient rage and a longer-lasting sulk before I realized hers was the only appropriate response.

"Silly, silly," she said. "A watered-down Byronic character, full of self-pity and sloppy self-adulation." She blocked my exit from the kitchen and said millimeters from my face, "It's not as though you're waking up at thirty to discover that only fifty-six people have heard of you."

I stuttered over a weak retort.

"Fifty-seven?" She laughed; I laughed.

Then I was forty and went through the same pseudo-menopausal trauma. Admittedly, I hadn't done any work at all for nearly a year, and any *good* work for two. Lisa didn't laugh this time; she did what she could, which was mainly to stay out of my way while I alternately moped and raged around the coast house southwest of Portland. Royalties from the book I'd done on the fusion breakthrough kept us in groceries and mortgage payments.

"Listen, maybe if I'd go away for a while—" she said. "Maybe it would help for you to be alone." Temporary separations weren't alien to our marriage; we'd once figured that our relationship got measurably rockier if we spent more than about sixty percent of our time together. It had been a long winter and we were overdue; but then Lisa looked intently at my face and decided not to leave. Two months later I worked through the problems in my skull, and asked her for solitude. She knew me well—well enough to laugh again because she knew I was waking out of another mental hibernation.

She got onto a jetliner on a gray winter day and headed east for my parents' old place in southern Colorado. The jetway for the flight was out of commission that afternoon, so the airline people had to roll out one of the old wheeled stairways. Just before she stepped into the cabin, Lisa paused and waved back from the head of the stairs; her dark hair curled about her face in the wind.

Two months later I'd roughed out most of the first draft for my initial book about the reproductive revolution. At least once a week I would call Lisa and she'd tell me about the photos she was taking river-running on an icy Colorado or Platte. Then I'd use her as a sounding board for speculations about ectogenesis, heterogynes, or the imminent emergence of an exploited human host-mother class.

"So what'll we do when you finish the first draft, Nick?"

"Maybe we'll take a leisurely month on the Trans-Canadian Railroad."

"Spring in the provinces . . ."

Then the initial draft was completed and so was Lisa's Colorado adventure. "Do you know how badly I want to see you?" she said.

"Almost as badly as I want to see you."

"Oh, no," she said. "Let me tell you—"

What she told me no doubt violated state and federal laws and probably telephone company tariffs as well. The frustration of only hearing her voice through the wire made me twine my legs like a contortionist.

"Nick, I'll book a flight out of Denver. I'll let you know."

I think she wanted to surprise me. Lisa didn't tell me when she booked the flight. The airline let me know.

And now I'm fifty-one. The pendulum has swung and I again bitterly resent not having achieved more. There is so much work left undone; should I live for centuries, I still could not complete it all. That, however, will not be a problem.

I am told that the goddamned level of acid phosphatase in my goddamned blood is elevated. How banal that single fact sounds, how sterile; and how self-pitying the phraseology. Can't I afford a luxurious tear, Lisa?

Lisa?

Death: I wish to determine my own time.

"Charming," I said much later. "End of the world."

My friend Denton, the young radio astronomer, said, "Christ almighty! Your damned jokes. How can you make a pun about this?"

"It keeps me from crying," I said quietly. "Wailing and breast-beating won't make a difference."

"Calm, so calm." She looked at me peculiarly.

"I've seen the enemy," I said. "I've had time to consider it."

Her face was thoughtful, eyes focused somewhere beyond this cluttered office. "*If* you're right," she said, "it could be the most fantastic event a scientist could observe and record." Her eyes refocused and met mine. "Or it might be the most frightening, a final horror."

"Choose one," I said.

"If I believed you at all."

"I'm dealing in speculations."

"Fantasies," she said.

"However you want to term it." I got up and moved to the door. "I don't think there's much time. You've never seen where I live. Come"—I hesitated—"visit me if you care to. I'd like that—to have you there."

"Maybe," she said.

I should not have left the situation ambiguous.

I didn't know that in another hour, after I had left her office, pulled my car out of the Gamow Peak parking lot and driven down to the valley, Denton would settle herself behind the wheel of her sports car and gun it onto the Peak road. Tourists saw her go off the switchback. A Highway Department crew pried her loose from the embrace of Lotus and lodgepole.

When I got the news I grieved for her, wondering if this were the price of belief. I drove to the hospital and, because no next of kin had been found and Amanda intervened, the doctors let me stand beside the bed.

I had never seen such still features, never such stasis short of actual death. I waited an hour, seconds sweeping silently from the wall clock, until the urge to return home was overpowering.

I could wait no longer because daylight was coming and I would tell no one.

Toward the beginning:

I've tolerated doctors as individuals; as a class they terrify me. It's a dread like shark attacks or dying by fire. But eventually I made the appointment for an examination, drove to the sparkling white clinic on the appointed day and spent a surly half hour reading a year-old issue of *Popular Science* in the waiting room.

"Mr. Richmond?" the smiling nurse finally said. I followed her back to the examination room. "Doctor will be here in just a minute." She left. I sat apprehensively on the edge of the examination table. After two minutes I heard the rustling of my file being removed from the outside rack. Then the door opened.

"How's it going?" said my doctor. "I haven't seen you in a while."

"Can't complain," I said, reverting to accustomed medical ritual. "No flu so far this winter. The shot must have been soon enough."

Amanda watched me patiently. "You're not a hypochondriac. You don't need continual reassurance—or sleeping pills—any more. You're not a medical groupie, God knows. So what is it?"

"Uh," I said. I spread my hands helplessly.

"Nicholas." Get-on-with-it-I'm-busy-today sharpness edged her voice.

"Don't imitate my maiden aunt."

"All right, *Nick,*" she said. "What's wrong?"

"I'm having trouble urinating."

She jotted something down. Without looking up: "What kind of trouble?"

"Straining."

"For how long?"

"Six, maybe seven months. It's been a gradual thing."

"Anything else you've noticed?"

"Increased frequency."

"That's all?"

"Well," I said, "afterwards, I, uh, dribble."

She listed, as though by rote: "Pain, burning, urgency, hesitancy, change in stream of urine? Incontinence, change in size of stream, change in appearance of urine?"

"What?"

"Darker, lighter, cloudy, blood discharge from penis, VD exposure, fever, night sweats?"

I answered with a variety of nods or monosyllables.

"Mmh." She continued to write on the pad, then snapped it shut. "Okay, Nick, would you get your clothes off?" And when I had stripped: "Please lie on the table. On your stomach."

"The greased finger?" I said. "Oh shit."

Amanda tore a disposable glove off the roll. It crackled as she put it on. "You think I get a thrill out of this?" She's been my GP for a long time.

When it was over and I sat gingerly and uncomfortably on the edge of the examining table, I said, "Well?"

Amanda again scribbled on a sheet. "I'm sending you to a urologist. He's just a couple of blocks away. I'll phone over. Try to get an appointment in—oh, inside of a week."

"Give me something better," I said, "or I'll go to the library and check out a handbook of symptoms."

She met my eyes with a candid blue gaze. "I want a specialist to check out the obstruction."

"You found something when you stuck your finger in?"

"Crude, Nicholas." She half smiled. "Your prostate is hard—stony. There could be a number of reasons."

"What John Wayne used to call the Big C?"

"Prostatic cancer," she said, "is relatively infrequent in a man of your age." She glanced down at my records. "Fifty."

"Fifty-one," I said, wanting to shift the tone, trying, failing. "You didn't send me a card on my birthday."

"But it's not impossible," Amanda said. She stood. "Come on up to the front desk. I want an appointment with you after the urology results come back." As always, she patted me on the shoulder as she followed me out of the examination room. But this time there was slightly too much tension in her fingers.

I was seeing grassy hummocks and marble slabs in my mind and didn't pay attention to my surroundings as I exited the waiting room.

"Nick?" A soft Oklahoma accent.

I turned back from the outer door, looked down, saw tousled hair. Jackie Denton, one of the bright young minds out at the Gamow Peak Observatory, held the well-thumbed copy of *Popular Science* loosely in her lap. She honked and snuffled into a deteriorating Kleenex. "Don't get too close. Probably doesn't matter at this point. Flu. You?" Her green irises were red-rimmed.

I fluttered my hands vaguely. "I had my shots."

"Yeah." She snuffled again. "I was going to call you later on from work. See the show last night?"

I must have looked blank.

"Some science writer," she said. "Rigel went supernova."

"Supernova," I repeated stupidly.

"Blam, you know? *Blooie.*" She illustrated with her hands and the magazine flipped onto the carpet. "Not that you missed anything. It'll be around for a few weeks—biggest show in the skies."

A sudden ugly image of red-and-white aircraft warning lights merging in an actinic flare sprayed my retinas. I shook my head. After a moment I said, "First one in our galaxy in—how long? Three hundred and fifty years? I wish you'd called me."

"A little longer. Kepler's star was in 1604. Sorry about not calling—we were all a little busy, you know?"

"I can imagine. When did it happen?"

She bent to retrieve the magazine. "Just about midnight. Spooky. I was just coming off shift." She smiled. "Nothing like a little cosmic cataclysm to take my mind off jammed sinuses. Just as well; no sick leave tonight. That's why I'm here at the clinic. Kris says no excuses."

Krishnamurthi was the Gamov director. "You'll be going back up to the peak soon?" She nodded. "Tell Kris I'll be in to visit. I want to pick up a lot of material."

"For sure."

The nurse walked up to us. "Ms. Denton?"

"Mmph." She nodded and wiped her nose a final time. Struggling up from the soft chair, she said, "How come you didn't read about Rigel in the papers? It made every morning edition."

"I let my subscriptions lapse."

"But the TV news? The radio?"

"I didn't watch, and I don't have a radio in the car."

Before disappearing into the corridor to the examination rooms, she said, "That country house of yours must really be isolated."

The ice drips from the eaves as I drive up and park beside the garage. Unless the sky deceives me there is no new weather front moving in yet; no need to protect the car from another ten centimeters of fresh snow.

Sunset comes sooner at my house among the mountains; shadows stalk across the barren yard and suck heat from my skin. The peaks are, of course, deliberate barriers blocking off light and warmth from the coastal cities. Once I personified them as friendly giants, amiable *lummoxen* guarding us. No more. Now they are only mountains again, the Cascade Range.

For an instant I think I see a light flash on, but it is just a quick sunset reflection on a window. The house remains dark and silent. The poet from Seattle's been gone for three months. My coldness —her heat. I thought that transference would warm me. Instead she chilled. The note she left me in the vacant house was a sonnet about psychic frostbite.

My last eleven years have not been celibate, but sometimes they feel like it. Entropy ultimately overcomes all kinetic force.

Then I looked toward the twilight east and saw Rigel rising. Luna wouldn't be visible for a while, so the brightest object in the sky was the exploded star. It fixed me to this spot by my car with the intensity of an aircraft landing light. The white light that shone down on me had left the supernova five hundred years before (a detail to include in the inevitable article—a graphic illustration of interstellar distances never fails to awe readers).

Tonight, watching the 100-billion-degree baleful eye that was Rigel convulsed, I know *I* was awed. The cataclysm glared, brighter than any planet. I wondered whether Rigel—unlikely, I knew—had had a planetary system, whether guttering mountain ranges and boiling seas had preceded worlds frying. I wondered whether, five centuries before, intelligent beings had watched stunned as the stellar fire engulfed their skies. Had they time to rail at the injustice? There are 100 billion stars in our galaxy; only an estimated three stars go supernova per thousand years. Good odds: Rigel lost.

Almost hypnotized, I watched until I was abruptly rocked by the wind rising in the darkness. My fingers were stiff with cold. But as I started to enter the house I looked at the sky a final time. Terrifying Rigel, yes—but my eyes were captured by another phenomenon in the north. A spark of light burned brighter than the surrounding stars. At first I thought it was a passing aircraft, but its position remained stationary. Gradually, knowing the odds and unwilling to believe, I recognized the new supernova for what it was.

In five decades I've seen many things. Yet watching the sky I felt like I was a primitive, shivering in uncured furs. My teeth chattered from more than the cold. I wanted to hide from the universe. The door to my house was unlocked, which was lucky—I couldn't have fitted a key into the latch. Finally I stepped over the threshold. I turned on all the lights, denying the two stellar pyres burning in the sky.

My urologist turned out to be a dour black man named Sharpe, who treated me, I suspected, like any of the other specimens that turned up in his laboratory. In his early thirties, he'd read several of my books. I appreciated his having absolutely no respect for his elders or for celebrities.

"You'll give me straight answers?" I said.

"Count on it."

He also gave me another of those damned urological fingers. When I was finally in a position to look back at him questioningly, he nodded slowly and said, "There's a nodule."

Then I got a series of blood tests for an enzyme called acid phosphatase. "Elevated," Sharpe said.

Finally, at the lab, I was to get the cystoscope, a shiny metal tube which would be run up my urethra. The biopsy forceps would be inserted through it. "Jesus, you're kidding." Sharpe shook his head. I said, "If the biopsy shows a malignancy . . ."

"I can't answer a silence."

"Come on," I said. "You've been straight until now. What are the chances of curing a malignancy?"

Sharpe had looked unhappy ever since I'd walked into his office. Now he looked unhappier. "Ain't my department," he said. "Depends on many factors."

"Just give me a simple figure."

"Maybe thirty percent. All bets are off if there's a metastasis." He met my eyes while he said that, then busied himself with the cystoscope. Local anesthetic or not, my penis burned like hell.

I had finally gotten through to Jackie Denton on a private line the night of the second supernova. "I thought last night was a madhouse," she said. "You should see us now. I've only got a minute."

"I just wanted to confirm what I was looking at," I said. "I saw the damn thing actually blow."

"You're ahead of everybody at Gamow. We were busily focusing on Rigel—" Electronic *wheeps* garbled the connection. "Nick, are you still there?"

"I think somebody wants the line. Just tell me a final thing. Is it a full-fledged supernova?"

"Absolutely. As far as we can determine now, it's a genuine Type Two."

"Sorry it couldn't be the biggest and best of all."

"Big enough," she said. "It's good enough. This time it's only about nine light-years away. Sirius A."

"Eight point seven light-years," I said automatically. "What's that going to mean?"

"Direct effects? Don't know. We're thinking about it." It sounded like her hand cupped the mouthpiece; then she came back on the line. "Listen, I've got to go. Kris is screaming for my head. Talk to you later."

"All right," I said. The connection broke. On the dead line I thought I heard the 21-centimeter basic hydrogen hiss of the universe. Then the dial tone cut in and I hung up the receiver.

Amanda did not look at all happy. She riffled twice through what I guessed were my laboratory test results. "All right," I said from the patient's side of the wide walnut desk. "Tell me."

"Mr. Richmond? Nicholas Richmond?"

"Speaking."

"This is Mrs. Kurnick, with Trans-West Airways. I'm calling from Denver."

"Yes?"

"We obtained this number from a charge slip. A ticket was issued to Lisa Richmond—"

"My wife. I've been expecting her sometime this weekend. Did she ask you to phone ahead?"

"Mr. Richmond, that's not it. Our manifest shows your wife boarded our Flight 903, Denver to Portland, tonight."

"So? What is it? What's wrong? Is she sick?"

"I'm afraid there's been an accident."

Silence choked me. *"How bad?"* The freezing began.

"Our craft went down about ten miles northwest of Glenwood Springs, Colorado. The ground parties at the site say there are no survivors. I'm sorry, Mr. Richmond."

"No one?" I said, *"I mean—"*

"I'm truly sorry," said Mrs. Kurnick. *"If there's any change in the situation, we will be in touch immediately."*

Automatically I said, "Thank you."

I had the impression that Mrs. Kurnick wanted to say something else; but after a pause, she only said, "Good night."

On a snowy Colorado mountainside I died.

"The biopsy was malignant," Amanda said.

"Well," I said. "That's pretty bad." She nodded. "Tell me about my alternatives." *Ragged bits of metal slammed into the mountainside like teeth.*

My case was unusual only in a relative sense. Amanda told me that prostatic cancer is the penalty men pay for otherwise good health. If they avoid every other health hazard, twentieth-century men eventually get zapped by their prostates. In my case, the problem was about twenty years early; my bad luck. *Cooling metal snapped and sizzled in the snow, was silent.*

Assuming that the cancer hadn't already metastasized, there were several possibilities; but Amanda had, at this stage, little hope for either radiology or chemotherapy. She suggested a radical prostatectomy.

"I wouldn't suggest it if you didn't have a hell of a lot of valuable years left," she said. "It's not usually advised for older patients. But you're in generally good condition; you could handle it."

Nothing moved on the mountainside. "What all would come out?" I said.

"You already know the ramifications of 'radical.'"

I didn't mind so much the ligation of the spermatic tubes—I should have done that a long time before. At fifty-one I could handle sterilization with equanimity, but—

"Sexually dysfunctional?" I said. "Oh my God." I was aware of my voice starting to tighten. "I can't do that."

"You sure as hell can," said Amanda firmly. "How long have I known you?" She answered her own question. "A long time. I know you well enough to know that what counts isn't all tied up in your penis."

I shook my head silently.

"Listen, damn it, cancer death is worse."

"No," I said stubbornly. "Maybe. Is that the whole bill?"

It wasn't. Amanda reached my bladder's entry on the list. It would be excised as well.

"Tubes protruding from me?" I said. *"If* I live, I'll have to spend the rest of my life toting a plastic bag as a drain for my urine?"

Quietly she said, "You're making it too melodramatic."

"But am I right?"

After a pause, "Essentially, yes."

And all that was the essence of it: the *good* news, all assuming that the carcinoma cells wouldn't jar loose during surgery and migrate off to other organs. "No," I said. The goddamned lousy, loathsome unfairness of it all slammed home. "Goddamn it, no. It's my choice; I won't live that way. If I just die, I'll be done with it."

"Nicholas! Cut the self-pity."

"Don't you think I'm entitled to some?"

"Be reasonable."

"You're supposed to comfort me," I said. "Not argue. You've taken all those death-and-dying courses. *You* be reasonable."

The muscles tightened around her mouth. "I'm giving you suggestions," said Amanda. "You can do with them as you damned well please." It had been years since I'd seen her angry.

We glared at each other for close to a minute. "Okay," I said. "I'm sorry."

She was not mollified. "Stay upset, even if it's whining. Get angry, be furious. I've watched you in a deep-freeze for a decade."

I recoiled internally. "I've survived. That's enough."

"No way. You've been sitting around for eleven years in suspended animation, waiting for someone to chip you free of the glacier. You've let people carom past, occasionally bouncing off you with no effect. Well, now it's not some*one* that's shoving you to the wall—it's some*thing*. Are you going to lie down for it? Lisa wouldn't have wanted that."

"Leave her out," I said.

"I can't. You're even more important to me because of her. She was my closest friend, remember?"

"Pay attention to her," Lisa had once said. *"She's more sensible than either of us." Lisa had known about the affair; after all, Amanda had introduced us.*

"I know." I felt disoriented; denial, resentment, numbness—the roller coaster clattered toward a final plunge.

"Nick, you've got a possibility for a healthy chunk of life left. I want you to have it, and if it takes using Lisa as a wedge, I will."

"I don't want to survive if it means crawling around as a piss-dripping cyborg eunuch." The roller coaster teetered on the brink.

Amanda regarded me for a long moment, then said earnestly, "There's an outside chance, a long shot. I heard from a friend there that the New Mexico Meson Physics Facility is scouting for a subject."

I scoured my memory. "Particle beam therapy?"

"Pions."

"It's chancy," I said.

"Are you arguing?" She smiled.

I smiled too. "No."

"Want to give it a try?"

My smile died. "I don't know. I'll think about it."

"That's encouragement enough," said Amanda. "I'll make some calls and see if the facility's as interested in you as I expect you'll be in them. Stick around home? I'll let you know."

"I haven't said 'yes.' We'll let each other know." I didn't tell Amanda, but I left her office thinking only of death.

Melodramatic as it may sound, I went downtown to visit the hardware stores and look at their displays of pistols. After two hours, I tired of handling weapons. The steel seemed uniformly cold and distant.

When I returned home late that afternoon, there was a single message on my phone-answering machine:

"Nick, this is Jackie Denton. Sorry I haven't called for a while, but you know how it's been. I thought you'd like to know that Kris is going to have a press conference early in the week—probably Monday afternoon. I think he's worried because he hasn't come up with a good theory to cover the three Type Two supernovas and the half-dozen standard novas that have occurred in the last few weeks. But then nobody I know has. We're all spending so much time awake nights, we're turning into vampires. I'll get back to you when I know the exact time of the conference. I think it must be about thirty seconds now, so I—" The tape ended.

I mused with winter bonfires in my mind as the machine rewound and reset. Three Type II supernovas? One is merely nature, I paraphrased. Two mean only coincidence. Three make a conspiracy.

Impulsively I slowly dialed Denton's home number; there was no answer. Then the lines to Gamow Peak were all busy. It seemed logical to me that I needed Jackie Denton for more than being my sounding board, or for merely news about the press conference. I needed an extension of her friendship. I thought I'd like to borrow the magnum pistol I knew she kept in a locked desk drawer at her observatory office. I knew I could ask her a favor. She ordinarily used the pistol to blast targets on the peak's rocky flanks after work.

The irritating regularity of the busy signal brought me back to sanity. Just a second, I told myself. Richmond, what the hell are you proposing?

Nothing, was the answer. Not yet. Not . . . quite.

Later in the night, I opened the sliding glass door and disturbed the skiff of snow on the second-story deck. I shamelessly allowed myself the luxury of leaving the door partially open so that warm air would spill out around me while I watched the sky. The stars were intermittently visible between the towering banks of stratocumulus scudding over the Cascades. Even so, the three supernovas dominated the night. I drew imaginary lines with my eyes; connect the dots and solve the puzzle. How many enigmas can you find in this picture?

I reluctantly took my eyes away from the headline phenomena and searched for old standbys. I picked out the red dot of Mars.

Several years ago I'd had a cockamamie scheme that sent me to a Mesmerist—that's how she'd billed herself—down in Eugene. I'd been driving up the coast after covering an aerospace medical conference in Oakland. Somewhere around Crescent City, I

capped a sea-bass dinner by getting blasted on prescribed pills and
proscribed Scotch. Sometime during the evening, I remembered
the computer-enhancement process JPL had used to sharpen the
clarity of telemetered photos from such projects as the Mariner
fly-bys and the Viking Mars lander. It seemed logical to me at the
time that memories from the human computer could somehow be
enhanced, brought into clarity through hypnosis. Truly stoned
fantasies. But they somehow sufficed as rationale and incentive to
wind up at Madame Guzmann's "Advice/Mesmerism/Health" es-
tablishment across the border in Oregon. Madame Guzmann had
skin the color of her stained hardwood door; she made a point of
looking and dressing the part of a stereotype we *gajos* would think
of as Gypsy. The scarf and crystal ball strained the image. I think
she was Vietnamese. At any rate she convinced me she could
hypnotize, and then she nudged me back through time.

*Just before she ducked into the cabin, Lisa paused and waved
back from the head of the stairs; her dark hair curled about her
face in the wind.*

I should have taken to heart the lesson of stasis; entropy is not
so easily overcome.

What Madame Guzmann achieved was to freeze-frame that last
image of Lisa. Then she zoomed me in so close it was like standing
beside Lisa. I sometimes still see it in my nightmares. Her eyes
focus distantly. Her skin has the graininess of a newspaper photo.
I look but cannot touch. I can speak but she will not answer. I
shiver with the cold—

—and slid the glass door further open.

There! An eye opened in space. A glare burned as cold as a
refrigerator light in a night kitchen. Mars seemed to disappear,
swallowed in the glow from the nova distantly behind it. Another
one, I thought. The new eye held me fascinated, pinned as securely as a child might fasten a new moth in the collection.

Nick?

Who is it?

Nick . . .

You're an auditory hallucination.

There on the deck the sound of laughter spiraled around me. I thought it would shake loose the snow from the trees. The mountain stillness vibrated.

The secret, Nick.

What secret?

You're old enough at fifty-one to decipher it.

Don't play with me.

Who's playing? Whatever time is left—

Yes?

You've spent eleven years now dreaming, drifting, letting others act on you.

I know.

Do you? Then act on that. Choose your actions. No lover can tell you more. Whatever time is left—

Shivering uncontrollably, I gripped the rail of the deck. A fleeting pointillist portrait in black and white dissolved into the trees. From branch to branch, top bough to bottom, crusted snow broke and fell, gathering momentum. The trees shed their mantle. Powder swirled up to the deck and touched my face with stinging diamonds.

Eleven years was more than half what Rip Van Winkle slept. "Damn it," I said. "Damn you." We prize our sleep. The grave rested peacefully among the trees. "Damn you," I said again, looking up at the sky.

On a snowy Oregon mountainside I was no longer dead.

And yes, Amanda. Yes.

After changing planes at Albuquerque, we flew into Los Alamos on a small feeder line called Ross Airlines. I'd never flown before on so ancient a DeHavilland Twin Otter, and I hoped never to again; I'd take a Greyhound out of Los Alamos first. The flight attendant and half the other sixteen passengers were throwing up in the turbulence as we approached the mountains. I hadn't expected the mountains. I'd assumed Los Alamos would lie in the same sort of southwestern scrub desert surrounding Albuquerque. Instead I found a small city nestled a couple of kilometers up a wooded mountainside.

The pilot's unruffled voice came on the cabin intercom to announce our imminent landing, the airport temperature, and the fact that Los Alamos has more Ph.D.'s per capita than any other American city. "Second only to Akademgorodok," I said, turning away from the window toward Amanda. The skin wrinkled around her closed eyes. She hadn't had to use her airsick bag. I had a feeling that despite old friendships, a colleague and husband who was willing to oversee the clinic, the urgency of helping a patient, and the desire to observe the exotic experiment, Amanda might be regretting accompanying me to what she'd termed "the meson factory."

The Twin Otter made a landing approach like a strafing run and then we were down. As we taxied across the apron I had a sudden sensation of déjà vu: the time a year ago when a friend had flown me north in a Cessna. The airport in Los Alamos looked much like the civil air terminal at Sea-Tac where I'd met the Seattle poet. It happened that we were both in line at the snack counter. I'd commented on her elaborate Haida-styled medallion. We took the same table and talked; it turned out she'd heard of me.

"I really admire your stuff," she said.

So much for my ideal poet using only precise images. Wry thought. She was—is—a first-rate poet. I rarely think of her as anything but "the poet from Seattle." Is that kind of depersonalization a symptom?

Amanda opened her eyes, smiled wanly, said, "I could use a doctor." The flight attendant cracked the door and thin New Mexican mountain air revived us both.

Most of the New Mexico Meson Physics Facility was buried beneath a mountain ridge. Being guest journalist as well as experimental subject, I think we were given a more exhaustive tour than would be offered most patients and their doctors. Everything I saw made me think of expensive sets for vintage science fiction movies: the interior of the main accelerator ring, glowing eggshell white and curving away like the space-station corridors in *2001;* the linac and booster areas; the straightaway tunnel to the meson medical channel; the five-meter bubble chamber looking like some sort of time machine.

I'd visited both FermiLab in Illinois and CERN in Geneva, so I had a general idea of what the facilities were all about. Still I had a difficult time trying to explain to Amanda the *Alice in Wonderland* mazes that constituted high-energy particle physics. But then so did Delaney, the young woman who was the liaison biophysicist for my treatment. It became difficult sorting out the mesons, pions, hadrons, leptons, baryons, J's, fermions and quarks, and such quantum qualities as strangeness, color, baryonness and charm. Especially charm, that ephemeral quality accounting for why certain types of radioactive decay should happen but don't. I finally bogged down in the midst of quarks, antiquarks, charmed quarks, neoquarks and quarklets.

Some wag had set a sign on the visitors' reception desk in the administration center reading "Charmed to meet you." "It's a joke, right?" said Amanda tentatively.

"It probably won't get any funnier," I said.

Delaney, who seemed to load every word with deadly earnestness, didn't laugh at all. "Some of the technicians think it's funny. I don't."

We rehashed the coming treatment endlessly. Optimistically I took notes for the book: *The primary problem with a radiological approach to the treatment of cancer is that hard radiation not only kills the cancerous cells, it also irradiates the surrounding*

healthy tissue. But in the mid-nineteen seventies, cancer research-
ers found a more promising tool: shaped beams of subatomic par-
ticles which can be selectively focused on the tissue of tumors.

Delaney had perhaps two decades on Amanda; being younger
seemed to give her a perverse satisfaction in playing the peda-
gogue. "Split atomic nuclei on a small scale—"

"Small?" said Amanda innocently.

"—smaller than a fission bomb. Much of the binding force of the
nucleus is miraculously transmuted to matter."

"Miraculously?" said Amanda. I looked up at her from the easy
cushion shot I was trying to line up on the green velvet. The three
of us were playing rotation in the billiards annex of the NMMPF
recreation lounge.

"Uh," said Delaney, the rhythm of her lecture broken. "Physics
shorthand."

"Reality shorthand," I said, not looking up from the cue now.
"Miracles are as exact a quality as charm."

Amanda chuckled. "That's all I wanted to know."

The miracle pertinent to my case was atomic glue, mesons, one
of the fission-formed particles. More specifically, my miracle was
the negatively charged pion, a subclass of meson. Electromagnetic
fields could focus pions into a controllable beam and fire it into a
particular target—me.

"There are no miracles in physics," said Delaney seriously. "I
used the wrong term."

I missed my shot. A gentle stroke, and gently the cue ball rolled
into the corner pocket, missing the eleven. I'd set things up nicely,
if accidentally, for Amanda.

She assayed the table and smiled. "Don't come unglued."

"That's very good," I said. Atomic glue does become unstuck,
thanks to pions' unique quality. When they collide and are captured by the nucleus of another atom, they reconvert to pure
energy—a tiny nuclear explosion.

Amanda missed her shot too. The corners of Delaney's mouth

curled in a small gesture of satisfaction. She leaned across the table, hands utterly steady. "Multiply pions, multiply target nuclei, and you have a controlled aggregate explosion releasing considerably more energy than the entering pion beam. *Hah!*"

She sank the eleven and twelve; then ran the table. Amanda and I exchanged glances. "Rack 'em up," said Delaney.

"Your turn," Amanda said to me.

In my case the NMMPF medical channel would fire a directed pion beam into my recalcitrant prostate. If all went as planned, the pions intercepting the atomic nuclei of my cancer cells would convert back into energy in a series of atomic flares. The cancer cells being more sensitive, tissue damage should be restricted, localized in my carcinogenic nodule.

Thinking of myself as a nuclear battlefield in miniature was wondrous. Thinking of myself as a new Stagg Field or an Oak Ridge was ridiculous.

Delaney turned out to be a pool shark *par excellence.* Winning was all-important and she won every time. I decided to interpret that as a positive omen.

"It's time," Amanda said.

"You needn't sound as though you're leading a condemned man to the electric chair." I tied the white medical smock securely about me, pulled on the slippers.

"I'm sorry. Are you worried?"

"Not so long as Delaney counts me as part of the effort toward a Nobel Prize."

"She's good." Her voice rang too hollow in the sterile tiled room. We walked together into the corridor.

"Me, I'm bucking for a Kalinga Prize," I said.

Amanda shook her head. Cloudy hair played about her face. "I'll just settle for a positive prognosis for my patient." Beyond the door, Delaney and two technicians with a gurney waited for me.

There is a state beyond indignity that defines being draped
naked on my belly over a bench arrangement, with my rear
spread and facing the medical channel. Rigidly clamped, a ce-
ramic target tube opened a separate channel through my anus to
the prostate. Monitoring equipment and shielding shut me in. I
felt hot and vastly uncomfortable. Amanda had shot me full of
chemicals, not all of whose names I'd recognized. Now dazed, I
couldn't decide which of many discomforts was the most irritating.

"Good luck," Amanda had said. "It'll be over before you know
it." I'd felt a gentle pat on my flank.

I thought I heard the phasing-up whine of electrical equipment.
I could tell my mind was closing down for the duration; I couldn't
even remember how many billion electron-volts were about to
route a pion beam up my backside. I heard sounds I couldn't
identify; perhaps an enormous metal door grinding shut.

My brain swam free in a chemical river; I waited for something
to happen.

*I thought I heard machined ball bearings rattling down a chute;
no, particles screaming past the giant bending magnets into the
medical channel at 300,000 kilometers per second; flashing toward me through the series of adjustable filters; slowing, slowing,
losing energy as they approach; then through the final tube and
into my body. Inside . . .*

*The pion sails the inner atomic seas for a relativistically finite
time. Then the perspective inhabited by one is inhabited by two.
The pion drives toward the target nucleus. At a certain point the
pion is no longer a pion; what was temporarily matter transmutes
back to energy. The energy flares, expands, expends and fades.
Other explosions detonate in the spaces within the patterns underlying larger patterns.*

Darkness and light interchange.

*The light coalesces into a ball—massive, hot, burning against
the darkness. Pierced, somehow stricken, the ball begins to collapse in upon itself. Its internal temperature climbs to a critical*

*level. At 600 million degrees, carbon nuclei fuse. Heavier elements
form. When the fuel is exhausted, the ball collapses further; again
the temperature is driven upward; again heavier elements form
and are in turn consumed. The cycle repeats until the nuclear
furnace manufactures iron. No further nuclear reaction can be
triggered; the heart's fire is extinguished. Without the outward
balance of fusion reaction, the ball initiates the ultimate collapse.
Heat reaches 100 billion degrees. Every conceivable nuclear reaction is consummated.*

*The ball explodes in a final convulsive cataclysm. Its energy
flares, fades, is eaten by entropy. The time it took is no more than
the time it takes Sol-light to reach and illuminate the Earth.*

"How do you feel?" Amanda leaned into my field of vision,
eclipsing the fluorescent rings overhead.

"Feel?" I seemed to be talking through a mouthful of cotton
candy.

"Feel."

"Compared to what?" I said.

She smiled. "You're doing fine."

"I had one foot on the accelerator," I said.

She looked puzzled, then started to laugh. "It'll wear off soon."
She completed her transit and the lights shone back in my face.

"No hand on the brake," I mumbled. I began to giggle. Something pricked my arm.

I think Delaney wanted to keep me under observation in New
Mexico until the anticipated ceremonies in Stockholm; I didn't
have time for that. I suspected none of us did. Amanda began to
worry about my moody silences; she ascribed them at first to my
medication and then to the two weeks' tests Delaney and her
colleagues were inflicting on me.

"To hell with this," I said. "We've got to get out of here."
Amanda and I were alone in my room.

"What?"

"Give me a prognosis."

She smiled. "I think you may as well shoot for the Kalinga."

"Maybe." I quickly added, "I'm not a patient any more; I'm an experimental subject."

"So? What do we do about it?"

We exited NMMPF under cover of darkness and struggled a half kilometer through brush to the highway. There we hitched a ride into town.

"This is crazy," said Amanda, picking thistle out of her sweater.

"It avoids a strong argument," I said as we neared the lights of Los Alamos.

The last bus of the day had left. I wanted to wait until morning. Over my protests, we flew out on Ross Airlines. "Doctor's orders," said Amanda, teeth tightly together, as the Twin Otter bumped onto the runway.

I dream of pions. I dream of colored balloons filled with hydrogen, igniting and flaming up in the night. I dream of Lisa's newsprint face. Her smile is both proud and sorrowful.

Amanda had her backlog of patients and enough to worry about, so I took my nightmares to Jackie Denton at the observatory. I told her of my hallucinations in the accelerator chamber. We stared at each other across the small office.

"I'm glad you're better, Nick, but—"

"That's not it," I said. "Remember how you hated my article about poetry glorifying the new technology? Too fanciful?" I launched into speculation, mixing with abandon pion beams, doctors, supernovas, irrational statistics, carcinogenic nodes, fire balloons and gods.

"Gods?" she said. *"Gods?* Are you going to put that in your next column?"

I nodded.

She looked as though she were inspecting a newly found-out psychopath. "No one needs that in the press now, Nick. The whole planet's upset already. The possibility of nova radiation damaging the ozone layer, the potential for genetic damage, all that's got people spooked."

"It's only speculation."

She said, "You don't yell 'fire' in a crowded theater."

"Or in a crowded world?"

Her voice was unamused. "Not now."

"And if I'm right?" I felt weary. "What about it?"

"A supernova? No way. Sol simply doesn't have the mass."

"But a nova?" I said.

"Possibly," she said tightly. "But it shouldn't happen for a few billion years. Stellar evolution—"

"—is theory," I said. *"Shouldn't* isn't *won't.* Tonight look again at that awesome sky."

Denton said nothing.

"Could you accept a solar flare? A big one?"

I read the revulsion in her face and knew I should stop talking; but I didn't. "Do you believe in God? Any god?" She shook her head. I had to get it all out. "How about concentric universes, one within the next like Chinese carved ivory spheres?" Her face went white. "Pick a card," I said, "any card. A wild card."

"God damn you, shut up." On the edge of the desk, her knuckles were as white as her lips.

"Charming," I said, ignoring the incantatory power of words, forgetting what belief could cost. I do not think she deliberately drove her Lotus off the Peak road. I don't want to believe that. Surely she was coming to join me.

Maybe, she'd said.

Nightmares should be kept home. So here I stand on my sundeck at high noon for the Earth. No need to worry about destruction of the ozone layer and the consequent skin cancer. There will be no problem with mutational effects and genetic damage. I need not worry about deadlines or contractual commitments. I regret that no one will ever read my book about pion therapy.

All that—maybe.

The sun shines bright—the tune plays dirgelike in my head.

Perhaps I am wrong. The flare may subside. Maybe I am not dying. No matter.

I wish Amanda were with me now, or that I were at Jackie Denton's bedside, or even that I had time to walk to Lisa's grave among the pines. Now there is no time.

At least I've lived as long as I have now by choice.

That's the secret, Nick . . .

The glare illuminates the universe.

SPIDER and JEANNE ROBINSON

❧ *Stardance*

Spider? Yes, he's very thin; he has a few feet of hair hanging from his head; and he's one of the folk I can describe, with no irony at all, as intensely nice to be around. Unhappily, I've never met Jeanne, who co-wrote this winning novella. I know she's an actress. And I certainly wouldn't be surprised if, as well as writing up a storm, she dances.

❧Nebula Award of the Science Fiction Writers of America for Best Novella, 1977.

I can't really say that I knew her, certainly not the way Seroff knew Isadora. All I know of her childhood and adolescence are the anecdotes she chanced to relate in my hearing—just enough to make me certain that all three of the contradictory biographies on the current best-seller list are fictional. All I know of her adult life are the hours she spent in my presence and on my monitors— more than enough to tell me that every newspaper account I've seen is fictional. Carrington probably believed he knew her better than I, and in a limited sense he was correct—but he would never have written of it, and now he is dead.

But I was her video man since the days when you touched the camera with your hands, and I knew her backstage: a type of relationship like no other on Earth or off it. I don't believe it can be described to anyone not of the profession—you might think of it as somewhere between co-workers and combat buddies. I was with her the day she came to Skyfac, terrified and determined, to stake her life upon a dream. I watched her work and worked with her for that whole two months, through endless rehearsals, and I have saved every tape and they are not for sale.

And, of course, I saw the Stardance. I was there; I taped it.

I guess I can tell you some things about her.

To begin with, it was not, as Cahill's *Shara* and Von Derski's *Dance Unbound: The Creation of New Modern* suggest, a life-long fascination with space and space travel that led her to become the race's first zero-gravity dancer. Space was a means to her, not an end, and its vast empty immensity scared her at first. Nor was it, as Melberg's hardcover tabloid *The Real Shara Drummond* claims, because she lacked the talent to make it as a dancer on Earth. If you think free-fall dancing is easier than conventional dance, you try it. Don't forget your dropsickness bag.

But there is a grain of truth in Melberg's slander, as there is in all the best slanders. She could *not* make it on Earth—but not through lack of talent.

I first saw her in Toronto in July of 1984. I headed Toronto Dance Theater's video department at that time, and I hated every minute of it. I hated everything in those days. The schedule that day called for spending the entire afternoon taping students, a waste of time and tape which I hated more than anything except the phone company. I hadn't seen the year's new crop yet and was not eager to. I love to watch dance done well—the efforts of a tyro are usually as pleasing to me as a first-year violin student in the next apartment is to you.

My leg was bothering me even more than usual as I walked into the studio. Norrey saw my face and left a group of young hopefuls to come over. "Charlie. . . ."

"I know, I know. 'They're tender fledglings, Charlie, with egos as fragile as an Easter egg in December. Don't bite them, Charlie. Don't even bark at them if you can help it, Charlie.' "

She smiled. "Something like that. Leg?"

"Leg."

Norrey Drummond is a dancer who gets away with looking like a woman because she's small. There's about a hundred and fifteen pounds of her, and most of it is heart. She stands about five-four, and is perfectly capable of seeming to tower over the tallest student. She has more energy than the North American Grid and uses it as efficiently as a vane pump. (Have you ever studied the principle of a standard piston-type pump? Go look up the principle of a vane pump. I wonder what the original conception of *that* notion must have been like, as an emotional experience.) There's a signaturelike uniqueness to her dance, the only reason I can see why she got so few of the really juicy parts in company productions until modern gave way to new modern. I liked her because she didn't pity me.

"It's not only the leg," I admitted. "I hate to see the tender fledglings butcher your choreography."

"Then you needn't worry. The piece you're taping today is by . . . one of the students."

"Oh, fine. I knew I should have called in sick." She made a face. "What's the catch?"

"Eh?"

"Why did the funny thing happen to your voice just as you got to 'one of the students'?"

She blushed. "Damn it, she's my sister."

My eyebrows rose. "She must be good then."

"Why, thank you, Charlie."

"Bullshit. I give compliments right-handed or not at all—I'm not talking about heredity. I mean that you're so hopelessly ethical you'd bend over backward to avoid nepotism. For you to give your own sister a feature like that, she must be *terrific.*"

"Charlie, she is," Norrey said simply.

"We'll see. What's her name?"

"Shara." Norrey pointed her out, and I understood the rest of the catch. Shara Drummond was ten years younger than her sister —and seven inches taller, with thirty or forty more pounds. I noted absently that she was stunningly beautiful, but it didn't deter my dismay. In her best years, Sophia Loren could never have become a modern dancer. Where Norrey was small, Shara was big; and where Norrey was big, Shara was bigger. If I'd seen

her on the street I might have whistled appreciatively—but in the
studio I frowned.

"My God, Norrey, she's enormous."

"Mother's second husband was a football player," she said
mournfully. "She's awfully good."

"If she *is* good, that *is* awful. Poor girl. Well, what do you want
me to do?"

"What makes you think I want you to do anything?"

"You're still standing here."

"Oh. I guess I am. Well . . . have lunch with us, Charlie?"

"Why?" I knew perfectly well why, but I expected a polite lie.
Not from Norrey Drummond. "Because you two have something in common, I think."

I paid her honesty the compliment of not wincing. "I suppose
we do."

"Then you will?"

"Right after the session."

She twinkled and was gone. In a remarkably short time she had
organized the studio full of wandering, chattering young people
into something that resembled a dance ensemble if you squinted.
They warmed up during the twenty minutes it took me to set up
and check out my equipment. I positioned one camera in front of
them, one behind, and kept one in my hands for walk-around
close-up work. I never triggered it.

There's a game you play in your mind. Every time someone
catches or is brought to your attention, you begin making guesses
about them. You try to extrapolate their character and habits from
their appearance. Him? Surly, disorganized—leaves the cap off
the toothpaste and drinks boilermakers. Her? Art student type,
probably uses a diaphragm and writes letters in a stylized calligra-
phy of her own invention. Them? They look like schoolteachers
from Miami, probably here to see what snow looks like, attend a
convention. Sometimes I come pretty close. I don't know how I
typecast Shara Drummond, in those first twenty minutes. The

moment she began to dance, all preconceptions left my mind. She became something elemental, something unknowable, a living bridge between our world and the one the Muses live in.

I know, on an intellectual and academic level, all there is to know about dance, and I could not categorize or classify or even really comprehend the dance she danced that afternoon. I saw it, I even appreciated it, but I was not equipped to understand it. My camera dangled from the end of my arm, next to my jaw. Dancers speak of their "center," the place their motion centers around, often quite near the physical center of gravity. You strive to "dance from your center" and the "contraction-and-release" idea which underlies much of modern dance depends on the center for its focus of energy. Shara's center seemed to move about the room under its own power, trailing limbs that attached to it by choice rather than necessity. What's the word for the outermost part of the sun, the part that still shows in an eclipse? Corona? That's what her limbs were: four lengthy tongues of flame that followed the center in its eccentric, whirling orbit, writhing fluidly around its surface. That the lower two frequently contacted the floor seemed coincidental —indeed the other two touched the floor nearly as regularly.

There were other students dancing. I know this because the two automatic videocameras, unlike me, did their job and recorded the piece as a whole. It was called *Birthing* and depicted the formation of a galaxy that ended up resembling Andromeda. It was only vaguely accurate, literally, but it wasn't intended to be. Symbolically, it felt like the birth of a galaxy.

In retrospect. At the time I was aware only of the galaxy's heart: Shara. Students occluded her from time to time, and I simply never noticed. It hurt to watch her.

If you know anything about dance, this must all sound horrid to you. A dance about a *nebula?* I know, I know. It's a ridiculous notion. And it worked. In the most gut-level, cellular way it worked—save only that Shara was too good for those around her. She did not belong in that eager crew of awkward half-trained

apprentices. It was like listening to the late Stephen Wonder trying to work with a pick-up band in a Montreal bar.

But that wasn't what hurt.

Le Maintenant was shabby, but the food was good and the house
brand of grass was excellent. Show a Diners Club card in there and
they'd show you a galley full of dirty dishes. It's gone now. Norrey
and Shara declined a toke, but in my line of work it helps. Besides,
I needed a few hits. How to tell a lovely lady her dearest dream
is hopeless?

I didn't need to ask Shara to know that her dearest dream was
to dance. More: to dance professionally. I have often speculated on
the motives of the professional artist. Some seek the narcissistic
assurance that others will actually pay cash to watch or hear them.
Some are so incompetent or disorganized that they can support
themselves in no other way. Some have a message which they feel
needs expressing. I suppose most artists combine elements of all
three. This is no complaint—what they do for us is necessary. We
should be grateful that there *are* motives.

But Shara was one of the rare ones. She danced because she
needed to. She needed to say things which could be said in no
other way, and she needed to take her meaning and her living
from the saying of them. Anything else would have demeaned and
devalued the essential statement of her dance. I know this, from
watching that one dance.

Between toking up and keeping my mouth full and then toking
again (a mild amount to offset the slight down that eating brings),
it was over half an hour before I was required to say anything
beyond an occasional grunted response to the luncheon chatter of
the ladies. As the coffee arrived, Shara looked me square in the eye
and said, "Do you talk, Charlie?"

She was Norrey's sister, all right.

"Only inanities."

"No such thing. Inane people, maybe."

"Do you enjoy dancing, Miss Drummond?"

She answered seriously. "Define 'enjoy.' "

I opened my mouth and closed it, perhaps three times. You try it.

"And for God's sake tell me why you're so intent on not talking to me. You've got me worried."

"Shara!" Norrey looked dismayed.

"Hush. I want to know."

I took a crack at it. "Shara, before he died I had the privilege of meeting Bertram Ross. I had just seen him dance. A producer who knew and liked me took me backstage, the way you take a kid to see Santa Claus. I had expected him to look even older offstage, at rest. He looked younger, as if that incredible motion of his was barely in check. He talked to me. After a while I stopped opening my mouth, because nothing ever came out."

She waited, expecting more. Only gradually did she comprehend the compliment and its dimension. I had assumed it would be obvious. Most artists *expect* to be complimented. When she did twig, she did not blush or simper. She did not cock her head and say, "Oh, come on." She did not say, "You flatter me." She did not look away.

She nodded slowly and said, "Thank you, Charlie. That's worth a lot more than idle chatter." There was a suggestion of sadness in her smile, as if we shared a bitter joke.

"You're welcome."

"For heaven's sake, Norrey, what are you looking so upset about?"

The cat now had Norrey's tongue.

"She's disappointed in me," I said. "I said the wrong thing."

"That was the wrong thing?"

"It should have been 'Miss Drummond, I think you ought to give up dancing.' "

"It should have been *'Shara,* I think you ought' . . . *what?"*

"Charlie," Norrey began.

"I was supposed to tell you that we can't all be professional dancers, that they also surf who only sand and wade. Shara, I was supposed to tell you to dump the dance—before it dumps you."

In my need to be honest with her, I had been more brutal than was necessary, I thought. I was to learn that bluntness never dismayed Shara. She demanded it.

"Why you?" was all she said.

"We're inhabiting the same vessel, you and I. We've both got an itch that our bodies just won't let us scratch."

Her eyes softened. "What's your itch?"

"The same as yours."

"Eh?"

"The man was supposed to come and fix the phone on Thursday. My roommate Karen and I had an all-day rehearsal. We left a note. Mr. telephone man, we had to go out, and we sure couldn't call you, heh heh. Please get the key from the concierge and come on in; the phone's in the bedroom. The phone man never showed up. They never do." My hands seemed to be shaking. "We came home up the back stairs from the alley. The phone was still dead, but I never thought to take down the note on the front door. I got sick the next morning. Cramps. Vomiting. Karen and I were just friends, but she stayed home to take care of me. I suppose on a Friday night the note seemed even more plausible. He slipped the lock with a piece of plastic, and Karen came out of the kitchen as he was unplugging the stereo. He was so indignant he shot her. Twice. The noise scared him; by the time I got there he was halfway out the door. He just had time to put a slug through my hip joint, and then he was gone. They never got him. They never even came to fix the phone." My hands were under control now. "Karen was a damned good dancer, but I was better. In my head, I still am."

Her eyes were round. "You're not Charlie . . . Charles *Armstead.*"

I nodded.

"Oh my God. So *that's* where you went."

I was shocked by how she looked. It brought me back from the cold and windy border of self-pity. I began a little to pity her. I should have guessed the depth of her empathy. And in the way that really mattered, we were too damned alike—we *did* share the same bitter joke. I wondered why I had wanted to shock her.

"They couldn't repair the joint?" she asked softly.

"I can walk splendidly. Given a strong enough motivation, I can even run short distances. I can't dance worth a damn."

"So you became a video man."

"Three years ago. People who know both video and dance are about as common as garter belts these days. Oh, they've been taping dance since the Seventies—with the imagination of a network news cameraman. If you film a stage play with two cameras in the orchestra pit, is it a movie?"

"You do for dance what the movie camera did for drama?"

"Pretty fair analogy. Where it breaks down is that dance is more analogous to music than to drama. You can't stop and start it, or go back and retake a scene that didn't go in the can right, or reverse the chronology to get a tidy shooting schedule. The event happens and you record it. What I am is what the record industry pays top dollars for—a mixman with savvy enough to know which ax is wailing at the moment and mike it high—and the sense to have given the heaviest dudes the best mikes. There are a few others like me. I'm the best."

She took it the way she had the compliment to herself—at face value. Usually when I say things like that, I don't give a damn what reaction I get, or I'm being salty and hoping for outrage. But I was pleased at her acceptance, pleased enough to bother me. A faint irritation made me go brutal again, *knowing* it wouldn't work. "So what all this leads to is that Norrey was hoping I'd suggest some similar form of sublimation for you. Because I'll make it in dance before you will."

She stubborned up. "I don't buy that, Charlie. I know what

you're talking about. I'm not a fool, but I think I can beat it."

"Sure you will. *You're too damned big, lady.* You've got tits like both halves of a prize honeydew melon and an ass that any actress in Hollywood would sell her parents for, and in modern dance that makes you d-e-d dead; you haven't got a chance. Beat it? You'll beat your head in first. How'm I doing, Norrey?"

"For Christ's sake, Charlie!"

I softened. I can't work Norrey into a tantrum—I like her too much. "I'm sorry, hon. My leg's giving me the mischief, and I'm stinkin' mad. She *ought* to make it—and she won't. She's your sister, and so it saddens you. Well, I'm a total stranger, and it enrages me."

"How do you think it makes me feel?" Shara blazed, startling us both. I hadn't known she had so much voice. "So you want me to pack it in and rent me a camera, huh, Charlie? Or maybe sell apples outside the studio?" A ripple ran up her jaw. "Well, I will be damned by all the gods in Southern California before I'll pack it in. God gave me the large economy size, but there is not a surplus pound on it and it fits me like a glove and I can, by Jesus, *dance* it and I will. You may be right—I may beat my head in first. But I will get it done." She took a deep breath. "Now I thank you for your kind intentions, Char— Mr. Armst— Oh shit." The tears came and she left hastily, spilling a quarter-cup of cold coffee on Norrey's lap.

"Charlie," Norrey said through clenched teeth, "why do I like you so much?"

"Dancers are dumb." I gave her my handkerchief.

"Oh." She patted at her lap awhile. "How come you like me?"

"Video men are smart."

"Oh."

I spent the afternoon in my apartment reviewing the footage I'd shot that morning, and the more I watched, the madder I got.

Dance requires intense motivation at an extraordinarily early

age—a blind devotion, a gamble on the as-yet-unrealized poten-
tials of heredity and nutrition. You can begin, say, classical ballet
training at age six—and at fourteen find yourself broad-shoul-
dered, the years of total effort utterly wasted. Shara had set her
sights on modern dance—and found out too late that God had
dealt her the body of a woman.

She was not fat—you have seen her. She was tall, big-boned tall,
and on that great frame was built a rich, ripely female body. As
I ran and reran the tapes of *Birthing,* the pain grew in me until
I even forgot the ever-present aching of my own leg. It was like
watching a supremely gifted basketball player who stood four feet
tall.

To make it in modern dance, it is essential to get into a company.
You cannot be seen unless you are visible. Norrey had told me, on
the walk back to the studio, of Shara's efforts to get into a company
—and I could have predicted nearly every word.

"Merce *Cunningham* saw her dance, Charlie. Martha Graham
saw her dance, just before she died. Both of them praised her
warmly, for her choreography as much as for her technique. Neither offered her a position. I'm not even sure I blame them—I can
sort of understand."

Norrey could understand all right. It was her own defect mag-
nified a hundredfold: uniqueness. A company member must be
capable of excellent solo work—but she must also be able to blend
into group effort, in ensemble work. Shara's very uniqueness made
her virtually useless as a company member. She could not help but
draw the eye.

And once drawn, the male eye at least would never leave.
Modern dancers must sometimes work nude these days, and it
is therefore meet that they have the body of a fourteen-year-
old boy. We may have ladies dancing with few or no clothes on
up here, but by God it is Art. An actress or a musician or a
singer or a painter may be lushly endowed, deliciously rounded
—but a dancer must be nearly as sexless as a high-fashion

model. Perhaps God knows why. Shara could not have purged her dance of her sexuality even if she had been interested in trying, and as I watched her dance on my monitor and in my mind's eye, I knew she was not.

Why did her genius have to lie in the only occupation besides model and nun in which sexiness is a liability? It broke my heart, by empathic analogy.

"It's no good at all, is it?"

I whirled and barked, "Damn it, you made me bite my tongue."

"I'm sorry." She came from the doorway into my living room. "Norrey told me how to find the place. The door was ajar."

"I forgot to shut it when I came home."

"You leave it open?"

"I've learned the lesson of history. No junkie, no matter how strung out he is, will enter an apartment with the door ajar and the radio on. Obviously there's someone home. And you're right, it's no damn good at all. Sit down."

She sat on the couch. Her hair was down now, and I liked it better that way. I shut off the monitor and popped the tape, tossing it on a shelf.

"I came to apologize. I shouldn't have blown up at you at lunch. You were trying to help me."

"You had it coming. I imagine by now you've built up quite a head of steam."

"Five years' worth. I figured I'd start in the States instead of Canada. Go farther faster. Now I'm back in Toronto and I don't think I'm going to make it here either. You're right, Mr. Armstead —I'm too damned big. Amazons don't dance."

"It's still Charlie. Listen, something I want to ask you. That last gesture, at the end of *Birthing*—what was that? I thought it was a beckoning; Norrey says it was a farewell; and now that I've run the tape it looks like a yearning, a reaching out."

"Then it worked."

"Pardon?"

"It seemed to me that the birth of a galaxy called for all three. They're so close together in spirit it seemed silly to give each a separate movement."

"Mmm." Worse and worse. Suppose Einstein had aphasia. "Why couldn't you have been a rotten dancer? That'd just be irony. This"—I pointed to the tape—"is high tragedy."

"Aren't you going to tell me I can still dance for myself?"

"No. For you that'd be worse than not dancing at all."

"My God, you're perceptive. Or am I that easy to read?"

I shrugged.

"Oh Charlie," she burst out, "what am I going to do?"

"You'd better not ask me that." My voice sounded funny.

"Why not?"

"Because I'm already two-thirds in love with you. And because you're not in love with me and never will be. And so that is the sort of question you shouldn't ask me."

It jolted her a little, but she recovered quickly. Her eyes softened, and she shook her head slowly. "You even know why I'm not, don't you?"

"And why you won't be."

I was terribly afraid she was going to say, "Charlie, I'm sorry." But she surprised me again. What she said was "I can count on the fingers of one foot the number of grown-up men I've ever met. I'm grateful for you. I guess ironic tragedies come in pairs."

"Sometimes."

"Well, now all I have to do is figure out what to do with my life. That should kill the weekend."

"Will you continue your classes?"

"Might as well. It's never a waste of time to study. Norrey's teaching me things."

All of a sudden my mind started to percolate. Man is a rational animal, right? Right. "What if I had a better idea?"

"If you've got another idea, it's better. Speak."

"Do you have to have an audience? I mean, does it have to be *live?*"

"What do you mean?"

"Maybe there's a back way in. Home video machines are starting to sell—once people understood they could collect old movies and such like they do records, it was just a matter of making it cheap enough for the traffic to bear. It's just about there—you know, TDT's already thinking of entering the market, and the Graham company has."

"So?"

"So suppose we go freelance? You and me? You dance it and I'll tape it: a straight business deal. I've got a few connections, and maybe I can get more. I could name you ten acts in the music business right now that never go on tour—just record and record. Why don't you bypass the structure of the dance companies and take a chance on the public? Maybe word of mouth could . . ."

Her face was beginning to light up like a jack-o'-lantern. "Charlie, do you think it could work? Do you really think so?"

"I don't think it has a snowball's chance." I crossed the room, opened up the beer fridge, took out the snowball I keep there in the summer, and tossed it at her. She caught it, but just barely, and when she realized what it was, she burst out laughing. "I've got just enough faith in the idea to quit working for TDT and put my time into it. I'll invest my time, my tape, my equipment, and my savings. Ante up."

She tried to get sober, but the snowball froze her fingers and she broke up again. "A snowball in July. You madman. Count me in. I've got a little money saved. And . . . and I guess I don't have much choice, do I?"

"I guess not."

The next three years were some of the most exciting years of my life, of both our lives. While I watched and taped, Shara transformed herself from a potentially great dancer into something truly awesome. She did something I'm not sure I can explain.

She became dance's analogy of the jazzman.

Dance was, for Shara, self-expression, pure and simple, first, last, and always. Once she freed herself of the attempt to fit into the world of company dance, she came to regard choreography, per se, as an *obstacle* to her self-expression, as a preprogrammed rut, inexorable as a script and as limiting. And so she devalued it.

A jazzman may blow *Night in Tunisia* for a dozen consecutive nights, and each evening will be a different experience, as he interprets and reinterprets the melody according to his mood of the moment. Total unity of artist and his art: spontaneous creation. The melodic starting point distinguishes the result from pure anarchy.

In just this way Shara devalued preperformance choreography to a starting point, a framework on which to build whatever the moment demanded, and then jammed around it. She learned in those three busy years to dismantle the interface between herself and her dance. Dancers have always tended to sneer at improv dancing, even while they practiced it in the studio, for the looseness it gave. They failed to see that *planned* improv, improv around a theme fully thought out in advance, was the natural next step in dance. Shara took the step. You must be very, very good to get away with that much freedom. She was good enough.

There's no point in detailing our professional fortunes over those three years. We worked hard, we made some magnificent tapes, and we couldn't sell them for paperweights. A home video cassette industry indeed formed—and they knew as much about modern dance as the record industry knew about the blues when *they* started. The big outfits wanted credentials, and the little outfits wanted cheap talent. Finally we even got desperate enough to try the schlock houses—and learned what we already knew. They didn't have the distribution, the prestige, or the technical specs for the critics to pay any attention to them. Word-of-mouth advertising is like a gene pool—if it isn't a certain minimum size to start with, it doesn't get anywhere. "Spider" John Koerner is an incredibly talented musician and songwriter who has been making and selling his own records since 1972. How many of you have ever heard of him?

In May of 1987 I opened my mailbox in the lobby and found the letter from VisuEnt, Inc., terminating our option with deepest sorrow and no severance. I went straight over to Shara's apartment, and my leg felt like the bone marrow had been replaced with thermite and ignited. It was a very long walk.

She was working on *Weight Is a Verb* when I got there. Converting her big living room into a studio had cost time, energy, skull-sweat, and a fat bribe to the landlord, but it was cheaper than renting time in a studio, considering the sets we wanted. It looked like high mountain country that day, and I hung my hat on a fake alder when I entered.

She flashed me a smile and kept moving, building up to greater and greater leaps. She looked like the most beautiful mountain goat I ever saw. I was in a foul mood and I wanted to kill the music (McLaughlin and Miles together, leaping some themselves), but I never could interrupt Shara when she was dancing. She built it gradually, with directional counterpoint, until she seemed to hurl herself into the air, stay there until she was damned good and ready, and then hurl herself down again. Sometimes she rolled when she hit and sometimes she landed on her hands, and always the energy of falling was transmuted into something instead of being absorbed. It was total energy output, and by the time she was done I had calmed down enough to be almost philosophical about our mutual professional ruin.

She ended up collapsed in upon herself, head bowed, exquisitely humbled in her attempt to defy gravity. I couldn't help applauding. It felt corny, but I couldn't help it.

"Thank you, Charlie."

"I'll be damned. Weight *is* a verb. I thought you were crazy when you told me the title."

"It's one of the strongest verbs in dance—and you can make it do *anything.*"

"Almost anything."

"Eh?"

"VisuEnt gave us our contract back."

"Oh." Nothing showed in her eyes, but I knew what was behind them. "Well, who's next on the list?"

"There is no one left on the list."

"Oh." This time it showed. "Oh."

"We should have remembered. Great artists are never honored in their own lifetime. What we ought to do is drop dead—then we'd be all set."

In my way I was trying to be strong for her, and she knew it and tried to be strong for me.

"Maybe what we should do is go into death insurance, for artists," she said. "We pay the client premiums against a controlling interest in his estate, and we insure that he'll die."

"We can't lose. And if he becomes famous in his lifetime he can buy out."

"Terrific. Let's stop this before I laugh myself to death."

"Yeah."

She was silent for a long time. My own mind was racing efficiently, but the transmission seemed to be blown—it wouldn't *go* anywhere. Finally she got up and turned off the music machine, which had been whining softly ever since the tape ended. It made a loud *click.*

"Norrey's got some land on Prince Edward Island," she said, not meeting my eyes. "There's a house."

I tried to head her off with the punchline from the old joke about the kid shoveling out the elephant cage in the circus whose father offers to take him back and set him up with a decent job. "What? And leave show business?"

"Screw show business," she said softly. "If I went out to PEI now, maybe I could get the land cleared and plowed in time to get a garden in." Her expression changed. "How about you?"

"Me? I'll be okay. TDT asked me to come back."

"That was six months ago."

"They asked again. Last week."

"And you said no. Moron."

"Maybe so, maybe so."

"The whole damn thing was a waste of time. All that time. All that energy. All that work. I might as well have been farming in PEI—by now the soil'd be starting to bear well. What a waste, Charlie, what a stinking waste."

"No, I don't think so, Shara. It sounds glib to say that 'nothing is wasted,' but—well, it's like that dance you just did. Maybe you can't beat gravity—but it surely is a beautiful thing to *try.*"

"Yeah, I know. Remember the Light Brigade. Remember the Alamo. They tried." She laughed, a bitter laugh.

"Yes, and so did Jesus of Nazareth. Did you do it for material reward, or because it needed doing? If nothing else, we now have several hundred thousand feet of the most magnificent dance recordings on tape, commercial value zero, real value incalculable, and by me that is no waste. It's over now, and we'll both go do the next thing, but it was *not a waste.*" I discovered that I was shouting, and stopped.

She closed her mouth. After a while she tried a smile. "You're right, Charlie. It wasn't waste. I'm a better dancer than I ever was."

"Damn right. You've transcended choreography."

She smiled ruefully. "Yeah. Even Norrey thinks it's a dead end."

"It is *not* a dead end. There's more to poetry than haiku and sonnets. Dancers don't *have* to be robots, delivering memorized lines with their bodies."

"They do if they want to make a living."

"We'll try again in a few years. Maybe they'll be ready then."

"Sure. Let me get us some drinks."

I slept with her that night, for the first and last time. In the morning I broke down the set in the living room while she packed. I promised to write. I promised to come and visit when I could. I carried her bags down to the car and stowed them inside. I kissed her and waved goodbye. I went looking for a drink, and at four o'clock the next morning a mugger decided I looked drunk enough, and I broke his jaw, his nose, and two ribs and then sat down on him and cried. On Monday morning I showed up at the studio with my hat in my hand and a mouth like a bus-station ashtray and crawled back into my old job. Norrey didn't ask any questions. What with rising food prices, I gave up eating anything but bourbon, and in six months I was fired. It went like that for a long time.

I never did write to her. I kept getting bogged down after "Dear Shara . . ."

When I got to the point of selling my video equipment for booze, a relay clicked somewhere and I took stock of myself. The stuff was all the life I had left, and so I went to the local AlAnon instead of the pawn shop and got sober. After a while my soul got numb, and I stopped flinching when I woke up. A hundred times I began to wipe the tapes I still had of Shara— she had copies of her own—but in the end I could not. From time to time I wondered how *she* was doing, and I could not bear to find out. If Norrey heard anything, she didn't tell me about it. She even tried to get me my job back a third time, but it was hopeless. Reputation can be a terrible thing once you've blown it. I was lucky to land a job with an educational TV station in New Brunswick.

It was a long couple of years.

Vidphones were coming out by 1990 and I had breadboarded one of my own without the knowledge or consent of the phone company, which I still hated more than anything. When the peanut bulb that I had replaced the damned bell with started glowing softly on and off one evening in June, I put the receiver on the audio pickup and energized the tube, in case the caller was also equipped. "Hello?"

She was. When Shara's face appeared, I got a cold cube of fear in the pit of my stomach, because I had quit seeing her face everywhere when I quit drinking, and I had been thinking lately of hitting the sauce again. When I blinked and she was still there, I felt a little better and tried to speak. It didn't work.

"Hello, Charlie. It's been a long time."

The second time it worked. "Seems like yesterday. Somebody else's yesterday."

"Yes, it does. It took me *days* to find you. Norrey's in Paris, and no one else knew where you'd gone."

"Yeah. How's farming?"

"I . . . I've put that away, Charlie. It's even more creative than dancing, but it's not the same."

"Then what *are* you doing?"

"Working."

"Dancing?"

"Yes. Charlie, I need you. I mean, I have a job for you. I need your cameras and your eye."

"Never mind the qualifications. Any kind of need will do. *Where are you?* When's the next plane there? Which cameras do I pack?"

"New York, an hour from now, and none of them. I didn't mean 'your cameras' literally—unless you're using GLX-5000s and a Hamilton Board lately."

I whistled. It hurt my mouth. "Not on my budget. Besides, I'm old-fashioned—I like to hold 'em with my hands."

"For this job you'll use a Hamilton, and it'll be a twenty-input Masterchrome, brand new."

"You grew poppies on that farm? Or just struck diamonds with the roto-tiller?"

"You'll be getting paid by Bryce Carrington."

I blinked.

"Now will you catch that plane so I can tell you about it? The New Age, ask for the Presidential Suite."

"The hell with the plane, I'll walk. Quicker." I hung up.

According to the *Time* magazine in my dentist's waiting room, Bryce Carrington was the genius who had become a multimillionaire by convincing a number of giants of industry to underwrite Skyfac, the great orbiting complex that kicked the bottom out of the crystals market. As I recalled the story, some rare poliolike disease had wasted both his legs and put him in a wheelchair. But the legs had lost strength, not function—in lessened gravity, they worked well enough. So he created Skyfac, establishing mining crews on Luna to supply it with cheap raw materials, and lived in orbit under reduced gravity. His picture made him look like a reasonably successful author (as opposed to writer). Other than that I knew nothing about him. I paid little attention to news and none at all to space news.

The New Age was *the* hotel in New York in those days, built on the ruins of the Sheraton. Ultraefficient security, bulletproof windows, carpets thicker than the outside air, and a lobby of an architectural persuasion that John D. MacDonald once called "Early Dental Plate." It stank of money. I was glad I'd made the effort to locate a necktie, and I wished I'd shined my shoes. An incredible man blocked my way as I came in through the airlock. He moved and was built like the toughest, fastest bouncer I ever saw, and he dressed and acted like God's butler. He said his name was Perry. He asked if he could help me, as though he didn't think so.

"Yes, Perry. Would you mind lifting up one of your feet?"

"Why?"

"I'll bet twenty dollars you've shined your soles."

Half his mouth smiled, and he didn't move an inch. "Who did you wish to see?"

"Shara Drummond."

"Not registered."

"The Presidential Suite."

"Oh." Light dawned. "Mr. Carrington's lady. You should have said so. Wait here, please." While he phoned to verify that I was expected, keeping his eye on me and his hand near his pocket, I swallowed my heart and rearranged my face. It took some time. So that was how it was. All right then. That was how it was.

Perry came back and gave me the little button transmitter that would let me walk the corridors of the New Age without being cut down by automatic laser fire, and explained carefully that it would blow a largish hole in me if I attempted to leave the building without returning it. From his manner I gathered that I had just skipped four grades in social standing. I thanked him, though I'm damned if I know why.

I followed the green fluorescent arrows that appeared on the bulbless ceiling, and came after a long and scenic walk to the Presidential Suite. Shara was waiting at the door, in something like an angel's pajamas. It made all that big body look delicate. "Hello, Charlie."

I was jovial and hearty. "Hi, babe. Swell joint. How've you been keeping yourself?"

"I haven't been."

"Well, how's Carrington been keeping you, then?" Steady, boy.

"Come in Charlie."

I went in. It looked like where the Queen stayed when she was in town, and I'm sure she enjoyed it. You could have landed an airplane in the living room without waking anyone in the bedroom. It had two pianos. Only one fireplace, barely big enough to barbecue a buffalo—you have to scrimp somewhere, I guess. Roger Kellaway was on the quadio, and for a wild moment I thought he was actually in the suite, playing some unseen third piano. So this was how it was.

"Can I get you something, Charlie?"

"Oh, sure. Hash oil, Tangier Supreme. Dom Perignon for the pipe."

Without cracking a smile, she went to the cabinet, which looked like a midget cathedral, and produced precisely what I had ordered. I kept my own features impassive and lit up. The bubbles tickled my throat, and the rush was exquisite. I felt myself relaxing, and when we had passed the narghile's mouthpiece a few times I felt her relax. We looked at each other then—really looked at each other—then at the room around us and then at each other again. Simultaneously we roared with laughter, a laughter that blew all the wealth out of the room and let in richness. Her laugh was the same whooping, braying belly laugh I remembered so well, an unselfconscious and lusty laugh, and it reassured me tremendously. I was so relieved I couldn't stop laughing myself, and that kept *her* going, and just as we might have stopped she pursed her lips and blew a stuttered arpeggio. There's an old recording called the *Spike Jones Laughing Record,* where the tuba player tries to play "The Flight of the Bumblebee" and falls down laughing, and the whole band breaks up and horse-laughs for a full two minutes, and every time they run out of air the tuba player tries another flutter and roars and they all break up again, and once when Shara was blue I bet her ten dollars that she couldn't listen to that record without at least giggling and I won. When I understood now that she was quoting it, I shuddered and dissolved into great whoops of new laughter, and a minute later we had reached the stage where we literally laughed ourselves out of our chairs and lay on the floor in agonies of mirth, weakly pounding the floor and howling. I take that laugh out of my memory now and then and rerun it—but not often, for such records deteriorate drastically with play.

At last we dopplered back down to panting grins, and I helped her to her feet.

"What a perfectly dreadful place," I said, still chuckling.

She glanced around and shuddered. "Oh God, it *is,* Charlie. It must be awful to need this much front."

"For a horrid while I thought *you* did."

She sobered and met my eyes. "Charlie, I wish I could resent that. In a way I do need it."

My eyes narrowed. "Just what do you mean?"

"I need Bryce Carrington."

"This time you can trot out the qualifiers. *How* do you need him?"

"I need his money," she cried.

How can you relax and tense up at the same time? "Oh, *damn* it, Shara! Is *that* how you're going to get to dance? Buy your way in? What does a critic go for these days?"

"Charlie, stop it. I need Carrington to get seen. He's going to rent me a hall, that's all."

"If that's all, let's get out of the dump right now. I can bor— get enough cash to rent you any hall in the world, and I'm just as willing to risk my money."

"Can you get me Skyfac?"

"*Uh?*"

I couldn't for the life of me imagine why she proposed to go to Skyfac to dance. Why not Antarctica?

"Shara, you know even less about space than I do, but you must know that a satellite broadcast doesn't have to be made from a satellite?"

"Idiot. It's the setting I want."

I thought about it. "Moon'd be better, visually. Mountains. Light. Contrast."

"The visual aspect is secondary. I don't want one-sixth gee, Charlie. I want zero gravity."

My mouth hung open.

"And I want you to be my video man."

God, she was a rare one. What I needed then was to sit there with my mouth open and think for several minutes. She let me do just that, waiting patiently for me to work it all out.

"Weight isn't a verb anymore, Charlie," she said finally. "That dance ended on the assertion that you can't beat gravity—you said so yourself. Well, that statement is incorrect—obsolete. The dance of the twenty-first century will have to acknowledge that."

"And it's just what you need to make it. A new kind of dance for a new kind of dancer. Unique. It'll catch the public eye, and you should have the field entirely to yourself for years. I like it, Shara. I like it. But can you pull it off?"

"I thought about what you said: that you can't beat gravity but it's beautiful to try. It stayed in my head for months, and then one day I was visiting a neighbor with a TV and I saw newsreels of the crew working on Skyfac Two. I was up all night thinking, and the next morning came up to the States and got a job in Skyfac One. I've been up there for nearly a year, getting next to Carrington. I can do it, Charlie, I can make it work." There was a ripple in her jaw that I had seen before—when she told me off in Le Maintenant. It was a ripple of determination.

Still I frowned. "With Carrington's backing."

Her eyes left mine. "There's no such thing as a free lunch."

"What does he charge?"

She failed to answer, for long enough to answer me. In that instant I began believing in God again, for the first time in years, just to be able to hate Him.

But I kept my mouth shut. She was old enough to manage her own finances. The price of a dream gets higher every year. Hell, I'd half expected it from the moment she'd called me.

But only half.

"Charlie, don't just sit there with your face all knotted up. Say something. Cuss me out, call me a whore, *something.*"

"Nuts. You be your own conscience, I have trouble enough being my own. You want to dance, you've got a patron. So now you've got a video man."

I hadn't intended to say that last sentence at all.

Strangely, it almost seemed to disappoint her at first. But then she relaxed and smiled. "Thank you, Charlie. Can you get out of whatever you're doing right away?"

"I'm working for an educational station in Shediac. I even got to shoot some dance footage. A dancing bear from the London Zoo. The amazing thing was how well he danced." She grinned. "I can get free."

"I'm glad. I don't think I could pull this off without you."

"I'm working for you. Not for Carrington."

"All right."

"Where is the great man, anyway? Scuba diving in the bathtub?"

"No," came a quiet voice from the doorway. "I've been skydiving in the lobby."

His wheelchair was a mobile throne. He wore a four-hundred-dollar suit the color of strawberry ice cream, a powder blue turtleneck, and one gold earring. The shoes were genuine leather. The watch was that newfangled bandless kind that literally tells you the time. He wasn't tall enough for her, and his shoulders were absurdly broad, although the suit tried hard to deny both. His eyes were like twin blueberries. His smile was that of a shark wondering which part will taste best. I wanted to crush his head between two boulders.

Shara was on her feet. "Bryce, this is Charles Armstead. I told you—"

"Oh yes. The video chap." He rolled forward and extended an impeccably manicured hand. "I'm Bryce Carrington, Armstead."

I remained seated, hands in my lap. "Oh yes. The rich chap."

One eyebrow rose an urbane quarter-inch. "Oh my. Another rude one. Well, if you're as good as Shara says you are, you're entitled."

"I'm rotten."

The smile faded. "Let's stop fencing, Armstead. I don't expect manners from creative people, but I have far more significant contempt than yours available if I need any. Now I'm tired of this damned gravity and I've had a rotten day testifying for a friend and it looks like they're going to recall me tomorrow. Do you want the job or don't you?"

He had me there. I did. "Yeah."

"All right, then. Your room is 2772. We'll be going up to Skyfac in two days. Be here at eight A.M."

"I'll want to talk with you about what you'll be needing, Charlie," Shara said. "Give me a call tomorrow."

I whirled to face her, and she flinched from my eyes.

Carrington failed to notice. "Yes, make a list of your requirements by tomorrow, so it can go up with us. Don't scrimp—if you don't fetch it, you'll do without. Good night, Armstead."

I faced him. "Good night, Mr. Carrington." Suh.

He turned toward the narghile, and Shara hurried to refill the chamber and bowl. I turned away hastily and made for the door. My leg hurt so much I nearly fell on the way, but I set my jaw and made it. When I reached the door I said to myself, You will now open the door and go through it, and then I spun on my heel. "Carrington!"

He blinked, surprised to discover I still existed. "Yes?"

"Are you *aware* that she doesn't love you in the slightest? Does that matter to you in any way?" My voice was high, and my fists were surely clenched.

"Oh," he said, and then again, "Oh. So that's what it is. I didn't *think* success alone merited that much contempt." He put down the mouthpiece and folded his fingers together. "Let me tell you something, Armstead. No one has ever loved me, to my knowledge. This suite does not love me." His voice took on human feeling for the first time. "But it is *mine*. Now get out."

I opened my mouth to tell him where to put his job, and then I saw Shara's face, and the pain in it suddenly made me deeply ashamed. I left at once, and when the door closed behind me I vomited on a rug that was worth slightly less than a Hamilton Masterchrome board. I was sorry then that I'd worn a necktie.

The trip to Pike's Peak Spaceport, at least, was aesthetically pleasurable. I enjoy air travel, gliding among stately clouds, watching the rolling procession of mountains and plains, vast jigsaws of farmland, and intricate mosaics of suburbia unfolding below.

But the jump to Skyfac in Carrington's personal shuttle, *That First Step,* might as well have been an old Space Commando rerun. I *know* they can't put portholes in spaceships—but damn it, a shipboard video relay conveys no better resolution, color values, or presence than you get on your living room tube. The only differences are that the stars don't "move" to give the illusion of travel, and there's no director editing the POV to give you dramatically interesting shots.

Aesthetically speaking. The *experiential* difference is that they do not, while you are watching the Space Commando, sell hemorrhoid remedies, strap you into a couch, batter you with thunders, make you weigh better than half a ton for an unreasonably long time, and then drop you off the edge of the world into weightlessness. I had been half expecting nausea, but what I got was even more shocking: the sudden, unprecedented, total absence of pain in my leg. At that, Shara was hit worse than I was, barely managing to deploy her dropsickness bag in time. Carrington unstrapped and administered an anti-nausea injection with sure movements. It seemed to take forever to hit her, but when it did there was an enormous change—color and strength returned rapidly, and she was apparently fully recovered by the time the pilot announced that we were commencing docking and would everyone please strap in and shut up. I half expected Carrington to bark manners into him, but apparently the industrial magnate was not that sort of fool. He shut up and strapped himself down.

My leg didn't hurt in the slightest. Not at all.

The Skyfac complex looked like a disorderly heap of bicycle tires and beach balls of various sizes. The one our pilot made for was more like a tractor tire. We matched course, became its axle, and matched spin, and the damned thing grew a spoke that caught us square in the airlock. The airlock was "overhead" of our couches, but we entered and left it feet first. A few yards into the spoke, the direction we traveled became "down," and handholds became a ladder. Weight increased with every step, but even when we had emerged in a rather large cubical compartment it was far less than Earth-normal. Nonetheless, my leg resumed biting me.

The room tried to be a classic reception room, high level ("Please be seated. His Majesty will see you shortly."), but the low gee and the p-suits racked along two walls spoiled the effect. Unlike the Space Commando's armor, a real pressure suit looks like nothing so much as a people-shaped baggie, and they look particularly silly in repose. A young dark-haired man in tweed rose from behind a splendidly gadgeted desk and smiled. "Good to see you, Mr. Carrington, I hope you had a pleasant jump."

"Fine thanks, Tom. You remember Shara, of course. This is Charles Armstead. Tom McGillicuddy." We both displayed our teeth and said we were delighted to meet one another. I could see that beneath the pleasantries McGillicuddy was upset about something.

"Nils and Mr. Longmire are waiting in your office, sir. There's . . . there's been another sighting."

"God *damn* it," Carrington began and cut himself off. I stared at him. The full force of my best sarcasm had failed to anger this man. "All right. Take care of my guests while I go hear what Longmire has to say." He started for the door, moving like a beach ball in slow motion but under his own power. "Oh yes—the *Step* is loaded to the gun'ls with bulky equipment, Tom. Have her brought around to the cargo bays. Store the equipment in Six. He left, looking worried. McGillicuddy activated his desk and gave the necessary orders.

"What's going on, Tom?" Shara asked when he was through.

He looked at me before replying. "Pardon my asking, Mr. Armstead, but—are you a newsman?"

"Charlie. No, I'm not. I am a video man, but I work for Shara."

"Mmmm. Well, you'll hear about it sooner or later. About two weeks ago, an object appeared on radar within the orbit of Neptune, just appeared out of nowhere. There were . . . certain other anomalies. It stayed put for half a day and then vanished again. The Space Command slapped a hush on it, but it's common knowledge on board Skyfac."

"And the thing has been sighted again?" Shara asked.

"Just beyond the orbit of Jupiter."

I was only mildly interested. No doubt there was an explanation for the phenomenon, and since Isaac Asimov wasn't around I would doubtless never understand a word of it. Most of us gave up on intelligent nonhuman life when the last intersystem probe came back empty. "Little green men, I suppose. Can you show us the Lounge, Tom? I understand it's just like the one we'll be working in."

He seemed to welcome the change of subject. "Sure thing."

McGillicuddy led us through a p-door opposite the one Carrington had used, through long halls whose floors curved up ahead of and behind us. Each was outfitted differently, each was full of busy, purposeful people, and each reminded me somehow of the lobby of the New Age, or perhaps of the old movie *2001*. Futuristic Opulence, so understated as to fairly shriek. Wall Street lifted bodily into orbit—the *clocks* were on Wall Street time. I tried to make myself believe that cold, empty space lay a short distance away in any direction, but it was impossible. I decided it was a good thing spacecraft didn't have portholes—once he got used to the low gravity, a man might forget and open one to throw out a cigar.

I studied McGillicuddy as we walked. He was immaculate in every respect, from necktie down to nail polish, and he wore no jewelry at all. His hair was short and black, his beard inhibited, and his eyes surprisingly warm in a professionally sterile face. I wondered what he had sold his soul for. I hoped he had gotten his price.

We had to descend two levels to get to the Lounge. The gravity on the upper level was kept at one-sixth normal, partly for the convenience of the Lunar personnel who were Skyfac's only regular commuters, and mostly (of course) for the convenience of Carrington. But descending brought a subtle increase in weight, to nearly a quarter normal. My leg complained bitterly, but I found to my surprise that I preferred the pain to its absence. It's a little scary when an old friend goes away like that.

The Lounge was a larger room than I had expected, quite big enough for our purposes. It encompassed all three levels, and one whole wall was an immense video screen across which stars wheeled dizzily, joined with occasional regularity by a slice of mother Terra. The floor was crowded with chairs and tables in various groupings, but I could see that, stripped, it would provide Shara with entirely adequate room to dance; equally important, my feet told me that it would make a splendid dancing surface. Then I remembered how little use the floor was liable to get.

"Well," Shara said to me with a smile, "this is what home will look like for the next six months. The Ring Two Lounge is identical to this one.

"Six?" McGillicuddy said. "Not a chance."

"What do you mean?" Shara and I said together.

He blinked at our combined volume. "Well, *you* might be good for that long, Charlie. But Shara's already had over a year of low gee, while she was in the typing pool."

"So what?"

"Look, you expect to be in free fall for long periods of time, if I understand this correctly?"

"Twelve hours a day," Shara agreed.

He grimaced. "Shara, I hate to say this . . . but I'll be surprised if you last a month. A body designed for a one-gee environment doesn't work properly in zero gee."

"But it will adapt, won't it?"

He laughed mirthlessly. "Sure. That's why we rotate all personnel Earthside every fourteen months. Your body will adapt. One way. No return. Once you've fully adapted, returning to Earth will stop your heart—if some other major systemic failure doesn't occur first. Look, you were just Earthside for three days—did you have any chest pains? Dizziness? Bowel trouble? Dropsickness on the way up?"

"All of the above," she admitted.

"There you go. You were close to the nominal fourteen-month limit when you left. And your body will adapt even faster under no gravity at all. The free-fall endurance record is ninety days, by the first Skylab crew—and *they* hadn't spent a year in one-sixth gee first, *and* they weren't straining their hearts the way you will be. Hell, there are four men on Luna now, from the original dozen in the first mining team, who will never see Earth again. Eight of their teammates tried. Don't you two know *any*thing about space?"

"But I've got to have at least four months. Four months of solid work, every day. I *must.*" She was dismayed but fighting hard for control.

McGillicuddy started to shake his head and then thought better of it. His warm eyes were studying Shara's face. I knew exactly what he was thinking, and I liked him for it.

He was thinking, *How to tell a lovely lady her dearest dream is hopeless?*

He didn't know the half of it. I *knew* how much Shara had already—irrevocably—invested in this dream, and something in me screamed.

And then I saw her jaw ripple and I dared to hope.

Dr. Panzarella was a wiry old man with eyebrows like two fuzzy caterpillars. He wore a tight-fitting jumpsuit which would not foul a p-suit's seals should he have to get into one in a hurry. His shoulder-length hair, which should have been a mane on the great skull, was tied tightly back against a sudden absence of gravity. A cautious man. To employ an obsolete metaphor, he was a suspenders-*and*-belt type. He looked Shara over, ran tests, and gave her just under a month and a half. Shara said some things. I said some things. McGillicuddy said some things. Panzarella shrugged, made further very careful tests, and reluctantly cut loose of the suspenders. Two months. Not a day over. Possibly less, depending on subsequent monitoring of her body's reactions to extended weightlessness. Then a year Earthside before risking it again. Shara seemed satisfied.

I didn't see how we could do it.

McGillicuddy had assured us that it would take Shara at least a month simply to learn to handle herself competently in zero gee, much less dance. Her familiarity with one-sixth gee would, he predicted, be a liability rather than an asset. Then figure three weeks of choreography and rehearsal, a week of taping and just maybe we could broadcast one dance before Shara had to return to Earth. Not good enough. She and I had calculated that we would need three successive shows, each well received, to make a big enough dent in the dance world for Shara to squeeze into it. A year was far too big a spacing—and *who knew how soon Carrington would tire of her?* So I hollered at Panzarella.

"Mr. Armstead," he said hotly, "I am specifically contractually forbidden to allow this young lady to commit suicide." He grimaced sourly. "I'm told it's terrible public relations."

"Charlie, it's okay," Shara insisted. "I can fit in three dances. We may lose some sleep, but we can do it."

"I once told a man nothing was impossible. He asked me if I could ski through a revolving door. You haven't got . . ."

My brain slammed into hyperdrive, thought about things, kicked itself in the ass a few times, and returned to realtime in time to hear my mouth finish without a break: ". . . much choice, though. Okay, Tom, have that damned Ring Two Lounge cleaned out. I want it naked and spotless, and have somebody paint over that damned video wall, the same shade as the other three and I mean *the same.* Shara, get out of those clothes and into your leotard. Doctor, we'll be seeing you in twelve hours. Quit gaping and *go*, Tom—we'll be going over there at once. *Where the hell are my cameras?*"

McGillicuddy sputtered.

"Get me a torch crew—I'll want holes cut through the walls, cameras behind them, one-way glass, six locations, a room adjacent to the Lounge for a mixer console the size of a jetliner cockpit, and bolt a coffee machine next to the chair. I'll need another room for editing, complete privacy, and total darkness, size of an efficiency kitchen, another coffee machine."

McGillicuddy finally drowned me out. "Mr. *Armstead*, this is the Main Ring of the Skyfac One complex, the administrative offices of one of the wealthiest corporations in existence. If you think this whole Ring is going to stand on its head for you . . ."

So we brought the problem to Carrington. He told McGillicuddy that henceforth, Ring Two was *ours*, as well as any assistance whatsoever that we requested. He looked rather distracted. McGillicuddy started to tell him by how many weeks all this would put off the opening of the Skyfac Two complex. Carrington replied very quietly that he could add and subtract quite well, thank you, and McGillicuddy got white and quiet.

I'll give Carrington that much. He gave us a free hand.

Panzarella ferried over to Skyfac Two with us. We were chauffeured by lean-jawed astronaut types on vehicles looking, for all the world, like pregnant broomsticks. It was as well that we had the doctor with us—Shara fainted on the way over. I nearly did myself, and I'm sure that broomstick has my thigh prints on it yet —falling through space is a scary experience the first time. Shara responded splendidly once we had her inboard again, and fortunately her dropsickness did not return—nausea can be a nuisance in free fall, a disaster in a p-suit. By the time my cameras and mixer had arrived, she was on her feet and sheepish. And while I browbeat a sweating crew of borrowed techs into installing them faster than was humanly possible, Shara began learning how to move in zero gee.

We were ready for the first taping in three weeks.

Living quarters and minimal life support were rigged for us in Ring Two so that we could work around the clock if we chose, but we spent nearly half of our nominal "off hours" in Skyfac One. Shara was required to spend half of three days a week there with Carrington, and spent a sizable portion of her remaining putative sack time out in space, in a p-suit. At first it was a conscious attempt to overcome her gut-level fear of all that emptiness. Soon it became her meditation, her retreat, her artistic reverie—an attempt to gain from contemplation of the cold black depths enough insight into the meaning of extraterrestrial existence to dance of it.

I spent my own time arguing with engineers and electricians and technicians and a damn fool union legate who insisted that the Second Lounge, finished or not, belonged to the hypothetical future crew and administrative personnel. Securing his permission to work there wore the lining off my throat and the insulation off my nerves. Far too many nights I spent slugging instead of sleeping. Minor example: every interior wall in the whole damned Second Ring was painted the identical shade of turquoise—and they couldn't duplicate it to cover that godforsaken video wall in the Lounge. It was McGillicuddy who saved me from gibbering apoplexy—at his suggestion I washed off the third latex job, unshipped the outboard camera that fed the wall screen, brought it inboard, and fixed it to scan an interior wall in an adjoining room. That made us friends again.

It was all like that: jury-rig, improvise, file to fit, and paint to cover. If a camera broke down, I spent sleep time talking with off-shift engineers, finding out what parts in stock could be adapted. It was simply too expensive to have anything shipped up from Earth's immense gravity well, and Luna didn't have what I needed.

At that, Shara worked harder than I did. A body must totally recoordinate itself to function in the absence of weight—she had to forget literally everything she had ever known or learned about

dancing and acquire a whole new set of skills. This turned out to
be even harder than we had expected. McGillicuddy had been
right: what Shara had learned in her year of one-sixth gee was an
exaggerated attempt to *retain* terrestrial patterns of coordination
—rejecting them altogether was actually easier for *me.*

But I couldn't keep up with her—I had to abandon any thought
of handheld camera work and base my plans solely on the six fixed
cameras. Fortunately GLX-5000s have a ball-and-socket mount:
even behind that damned one-way glass I had about forty degrees
of traverse on each one. Learning to coordinate all six simultaneously on the Hamilton Board did a truly extraordinary thing to me
—it lifted me that one last step to unity with my art. I found that
I could learn to be aware of all six monitors with my mind's eye,
to perceive almost spherically, to—not share my attention among
the six—to *encompass* them all, seeing like a six-eyed creature
from many angles at once. My mind's eye became holographic, my
awareness multilayered. I began to really understand, for the first
time, three-dimensionality.

It was that fourth dimension that was the kicker. It took Shara
two days to decide that she could not possibly become proficient
enough in free-fall maneuvering to sustain a half-hour piece in the
time required. So she rethought her work plan too, adapting her
choreography to the demands of exigency. She put in six hard days
under normal Earth weight.

And for her, too, the effort brought her that one last step toward
apotheosis.

On Monday of the fourth week we began taping *Liberation.*

Establishing shot:
A great turquoise box, seen from within. Dimensions unknown,
but the color somehow lends an impression of immensity, of vast
distances. Against the far wall, a swinging pendulum attests that
this is a standard-gravity environment; but the pendulum swings
so slowly and is so featureless in construction that it is impossible

to estimate its size and so extrapolate that of the room.

Because of this trompe l'oeil effect, the room seems rather smaller than it really is when the camera pulls back and we are wrenched into proper perspective by the appearance of Shara, prone, inert, face down on the floor, facing us.

She wears beige leotard and tights. Hair the color of fine mahogany is pulled back into a loose ponytail which fans across one shoulder blade. She does not appear to breathe. She does not appear to be alive.

Music begins. The aging Mahavishnu, on obsolete nylon acoustic, establishes a minor E in no hurry at all. A pair of small candles in simple brass holders appear, inset on either side of the room. They are larger than life, though small beside Shara. Both are unlit.

Her body . . . there is no word. It does not move, in the sense of motor activity. One might say that a ripple passes through it, save that the motion is clearly all outward from her center. She *swells,* as if the first breath of life was being taken by her whole body at once. She lives.

The twin wicks begin to glow, oh, softly. The music takes on quiet urgency.

Shara raises her head to us. Her eyes focus somewhere beyond the camera yet short of infinity. Her body writhes, undulates, and the glowing wicks are coals (that this brightening takes place in slow motion is not apparent).

A violent contraction raises her to a crouch, spilling the ponytail across her shoulder. Mahavishnu begins a cyclical cascade of runs, in increasing tempo. Long, questing tongues of yellow-orange flame begin to blossom *downward* from the twin wicks, whose coals are turning to blue.

The contraction's release flings her to her feet. The twin skirts of flame about the wicks curl up over themselves, writhing furiously, to become conventional candle flames, flickering now in normal time. Tablas, tambouras, and a bowed string bass join the guitar, and they segue into an energetic interplay around a minor seventh that keeps trying, fruitlessly, to find resolution in the sixth. The candles stay in perspective but dwindle in size until they vanish.

Shara begins to explore the possibilities of motion. First she moves only perpendicular to the camera's line of sight, exploring that dimension. Every motion of arms or legs or head is clearly seen to be a defiance of gravity, of a force as inexorable as radioactive decay, as entropy itself. The most violent surges of energy succeed only for a time—the outflung leg falls, the outthrust arm drops. She must struggle or fall. She pauses in thought.

Her hands and arms reach out toward the camera, and at the instant they do we cut to a view from the left-hand wall. Seen from the right side, she reaches out into this new dimension and soon begins to move in it. (As she moves backward out of the camera's field, its entire image shifts right on our screen, butted out of the way by the incoming image of a second camera, which picks her up as the first loses her without a visible seam.)

The new dimension too fails to fulfill Shara's desire for freedom from gravity. Combining the two, however, presents so many permutations of movement that for a while, intoxicated, she flings herself into experimentation. In the next fifteen minutes, Shara's entire background and history in dance are recapitulated in a blinding tour de force that incorporates elements of jazz, modern, and the more graceful aspects of Olympic-level mat gymnastics. Five cameras come into play, singly and in pairs on split-screen, as the "bag of tricks" amassed in a lifetime of study and improvisation are rediscovered and performed by a superbly trained and versatile body, in a pyrotechnic display that would shout of joy if her expression did not remain aloof, almost arrogant. *This is the offering,* she seems to say, *which you would not accept. This, by itself, was not good enough.*

And it is not. Even in its raging energy and total control, her body returns again and again to the final compromise of mere erectness, that last simple refusal to fall.

Clamping her jaw, she works into a series of leaps, ever longer, ever higher. She seems at last to hang suspended for full seconds, straining to fly. When, inevitably, she falls, she falls reluctantly, only at the last possible instant tucking and rolling back onto her feet. The musicians are in a crescendoing frenzy. We see her now only with the single original camera, and the twin candles have returned, small but burning fiercely.

The leaps begin to diminish in intensity and height, and she takes longer to build to each one. She has been dancing flat out for nearly twenty minutes: as the candle flames begin to wane, so does her strength. At last she retreats to a place beneath the indifferent pendulum, gathers herself with a final desperation, and races forward toward us. She reaches incredible speed in a short space, hurls herself into a double roll, and bounds up into the air off one foot, seeming a full second later to push off against empty air for a few more inches of height. Her body goes rigid, her eyes and mouth gape wide, the flames reach maximum brilliance, the music peaks with the tortured wail of an electric guitar, and—she falls, barely snapping into a roll in time, rising only as far as a crouch. She holds there for a long moment, and gradually her head and shoulders slump, defeated, toward the floor. The candle flames draw in upon themselves in a curious way and appear to go out. The string bass saws on, modulating down to D.

Muscle by muscle, Shara's body gives up the struggle. The air seems to tremble around the wicks of the candles, which have now grown nearly as tall as her crouching form.

Shara lifts her face to the camera with evident effort. Her face is anguished, her eyes nearly shut. A long beat.

All at once she opens her eyes wide, squares her shoulders, and contracts. It is the most exquisite and total contraction ever dreamed of, filmed in realtime but seeming almost to be in slow motion. She holds it. Mahavishnu comes back in on guitar, building in increasing tempo from a downtuned bass string to a D with a flatted fourth. Shara holds.

We shift for the first time to an overhead camera, looking down on her from a great height. As Mahavishnu's picking increases to the point where the chord seems a sustained drone, Shara slowly lifts her head, still holding the contraction, until she is staring directly up at us. She poises there for an eternity, like a spring wound to the bursting point . . .

. . . and explodes upward toward us, rising higher and faster than she possibly can in a soaring flight that *is* slow motion now, coming closer and closer until her hands disappear off either side and her face fills the screen, flanked by two candles which have bloomed into gouts of yellow flame in an instant. The guitar and bass are submerged in an orchestra.

Almost at once she whirls away from us, and the POV switches to the original camera, on which we see her fling herself down ten meters to the floor, reversing her attitude in midflight and twisting. She comes out of her roll in an absolutely flat trajectory that takes her the length of the room. She hits the far wall with a crash audible even over the music, shattering the still pendulum. Her thighs soak up the kinetic energy and then release it, and once again she is racing toward us, hair streaming straight out behind her, a broad smile of triumph growing larger in the screen.

In the next five minutes all six cameras vainly try to track her as she caroms around the immense room like a hummingbird trying to batter its way out of a cage, using the walls, floor, and ceiling the way a jai alai master does, *existing in three dimensions.* Gravity is defeated. The basic assumption of all dance is transcended.

Shara is transformed.

She comes to rest at last at vertical center in the forefront of the turquoise cube, arms-legs-fingers-toes-face straining *outward,* turning gently end over end. All four cameras that bear on her join

in a four-way split-screen, the orchestra resolves into its final E
major, and—fadeout.

I had neither the time nor the equipment to create the special
effects that Shara wanted. So I figured out ways to warp reality to
my need. The first candle segment was a twinned shot of a candle
being blown out from above—in ultraslow motion, and in reverse.
The second segment was a simple recording of reality. I had lit the
candle, started taping—and had the Ring's spin killed. A candle
behaves oddly in zero gee. The low-density combustion gases do
not rise up from the flame, allowing air to reach it from beneath.
The flame does not go out: it becomes dormant. Restore gravity
within a minute or so, and it blooms back to life again. All I did was
monkey with speeds a bit to match in with the music and Shara's
dance. I got the idea from the foreman of the metal shop where we
were designing things Shara would need for the next dance.

I set up a screen in the Ring One Lounge, and everyone in
Skyfac who could cut work crowded in for the broadcast. They saw
exactly what was being sent out over worldwide satellite hookup
(Carrington had sufficient pull to arrange twenty-five minutes
without commercial interruption) almost a full half-second before
the world did.

I spent the broadcast in the Communications Room chewing my
fingernails. But it went without a hitch, and I slapped my board
dead and made it to the Lounge in time to see the last half of the
standing ovation. Shara stood before the screen, Carrington sitting
beside her, and I found the difference in their expressions instruc-
tive. Her face showed no surprise or modesty. She had had faith
in herself throughout, had approved this tape for broadcast—she
was aware, with that incredible detachment of which so few artists
are capable, that the wild applause was only what she deserved.
But her face showed that she was deeply surprised—and deeply
grateful—to be given what she deserved.

Carrington, on the other hand, registered a triumph strangely mingled with relief. He too had faith in Shara, backing it with a large investment—but his faith was that of a businessman in a gamble he believes will pay off, and as I watched his eyes and the glisten of sweat on his forehead, I realized that no businessman ever takes an expensive gamble without worrying that it may be the fiasco that will begin the loss of his only essential commodity: face.

Seeing his kind of triumph next to hers spoiled the moment for me, and instead of thrilling for Shara I found myself almost hating her. She spotted me and waved me to join her before the cheering crowd, but I turned and literally flung myself from the room. I borrowed a bottle from the metal-shop foreman and got stinking.

The next morning my head felt like a fifteen-amp fuse on a forty-amp circuit, and I seemed to be held together only by surface tension.

Sudden movements frightened me. It's a long fall off that wagon, even at one-sixth gee.

The phone chimed—I hadn't had time to rewire it—and a young man I didn't know politely announced that Mr. Carrington wished to see me in his office. At once. I spoke of a barbed-wire suppository, and what Mr. Carrington might do with it, at once. Without changing expression, he repeated his message and disconnected.

So I crawled into my clothes, decided to grow a beard, and left. Along the way I wondered what I had traded my independence for, and why?

Carrington's office was oppressively tasteful, but at least the lighting was subdued. Best of all, its filter system would handle smoke—the sweet musk of pot lay on the air. I accepted a macrojoint of "Maoi-Zowie" from Carrington with something approaching gratitude and began melting my hangover.

Shara sat next to his desk, wearing a leotard and a layer of sweat. She had obviously spent the morning rehearsing for the next dance. I felt ashamed, and consequently snappish, avoiding her eyes and her hello. Panzarella and McGillicuddy came in on my heels, chattering about the latest sighting of the mysterious object from deep space, which had appeared this time in the neighborhood of Mercury. They were arguing over whether it displayed signs of sentience or not, and I wished they'd shut up.

Carrington waited until we had all seated ourselves and lit up, then rested a hip on his desk and smiled. "Well, Tom?"

McGillicuddy beamed. "Better than we expected, sir. All the ratings agree we had about 74 percent of the world audience."

"The hell with the Nielsens," I snapped. *"What did the critics say?"*

McGillicuddy blinked. "Well, the general reaction so far is that Shara was a smash. The *Times*—"

I cut him off again. "What was the less than general reaction?"

"Well, nothing is ever unanimous."

"Specifics. The dance press? Liz Zimmer? Migdalski?"

"Uh. Not as good. Praise, yes—only a blind man could've panned that show. But guarded praise. Uh, Zimmer called it a magnificent dance spoiled by a gimmicky ending."

"And Migdalski?" I insisted.

"He headed his review 'But What Do You Do for an Encore?' " McGillicuddy admitted. "His basic thesis was that it was a charming one-shot. But the *Times*—"

"Thank you, Tom," Carrington said quietly. "About what we expected, isn't it, my dear? A big splash, but no one's willing to call it a tidal wave yet."

She nodded. "But they will, Bryce. The next two dances will sew it up."

Panzarella spoke up. "Ms. Drummond, may I ask why you played it the way you did? Using the null-gee interlude only as a brief adjunct to conventional dance—surely you must have expected the critics to call it gimmickry."

Shara smiled and answered: "To be honest, Doctor, I had no choice. I'm learning to use my body in free fall, but it's still a conscious effort, almost a pantomime. I need another few weeks to make it second nature, and it *has* to be if I'm to sustain a whole piece in it. So I dug a conventional dance out of the trunk, tacked on a five-minute ending that used every zero-gee move I knew, and found to my extreme relief that they made thematic sense together. I told Charlie my notion, and he made it work visually and dramatically—that whole business of the candles was his, and it underlined what I was trying to say better than any set we could have built."

"So you have not yet completed what you came here to do?" Panzarella asked Shara.

"Oh, no. Not by any means. The next dance will show the world that dance is more than controlled falling. And the third . . . the third will be what this has all been for." Her face lit, became animated. "The third dance will be the one I have wanted to dance all my life. I can't entirely picture it, yet—but I know that when I become capable of dancing it, I will create it, and it will be my greatest dance."

Panzarella cleared his throat. "How long will it take you?"

"Not long," she said. "I'll be ready to tape the next dance in two weeks, and I can start on the last one almost at once. With luck, I'll have it in the can before my month is up."

"Ms. Drummond," Panzarella said gravely, "I'm afraid you don't have another month."

Shara went white as snow, and I half rose from my seat. Carrington looked intrigued.

"How much time?" Shara asked.

"Your latest tests have not been encouraging. I had assumed that the sustained exercise of rehearsal and practice would tend to slow your system's adaptation. But most of your work has been in total weightlessness, and I failed to realize the extent to which your body is accustomed to sustained exertion—in a terrestrial environment."

"How much time?"

"Two weeks. Possibly three, if you spend three separate hours a day at hard exercise in two gravities."

"That's ridiculous," I burst out. "We can't start and stop the Ring six times a day, and even if we could she could break a leg in two gees."

"I've got to have four weeks," Shara said.

"Ms. Drummond, I am sorry."

"I've got to have four weeks."

Panzarella had that same look of helpless sorrow that McGillicuddy and I had had in our turn, and I was suddenly sick to death of a universe in which people had to keep looking at Shara that way. "Dammit," I roared, "she needs four weeks."

Panzarella shook his shaggy head. "If she stays in zero gee for four working weeks, she may die."

Shara sprang from her chair. "Then I'll die," she cried. "I'll take that chance. I *have* to."

Carrington coughed. "I'm afraid I can't permit you to, darling."

She whirled on him furiously.

"This dance of yours is excellent PR for Skyfac," he said calmly, "but if it were to kill you it might boomerang, don't you think?"

Her mouth worked, and she fought desperately for control. My own head whirled. Die? Shara?

"Besides," he added, "I've grown quite fond of you."

"Then I'll stay up here in low-gee," she burst out.

"Where? The only areas of sustained weightlessness are factories, and you're not qualified to work in one."

"Then for God's sake give me one of the new pods, the small spheres. Bryce, I'll give you a higher return on your investment than a factory pod, and I'll . . ." Her voice changed. "I'll be available to you always."

He smiled lazily. "Yes, but I might not *want* you always, darling. My mother warned me strongly against making irrevocable decisions about women. Especially informal ones. Besides, I find zero-gee sex rather too exhausting as a steady diet."

I had almost found my voice and now I lost it again. I was glad

Carrington was turning her down—but the way he did it made me yearn to drink his blood.

Shara too was speechless for a time. When she spoke, her voice was low, intense, almost pleading. "Bryce, it's a matter of timing. If I broadcast two more dances in the next four weeks, I'll have a world to return to. If I have to go Earthside and wait a year or two, that third dance will sink without a trace—no one'll be looking, and they won't have the memory of the first two. This is my only option, Bryce—*let me take the chance.* Panzarella can't guarantee four weeks will kill me."

"I can't guarantee your survival," the doctor said.

"You can't guarantee that any one of us will live out the day," she snapped. She whirled back to Carrington, held him with her eyes. "Bryce, *let me risk it.*" Her face underwent a massive effort, produced a smile that put a knife through my heart. "I'll make it worth your while."

Carrington savored that smile and the utter surrender in her voice like a man enjoying a fine claret. I wanted to slay him with my hands and teeth, and I prayed that he would add the final cruelty of turning her down. But I had underestimated his true capacity for cruelty.

"Go ahead with your rehearsal, my dear," he said at last. "We'll make a final decision when the time comes. I shall have to think about it."

I don't think I've ever felt so hopeless, so . . . impotent in my life. Knowing it was futile, I said, "Shara, I can't let you risk your life—"

"I'm going to do this, Charlie," she cut me off, "with or without you. No one else knows my work well enough to tape it properly, but if you want out I can't stop you." Carrington watched me with detached interest. "Well?"

I said a filthy word. "You know the answer."

"Then let's get to work."

Tyros are transported on the pregnant broomsticks. Old hands
hang outside the airlock, dangling from handholds on the outer
surface of the spinning Ring. They face in the direction of the
spin, and when their destination comes under the horizon, they
just drop off. Thruster units built into gloves and boots supply
the necessary course corrections. The distances involved are
small. Shara and I, having spent more weightless hours than
some technicians who'd been in Skyfac for years, were old hands.
We made scant and efficient use of our thrusters, chiefly in can-
celing the energy imparted to us by the spin of the Ring we left.
We had throat mikes and hearing-aid-size receivers, but there
was no conversation on the way across the void. I spent the journey appreciating the starry emptiness through which I fell—I
had come, perforce, to understand the attraction of sky-diving—
and wondering whether I would ever get used to the cessation of
pain in my leg. It even seemed to hurt less under spin those
days.

We grounded, with much less force than a sky-diver does, on
the surface of the new studio. It was an enormous steel globe,
studded with sunpower screens and heat-losers, tethered to
three more spheres in various stages of construction on which
p-suited figures were even now working. McGillicuddy had told
me that the complex when completed would be used for "controlled density processing," and when I said, "How nice," he
added, "Dispersion forming and variable density casting," as if
that explained everything. Perhaps it did. Right at the moment, it was Shara's studio.

The airlock led to a rather small working space around a smaller
interior sphere some fifty meters in diameter. It too was pressur-
ized, intended to contain a vacuum, but its locks stood open. We
removed our p-suits, and Shara unstrapped her thruster bracelets
from a bracing strut and put them on, hanging by her ankles from
the strut while she did so. The anklets went on next. As jewelry
they were a shade bulky—but they had twenty minutes' continu-

ous use each, and their operation was not visible in normal atmosphere and lighting. Zero-gee dance without them would have been enormously more difficult.

As she was fastening the last strap I drifted over in front of her and grabbed the strut. "Shara . . ."

"Charlie, I can beat it. I'll exercise in *three* gravities, and I'll sleep in two, and I'll make this body last. I know I can."

"You could skip *Mass Is a Verb* and go right to the *Stardance.*"

She shook her head. "I'm not ready yet—and neither is the audience. I've got to lead myself and them through dance in a sphere first—in a contained space—before I'll be ready to dance in empty space, or for them to appreciate it. I have to free my mind, and theirs, from just about every preconception of dance, change the postulates. Even two stages is too few—but it's the irreducible minimum." Her eyes softened. "Charlie—I must."

"I know," I said gruffly and turned away. Tears are a nuisance in free fall—they don't *go* anywhere. I began hauling myself around the surface of the inner sphere toward the camera emplacement I was working on, and Shara entered the inner sphere to begin rehearsal.

I prayed as I worked on my equipment, snaking cables among the bracing struts and connecting them to drifting terminals. For the first time in years I prayed, prayed that Shara would make it. That we both would.

The next twelve days were the toughest of my life. Shara worked twice as hard as I did. She spent half of every day working in the studio, half of the rest in exercise under two and a quarter gravities (the most Dr. Panzarella would permit), and half of the rest in Carrington's bed, trying to make him contented enough to let her stretch her time limit. Perhaps she slept in the few hours left over. I only know that she never looked tired, never lost her composure or her dogged determination. Stubbornly, reluctantly, her body lost its awkwardness, took on grace even in an environment where grace required enormous concentration. Like a child learning to walk, Shara learned how to fly. I even began to get used to the absence of pain in my leg.

What can I tell you of *Mass* if you have not seen it? It cannot be described, even badly, in mechanistic terms, the way a symphony could be written out in words. Conventional dance terminology is, by its built-in assumptions, worse than useless, and if you are at all familiar with the new nomenclature you *must* be familiar with *Mass Is a Verb*, from which it draws *its* built-in assumptions.

Nor is there much I can say about the technical aspects of *Mass*. There were no special effects, not even music. Brindle's superb score was composed *from the dance* and added to the tape with my permission two years later, but it was for the original, silent version that I was given the Emmy. My entire contribution, aside from editing, and installing the two trampolines, was to camouflage batteries of wide-dispersion light sources in clusters around each camera eye and wire them so that they energized only when they were out of frame with respect to whichever camera was on at the time—ensuring that Shara was always lit from the front, presenting two (not always congruent) shadows. I made no attempt to employ flashy camera work; I simply recorded what Shara danced, changing POV only as she did.

No, *Mass Is a Verb* can be described only in symbolic terms, and then poorly. I can say that Shara demonstrated that mass and inertia are as able as gravity to supply the dynamic conflict essential to dance. I can tell you that from them she distilled a kind of dance that could only have been imagined by a group-head consisting of an acrobat, a stunt-diver, a sky-writer, and an underwater ballerina. I can tell you that she dismantled the last interface between herself and utter freedom of motion, subduing her body to her will and space itself to her need.

And still I will have told you next to nothing. For Shara sought more than freedom—she sought meaning. *Mass* was, above all, a spiritual event—its title pun paralleling its thematic ambiguity between the technological and the theological. Shara made the human confrontation with existence a transitive act, literally meeting God halfway. I do not mean to imply that her dance at any time addressed an exterior God, a discrete entity with or without white beard. Her dance addressed reality, gave successive expression to the Three Eternal Questions asked by every human being who ever lived.

Her dance observed her *self,* and asked, *"How have I come to be here?"*

Her dance observed the universe in which self existed, and asked, *"How did all this come to be here with me?"*

And at last, observing her self in relation to its universe, *"Why am I so alone?"*

And having asked these questions, having earnestly asked them with every muscle and sinew she possessed, she paused, hung suspended in the center of the sphere, her body and soul open to the universe, and when no answer came, she contracted. Not in a dramatic ceiling-spring sense, as she had in *Liberation,* a compressing of energy and tension. This was physically similar, but an utterly different phenomenon. It was a focusing inward, an act of introspection, a turning of the mind's (soul's?) eye in upon itself, to seek answers that lay nowhere else. Her body too, therefore, seemed to fold in upon itself, compacting her mass so evenly that her position in space was not disturbed.

And reaching within herself, she closed on emptiness. The camera faded out, leaving her alone, rigid, encapsulated, yearning. The dance ended, leaving her three questions unanswered, the tension of their asking unresolved. Only the expression of patient waiting on her face blunted the shocking edge of the non-ending, made it bearable, a small blessed sign whispering, "To be continued."

By the eighteenth day we had it in the can in rough form. Shara put it immediately out of her mind and began choreographing *Stardance,* but I spent two hard days of editing before I was ready to release the tape for broadcast. I had four days until the half-hour of prime time Carrington had purchased—but that wasn't the deadline I felt breathing down the back of my neck.

McGillicuddy came into my workroom while I was editing, and although he saw the tears running down my face he said no word. I let the tape run, and he watched in silence, and soon his face was wet, too. When the tape had been over for a long time he said, very softly, "One of these days I'm going to have to quit this stinking job."

I said nothing.

"I used to be a karate instructor. I was pretty good. I could teach again, maybe do exhibition work, make ten percent of what I do now."

I said nothing.

"The whole damned Ring's bugged, Charlie. The desk in my office can activate and tap any vidphone in Skyfac. Four at a time, actually."

I said nothing.

"I saw you both in the airlock, when you came back the last time. I saw her collapse. I saw you bringing her around. I heard her make you promise not to tell Dr. Panzarella."

I waited. Hope stirred.

He dried his face. "I came in here to tell you I was going to Panzarella, to tell him what I saw. He'd bully Carrington into sending her home right away."

"And now?" I said.

"I've seen that tape."

"And you know the *Stardance* will probably kill her?"

"Yes."

"And you know we have to let her do it?"

"Yes."

Hope died. I nodded. "Then get out of here and let me work."

He left.

On Wall Street and aboard Skyfac it was late afternoon when I finally had the tape edited to my satisfaction. I called Carrington, told him to expect me in half an hour, showered, shaved, dressed, and left.

A major of the Space Command was there with him when I arrived, but he was not introduced and so I ignored him. Shara was there too, wearing a thing made of orange smoke that left her breasts bare. Carrington had obviously made her wear it, as an urchin writes filthy words on an altar, but she wore it with a perverse and curious dignity that I sensed annoyed him. I looked her in the eye and smiled. "Hi, kid. It's a good tape."

"Let's see," Carrington said. He and the major took seats behind the desk, and Shara sat beside it.

I fed the tape into the video rig built into the office wall, dimmed the lights, and sat across from Shara. It ran twenty minutes, uninterrupted, no soundtrack, stark naked.

It was terrific.

Aghast is a funny word. To make you aghast, a thing must hit you in a place you haven't armored over with cynicism yet. I seem to have been born cynical; I have been aghast three times that I can remember. The first was when I learned, at the age of three, that there were people who could deliberately hurt kittens. The second was when I learned, at age seventeen, that there were people who could actually take LSD and then hurt other people for fun. The third was when *Mass Is a Verb* ended and Carrington said in perfectly conversational tones, "Very pleasant, very graceful. I like it"; then I learned, at age forty-five, that there were men, not fools or cretins but intelligent men, who could watch Shara Drummond dance and fail to *see*. We all, even the most cynical of us, always have some illusion which we cherish.

Shara simply let it bounce off her somehow, but I could see that the major was as aghast as I, controlling his features with a visible effort.

Suddenly welcoming a distraction from my horror and dismay,

I studied him more closely, wondering for the first time what he was doing here. He was my age, lean and more hard-bitten than I am, with silver fuzz on top of his skull and an extremely tidy mustache on the front. I'd taken him for a crony of Carrington's, but three things changed my mind. Something indefinable about his eyes told me that he was a military man of long combat experience. Something equally indefinable about his carriage told me that he was on duty at the moment. And something quite definable about the line his mouth made told me that he was disgusted with the duty he had drawn.

When Carrington went on, "What do you think, Major?" in polite tones, the man paused for a moment, gathering his thoughts and choosing his words. When he did speak, it was not to Carrington.

"Ms. Drummond," he said quietly, "I am Major William Cox, commander of S.C. *Champion,* and I am honored to meet you. That was the most profoundly moving thing I have ever seen."

Shara thanked him most gravely. "This is Charles Armstead, Major Cox. He made the tape."

Cox regarded me with new respect. "A magnificent job, Mr. Armstead." He stuck out his hand and I shook it.

Carrington was beginning to understand that we three shared a thing which excluded him. "I'm glad you enjoyed it, Major," he said with no visible trace of sincerity. "You can see it again on your television tomorrow night, if you chance to be off duty. And eventually, of course, cassettes will be made available. Now perhaps we can get to the matter at hand."

Cox's face closed as if it had been zippered up, became stiffly formal. "As you wish, sir."

Puzzled, I began what I thought was the matter at hand. "I'd like your own Comm Chief to supervise the actual transmission this time, Mr. Carrington. Shara and I will be too busy to—"

"My Comm Chief will supervise the broadcast, Armstead," Carrington interrupted, "but I don't think you'll be particularly busy."

I was groggy from lack of sleep; my uptake was rather slow.

He touched his desk delicately. "McGillicuddy, report at once," he said, and released it. "You see, Armstead, you and Shara are both returning to Earth. At once."

"What?"

"Bryce, you *can't,*" Shara cried. "You *promised.*"

"I promised I would think about it, my dear," he corrected.

"The hell you say. That was weeks ago. Last night you *promised.*"

"Did I? My dear, there were no witnesses present last night. Altogether for the best, don't you agree?"

I was speechless with rage.

McGillicuddy entered. "Hello, Tom," Carrington said pleasantly. "You're fired. You'll be returning to Earth at once, with Ms. Drummond and Mr. Armstead, aboard Major Cox's vessel. Departure in one hour, and don't leave anything you're fond of." He glanced from McGillicuddy to me. "From Tom's desk you can tap any vidphone in Skyfac. From my desk you can tap Tom's desk."

Shara's voice was low. "Bryce, two days. God damn you, name your price."

He smiled slightly. "I'm sorry, darling. When informed of your collapse, Dr. Panzarella became most specific. Not even one more day. Alive you are a distinct plus for Skyfac's image—you are my gift to the world. Dead you are an albatross around my neck. I cannot allow you to die on my property. I anticipated that you might resist leaving, and so I spoke to a friend in the"—he glanced at Cox—*"higher* echelons of the Space Command, who was good enough to send the major here to escort you home. You are not under arrest in the legal sense—but I assure you that you have no choice. Something like protective custody applies. Goodbye, Shara." He reached for a stack of reports on his desk, and I surprised myself considerably.

I cleared the desk entirely, tucked head catching him squarely in the sternum. His chair was belted to the deck and so it snapped clean. I recovered so well that I had time for one glorious right. Do you know how, if you punch a basketball squarely, it will bounce up from the floor? That's what his head did, in low-gee slow motion.

Then Cox had hauled me to my feet and shoved me into the far corner of the room. "Don't," he said to me, and his voice must have held a lot of that "habit of command" they talk about, because it stopped me cold. I stood breathing in great gasps while Cox helped Carrington to his feet.

The millionaire felt his smashed nose, examined the blood on his fingers, and looked at me with raw hatred. "You'll never work in video again, Armstead. You're through. Finished. Unemployed, you get that?"

Cox tapped him on the shoulder, and Carrington spun on him. "What the hell do you want?" he barked.

Cox smiled. "Carrington, my late father once said, 'Bill, make your enemies by choice, not by accident.' Over the years I have found that to be excellent advice. You suck."

"And not particularly well," Shara agreed.

Carrington blinked. Then his absurdly broad shoulders swelled and he roared, "Out, all of you! *Off my property at once!*"

By unspoken consent, we waited for McGillicuddy, who knew his cue. "Mr. Carrington, it is a rare privilege and a great honor to have been fired by you. I shall think of it always as a Pyrrhic defeat." And he half bowed and we left, each buoyed by a juvenile feeling of triumph that must have lasted ten seconds.

The sensation of falling that comes with zero gee is literal truth, but your body quickly learns to treat it as an illusion. Now, in zero gee for the last time, for the half hour before I would be back in Earth's own gravitational field, I felt I was falling. Plummeting into some bottomless gravity well, dragged down by the anvil that was my heart, the scraps of a dream that should have held me aloft fluttering overhead.

The *Champion* was three times the size of Carrington's yacht, which childishly pleased me until I recalled that he had summoned it here without paying for either fuel or crew. A guard at the airlock saluted as we entered. Cox led us to a compartment aft of the airlock where we were to strap in. He noticed along the way that I used only my left hand to pull myself along, and when we stopped, he said, "Mr. Armstead, my late father also told me, 'Hit the soft parts with your hand. Hit the hard parts with a utensil.' Otherwise I can find no fault with your technique. I wish I could shake your hand."

I tried to smile, but I didn't have it in me. "I admire your taste in enemies, Major."

"A man can't ask for more. I'm afraid I can't spare time to have your hand looked at until we've grounded. We begin re-entry immediately."

"Forget it."

He bowed to Shara, did *not* tell her how deeply sorry he was to, et cetera, wished us all a comfortable journey, and left. We strapped into our acceleration couches to await ignition. There ensued a long and heavy silence, compounded of a mutual sadness that bravado could only have underlined. We did not look at each other, as though our combined sorrow might achieve some kind of critical mass. Grief struck us dumb, and I believe that remarkably little of it was self-pity.

But then a whole lot of time seemed to have gone by. Quite a bit of intercom chatter came faintly from the next compartment, but ours was not in circuit. At last we began to talk, desultorily, discussing the probable critical reaction to *Mass Is a Verb,* whether analysis was worthwhile or the theater really dead, anything at all except future plans. Eventually there was nothing else to talk about, so we shut up again. I guess I'd say we were in shock.

For some reason I came out of it first. "What in hell is taking them so long?" I barked irritably.

McGillicuddy started to say something soothing, then glanced at his watch and yelped. "You're right. It's been nearly an hour."

I looked at the wall clock, got hopelessly confused until I realized it was on Greenwich time rather than Wall Street, and realized he was correct. "Chrissakes," I shouted, "the whole bloody *point* of this exercise is to protect Shara from overexposure to free fall! I'm going forward."

"Charlie, hold it." McGillicuddy, with two good hands, unstrapped faster than I. "Dammit, stay right there and cool off. I'll go find out what the holdup is."

He was back in a few minutes, and his face was slack. "We're not going anywhere. Cox has orders to sit tight."

"What? Tom, what the *hell* are you talking about?"

His voice was all funny. "Red fireflies. More like bees, actually. In a balloon."

He simply *could not* be joking with me, which meant he flat out *had* to have gone completely round the bend, which meant that somehow I had blundered into my favorite nightmare where everyone but me goes crazy and begins gibbering at me. So I lowered my head like an enraged bull and charged out of the room so fast the door barely had time to get out of my way.

It just got worse. When I reached the door to the bridge I was going much too fast to be stopped by anything short of a body block, and the crewmen present were caught flatfooted. There was a brief flurry at the door, and then I was on the bridge, and then I decided that I had gone crazy too, which somehow made everything all right.

The forward wall of the bridge was one enormous video tank—and just enough off center to faintly irritate me. Standing out against the black deep as clearly as cigarettes in a darkroom, there truly did swarm a multitude of red fireflies.

The conviction of unreality made it okay. But then Cox snapped me back to reality with a bellowed *"Off this bridge, mister."* If I'd been in a normal frame of mind it would have blown me out the door and into the farthest corner of the ship; in my current state it managed to jolt me into acceptance of the impossible situation. I shivered like a wet dog and turned to him.

"Major," I said desperately, "what is going on?"

As a king may be amused by an insolent varlet who refuses to kneel, he was bemused by the phenomenon of someone failing to obey him. It bought me an answer. "We are confronting intelligent alien life," he said concisely. "I believe them to be sentient plasmoids."

I had never for a moment believed that the mysterious object which had been leapfrogging around the solar system since I came to Skyfac was *alive*. I tried to take it in, then abandoned the task and went back to my main priority. "I don't care if they're eight tiny reindeer; you've got to get this can back to Earth *now*."

"Sir, this vessel is on Emergency Red Alert and on Combat Standby. At this moment the suppers of everyone in North America are getting cold. I will consider myself fortunate if I ever see Earth again. Now get off my bridge."

"But you don't *understand*. Sustained free fall might kill Shara. That's what you came up here to prevent, dammit. . . ."

"MISTER ARMSTEAD! This is a military vessel. We are facing nearly a dozen intelligent beings who appeared out of hyperspace near here twenty minutes ago, beings who therefore use a drive beyond my conception with no visible parts. If it makes you feel any better I am aware that I have a passenger aboard of greater intrinsic value to my species than this ship and everyone else on her, and if it is any comfort to you this knowledge already provides a distraction I need like an auxiliary anus, and I can no more leave this orbit than I can grow horns. Now will you get off this bridge or will you be dragged?"

I didn't get a chance to decide; they dragged me.

On the other hand, by the time I got back to our compartment, Cox had put our vidphone screen in circuit with the tank on the bridge. Shara and McGillicuddy were studying it with rapt attention. Having nothing better to do, I did too.

McGillicuddy had been right. They *did* act more like bees, in the swarming rapidity of their movement. I couldn't get an accurate count: forty or so. And they *were* in a balloon—a faint, barely tangible thing on the fine line between transparency and translucence. Though they darted like furious red gnats, it was only within the confines of the spheroid balloon—they never left it or seemed to touch its inner surface.

As I watched, the last of the adrenaline rinsed out of my kidneys, but it left a sense of frustrated urgency. I tried to grapple with the fact that these Space Commando special effects represented something that was more important than Shara. It was a primevally disturbing notion, but I could not reject it.

In my mind were two voices, each hollering questions at the top of their lungs, each ignoring the other's questions. One yelled, *Are those things friendly? Or hostile? Or do they even use those concepts? How big are they? How far away? From where?* The other voice was less ambitious but just as loud; all it said, over and over again, was *How much longer can Shara remain in free fall without dooming herself?*

Shara's voice was full of wonder. "They're . . . they're *dancing.*"

I looked closer. If there was a pattern to the flies-on-garbage swarm they made, I couldn't detect it. "Looks random to me."

"Charlie, look. All that furious activity, and they never bump into each other or the walls of that envelope they're in. They must be in orbits as carefully choreographed as those of electrons."

"Do atoms dance?"

She gave me an odd look. "Don't they, Charlie?"

"Laser beam," McGillicuddy said.

We looked at him.

"Those things have to be plasmoids—the man I talked to said they were first spotted on radar. That means they're ionized gases of some kind—the kind of thing that used to cause UFO reports." He giggled, then caught himself. "If you could slice through that envelope with a laser, I'll bet you could deionize them pretty good

—besides, that envelope has to hold their life support, whatever it is they metabolize."

I was dizzy. "Then we're not defenseless?"

"You're both talking like soldiers," Shara burst out. "I tell you they're dancing. Dancers aren't fighters."

"Come on, Shara," I barked. "Even if those things happen to be remotely like us, that's not true. Samurai, karate, kung fu—they're dance." I nodded to the screen. "All we know about these animated embers is that they travel interstellar space. That's enough to scare me."

"Charlie, look at them," she commanded.

I did.

By God, they didn't look threatening. They did, the more I watched, seem to move in a dancelike way, whirling in mad adagios just too fast for the eye to follow. Not like conventional dance—more analogous to what Shara had begun with *Mass Is a Verb.* I found myself wanting to switch to another camera for contrast of perspective, and that made my mind start to wake up at last. Two ideas surfaced, the second one necessary in order to sell Cox the first.

"How far do you suppose we are from Skyfac?" I asked McGillicuddy.

He pursed his lips. "Not far. There hasn't been much more than maneuvering acceleration. The damn things were probably attracted to Skyfac in the first place—it must be the most easily visible sign of intelligent life in this system." He grimaced. "Maybe they don't *use* planets."

I reached forward and punched the audio circuit. "Major Cox."

"Get off this circuit."

"How would you like a closer view of those things?"

"We're staying put. Now stop jiggling my elbow and get off this circuit or I'll—"

"Will you listen to me? I have four mobile cameras in space, remote control, self-contained power source and light, and better resolution than you've got. They were set up to tape Shara's next dance."

He shifted gears at once. "Can you patch them into my ship?"

"I think so. But I'll have to get back to the master board in Ring One."

"No good, then. I can't tie myself to a top—what if I have to fight or run?"

"Major—how far a walk is it?"

It startled him a bit. "A mile or two, as the crow flies. But you're a groundlubber."

"I've been in free fall for most of two months. Give me a portable radar and I can ground on Phobos."

"Mmmm. You're a civilian—but dammit, I need better video. Permission granted."

Now for the first idea. "Wait—one thing more. Shara and Tom must come with me."

"Nuts. This isn't a field trip."

"Major Cox—Shara *must* return to a gravity field as quickly as possible. Ring One'll do—in fact, it'd be ideal, if we enter through the 'spoke' in the center. She can descend very slowly and acclimatize gradually, the way a diver decompresses in stages, but in reverse. McGillicuddy will have to come along to stay with her —if she passes out and falls down the tube, she could break a leg even in one-sixth gee. Besides, he's better at EVA than either of us."

He thought it over. "Go."

We went.

The trip back to Ring One was far longer than any Shara or I had ever made, but under McGillicuddy's guidance we made it with minimal maneuvering. Ring, *Champion,* and aliens formed an equiangular triangle about a mile and a half on a side. Seen in perspective, the aliens took up about as much volume as Shea Stadium. They did not pause or slacken in their mad gyration, but somehow they seemed to watch us across the gap to Skyfac. I got an impression of a biologist studying the strange antics of a new species. We kept our suit radios off to avoid distraction, and it made me just a little bit more susceptible to suggestion.

I left McGillicuddy with Shara and dropped down the tube six rings at a time. Carrington was waiting for me in the reception room, with two flunkies. It was plain to see that he was scared silly and trying to cover it with anger. "God damn it, Armstead, those are my bloody cameras."

"Shut up, Carrington. If you put those cameras in the hands of the best technician available—me—and if I put their data in the hands of the best strategic mind in space—Cox—we *might* be able to save your damned factory for you. And the human race for the rest of us." I moved forward, and he got out of my way. It figured. Putting all humanity in danger might just be bad PR.

After all the practicing I'd done, it wasn't hard to direct four mobile cameras through space simultaneously by eye. The aliens ignored their approach. The Skyfac comm crew fed my signals to the *Champion* and patched me in to Cox on audio. At his direction I bracketed the balloon with the cameras, shifting POV at his command. Space Command Headquarters must have recorded the video, but I couldn't hear their conversation with Cox, for which I was grateful. I gave him slow-motion replay, close-ups, split screen—everything at my disposal. The movements of individual fireflies did not appear particularly symmetrical, but patterns began to repeat. In slow motion they looked more than ever as though they were dancing, and although I couldn't be sure, it seemed to me that they were increasing their tempo. Somehow the dramatic tension of their dance seemed to build.

And then I shifted POV to the camera which included Skyfac in the background, and my heart turned to hard vacuum and I screamed in pure primal terror—halfway between Ring One and the swarm of aliens, coming up on them slowly but inexorably, was a p-suited figure that had to be Shara.

With theatrical timing, McGillicuddy appeared in the doorway, leaning heavily on the chief engineer, his face drawn with pain. He stood on one foot, the other leg plainly broken.

"Guess I can't . . . go back to exhibition work . . . after all," he gasped. "Said . . . 'I'm sorry, Tom'. . . knew she was going to swing on me . . . wiped me out anyhow. Oh dammit, Charlie, I'm sorry." He sank into an empty chair.

Cox's voice came urgently. "What the hell is going on? Who is that?"

She *had* to be on our frequency. "Shara!" I screamed. "Get your ass back in here!"

"I can't, Charlie." Her voice was startlingly loud, and very calm. "Halfway down the tube my chest started to hurt like hell."

"Ms. Drummond," Cox rapped, "if you approach any closer to the aliens I will destroy you."

She laughed, a merry sound that froze my blood. "Bullshit, Major. You aren't about to get gay with laser beams near those things. Besides, you need me as much as you do Charlie."

"What do you mean?"

"These creatures communicate by dance. It's their equivalent of speech; it has to be a sophisticated kind of sign language, like hula."

"You can't know that."

"I *feel* it. I know it. Hell, how else do you communicate in airless space? Major Cox, I am the only qualified interpreter the human race has at the moment. Now will you kindly shut up so I can try to learn their 'language'?"

"I have no authority to . . ."

I said an extraordinary thing. I should have been gibbering, pleading with Shara to come back, even racing for a p-suit to *bring* her back. Instead I said, "She's right. Shut up, Cox."

"What are you trying to do?"

"Damn you, *don't waste her last effort.*"

He shut up.

Panzarella came in, shot McGillicuddy full of painkiller, and set his leg right there in the room, but I was oblivious. For over an hour I watched Shara watch the aliens. I watched them myself, in the silence of utter despair, and for the life of me I could not follow their dance. I strained my mind, trying to suck meaning from their crazy whirling, and failed. The best I could do to aid Shara was to record everything that happened, for a hypothetical posterity. Several times she cried out softly, small muffled exclamations, and I ached to call out to her in reply, but did not. With the last exclamation, she used her thrusters to bring her closer to the alien swarm, and hung there for a long time.

At last her voice came over the speaker, thick and slurred at first, as though she were talking in her sleep. "God, Charlie. Strange. So strange. I'm beginning to read them."

"How?"

"Every time I begin to understand a part of the dance, it . . . it brings us closer. Not telepathy, exactly. I just . . . know them better. Maybe it is telepathy, I don't know. By dancing what they feel, they give it enough intensity to make me understand. I'm getting about one concept in three. It's stronger up close."

Cox's voice was gentle but firm. "What have you learned, Shara?"

"That Tom and Charlie were right. They are warlike. At least, there's a flavor of arrogance to them—conviction of superiority. Their dance is a challenging, a dare. Tell Tom they *do* use planets."

"What?"

"I think at one stage of their development they're corporeal, planet-bound. Then when they have matured sufficiently, they . . . become these fireflies, like caterpillars becoming butterflies, and head out into space."

"Why?" from Cox.

"To find spawning grounds. They want Earth."

There was a silence lasting perhaps ten seconds. Then Cox spoke up quietly. "Back away, Shara. I'm going to see what lasers will do to them."

"No!" she cried, loud enough to make a really first-rate speaker distort.

"Shara, as Charlie pointed out to me, you are not only expendable, you are for all practical purposes expended."

"No!" This time it was me shouting.

"Major," Shara said urgently, "that's not the way. Believe me, they can dodge or withstand anything you or Earth can throw at them. I *know*."

"Hell and damnation, woman," Cox said, "what do you want me to do? Let them have the first shot? There are vessels from four countries on their way right now."

"Major, wait. Give me time."

He began to swear, then cut off. "How much time?"

She made no direct reply. "If only this telepathy thing works in reverse . . . it must. I'm no more strange to them than they are to me. Probably less so; I get the idea they've been around. Charlie?"

"Yeah."

"This is a take."

I knew. I had known since I first saw her in open space on my monitor. And I knew what she needed now, from the faint trembling of her voice. It took everything I had, and I was only glad I had it to give. With extremely realistic good cheer, I said, "Break a leg, kid," and killed my mike before she could hear the sob that followed.

And she danced.

It began slowly, the equivalent of one-finger exercises, as she sought to establish a vocabulary of motion that the creatures could comprehend. *Can you see,* she seemed to say, *that* this *movement is a reaching, a yearning? Do you see that* this *is a spurning,* this *an unfolding,* that *a graduated elision of energy? Do you feel the ambiguity in the way I distort this arabesque, or that the tension can be resolved* so?

And it seemed that Shara was right, that they had infinitely more experience with disparate cultures than we, for they were superb linguists of motion. It occurred to me later that perhaps they had selected motion for communication because of its very universality. At any rate as Shara's dance began to build, their own began to slow down perceptibly in speed and intensity, until at last they hung motionless in space watching her.

Soon after that Shara must have decided that she had sufficiently defined her terms, at least well enough for pidgin communication —for now she began to dance in earnest. Before she had used only her own muscles and the shifting masses of her limbs. Now she added thrusters, singly and in combination, moving within as well as in space. Her dance became a true dance: more than a collection of motions, a thing of substance and meaning. It was unquestionably the *Stardance,* just as she had prechoreographed it, as she had always intended to dance it. That it had something to say to utterly alien creatures, of man and his nature, was not at all a coincidence: it was the essential and ultimate statement of the greatest artist of her age, and it had something to say to God himself.

The camera lights struck silver from her p-suit, gold from the twin airtanks on her shoulders. To and fro against the black backdrop of space, she wove the intricacies of her dance, a leisurely movement that seemed somehow to leave echoes behind it. And the meaning of those great loops and whirls slowly became clear, drying my throat and clamping my teeth.

For her dance spoke of nothing more and nothing less than the tragedy of being alive, and being human. It spoke, most eloquently, of pain. It spoke, most knowingly, of despair. It spoke of the cruel humor of limitless ambition yoked to limited ability, of eternal hope invested in an ephemeral lifetime, of the driving need to try and create an inexorably predetermined future. It spoke of fear, and of hunger, and, most clearly, of the basic loneliness and alienation of the human animal. It described the universe through the eyes of man: a hostile environment, the embodiment of entropy, into which we are all thrown alone, forbidden by our nature to touch another mind save secondhand, by proxy. It spoke of the blind perversity which forces man to strive hugely for a peace which, once attained, becomes boredom. And it spoke of folly, of the terrible paradox by which man is simultaneously capable of reason and unreason, forever unable to cooperate even with himself.

It spoke of Shara and her life.

Again and again, cyclical statements of hope began, only to collapse into confusion and ruin. Again and again, cascades of energy strove for resolution, and found only frustration. All at once she launched into a pattern that seemed familiar, and in moments I recognized it: the closing movement of *Mass Is a Verb* recapitulated—not repeated but reprised, echoed, the Three Questions given a more terrible urgency by this new altar on which they were piled. And as before, it segued into that final relentless contraction, that ultimate drawing inward of all energies. Her body became derelict, abandoned, drifting in space, the essence of her being withdrawn to her center and invisible.

The quiescent aliens stirred for the first time.

And suddenly she exploded, blossoming from her contraction not as a spring uncoils, but as a flower bursts from a seed. The force of her release flung her through the void as though she were tossed like a gull in a hurricane by galactic winds. Her center appeared to hurl itself through space and time, yanking her body into a new dance.

And the new dance said, *This is what it is to be human: to see the essential existential futility of all action, all striving—and to act, to strive. This is what it is to be human: to reach forever beyond your grasp. This is what it is to be human: to live forever or die trying. This is what it is to be human: to perpetually ask the unanswerable questions, in the hope that the asking of them will somehow hasten the day when they will be answered. This is what*

*it is to be human: to strive in the face of the certainty of failure.
This is what it is to be human: to persist.*

It said all this with a soaring series of cyclical movements that
held all the rolling majesty of grand symphony, as uniquely different from each other as snowflakes, and as similar. And the new
dance *laughed,* and it laughed as much at tomorrow as it did at
yesterday, and it laughed most of all at today.

*For this is what it means to be human: to laugh at what another
would call tragedy.*

The aliens seemed to recoil from the ferocious energy, startled,
awed, and faintly terrified by Shara's indomitable spirit. They
seemed to wait for her dance to wane, for her to exhaust herself,
and her laughter sounded on my speaker as she redoubled her
efforts, became a pinwheel, a Catherine wheel. She changed the
focus of her dance, began to dance *around* them, in pyrotechnic
spatters of motion that came ever closer to the intangible spheroid
which contained them. They cringed inward from her, huddling
together in the center of the envelope, not so much physically
threatened as cowed.

This, said her body, *is what it means to be human: to commit
hara-kiri, with a smile, if it becomes needful.*

And before that terrible assurance, the aliens broke. Without
warning, fireflies and balloon vanished, gone, *elsewhere.*

I know that Cox and McGillicuddy were still alive, because I saw
them afterward, and that means they were probably saying and
doing things in my hearing and presence, but I neither heard nor
saw them then; they were as dead to me as everything except
Shara. I called out her name, and she approached the camera that
was lit, until I could make out her face behind the plastic hood of
her p-suit.

"We may be puny, Charlie," she puffed, gasping for breath. "But
by Jesus, we're tough."

"Shara—come on in now."

"You know I can't."

"Carrington'll *have* to give you a free-fall place to live now."

"A life of exile? For what? To dance? Charlie, *I haven't got anything more to say.*"

"Then I'll come out there."

"Don't be silly. Why? So you can hug a p-suit? Tenderly bump hoods one last time? Balls. It's a good exit so far—let's not blow it."

"*Shara!*" I broke completely, just caved in on myself and collapsed into great racking sobs.

"Charlie, listen now," she said softly, but with an urgency that reached me even in my despair. "Listen now, for I haven't much time. I have something to give you. I hoped you'd find it for yourself, but . . . will you listen?"

"Y-yes."

"Charlie, zero-gee dance is going to get awful popular all of a sudden. I've opened the door. But you know how fads are; they'll bitch it all up unless you move fast. I'm leaving it in your hands."

"What . . . what are you talking about?"

"About you, Charlie. You're going to dance again."

Oxygen starvation, I thought. But she can't be that low on air already. "Okay. Sure thing."

"For God's sake stop humoring me—I'm straight, I tell you. You'd have seen it yourself if you weren't so damned stupid. Don't you understand? *There's nothing wrong with your leg in free fall!*"

My jaw dropped.

"Do you hear me, Charlie? You can dance again!"

"No," I said, and searched for a reason why not. "I . . . you can't . . . it's . . . dammit, the leg's not strong enough for inside work."

"Forget for the moment that inside work'll be less than half of what you do. Forget it and remember that smack in the nose you gave Carrington. Charlie, when you leaped over the desk, *you pushed off with your right leg.*"

I sputtered for a while and shut up.

"There you go, Charlie. My farewell gift. You know I've never been in love with you ... but you must know that I've always loved you. Still do."

"I love you, Shara."

"So long, Charlie. Do it right."

And all four thrusters went off at once. I watched her go down. A while after she was too far to see, there was a long golden flame that arced above the face of the globe, waned, and then flared again as the airtanks went up.

There's a tired old hack plot about the threat of alien invasion unifying mankind overnight. It's about as realistic as Love Will Find a Way—if those damned fireflies ever come back, they'll find us just as disorganized as we were the last time. There you go.

Carrington, of course, tried to grab all the tapes and all the money—but neither Shara nor I had ever signed a contract, and her will was most explicit. So he tried to buy the judge, and he picked the wrong judge, and when it hit the papers and he saw how public and private opinion were going, he left Skyfac in a p-suit with no thrusters. I think he wanted to go the same way she had, but he was unused to EVA and let go too late. He was last seen heading in the general direction of Betelgeuse. The Skyfac board of directors picked a new man who was most anxious to wash off the stains, and he offered me continued use of all facilities.

And so I talked it over with Norrey, and she was free, and that's how the Shara Drummond Company of New Modern Dance was formed. We specialize in good dancers who couldn't cut it on Earth for one reason or another, and there are a surprising hell of a lot of them.

I enjoy dancing with Norrey. Together we're not as good as Shara was alone—but we mesh well. In spite of the obvious contraindications, I think our marriage is going to work.

That's the thing about us humans: we persist.

VONDA N. McINTYRE

Aztecs

Vonda N. McIntyre is another Clarion Workshop graduate (and later, Clarion West organizer). What I recall most distinctly about her from her student days was that she always managed to ask the question which, after I had filled up the silence with the obligatory verbiage teachers must, later—when I was out of class—made me *really* start to think. Now a highly accomplished writer (her novelette "Of Mist, and Grass, and Sand" won a Nebula Award in 1973), she has turned out the stimulating tale that follows: get ready to think again. . . .

She gave up her heart quite willingly.

After the operation, Laenea Trevelyan lived through what seemed an immense time of semiconsciousness, drugged so she would not feel the pain, kept almost insensible while her healing began. Those who watched her did not know she would have preferred consciousness and an end to her uncertainty. So she slept, shallowly, drifting toward awareness, driven back, existing in a world of nightmare. Her dulled mind suspected danger but could do nothing to protect her. She had been forced too often to sleep through danger. She would have preferred the pain.

Once Laenea almost woke: she glimpsed the sterile white walls and ceiling, blurrily, slowly recognizing what she saw. The green glow of monitoring screens flowed across her shoulder, over the scratchy sheets. Taped down, needles scraped nerves in her arm. She became aware of sounds, and heard the rhythmic thud of a beating heart.

She tried to cry out in anger and despair. Her left hand was heavy, lethargic, insensitive to her commands, but she moved it. It crawled like a spider to her right wrist and fumbled at the needles and tubes.

Air shushed from the room as the door opened. A gentle voice and a gentle touch reproved her, increased the flow of sedative, and cruelly returned her to sleep.

A tear slid back from the corner of her eye and trickled into her hair as she re-entered her nightmares, accompanied by the counterpoint of a basic human rhythm, the beating of a heart that she had hoped never to hear again.

Pastel light was Laenea's first assurance that she would live. It gave her no comfort. Intensive care was stark white, astringent in odor, but yellows and greens brightened this private room. The sedative wore off and she knew she would finally be allowed to wake. She did not fight the continuing drowsiness, but depression prevented anticipation of the return of her senses. She wanted only to live within her own mind, ignoring her body, ignoring failure. She did not even know what she would do in the future; perhaps she had none any more.

Yet the world impinged on her as she grew bored with lying still and sweaty and self-pitying. She had never been able to do simply *nothing.* Stubbornly she kept her eyes closed, but she could not avoid the sounds, the vibrations, for they went through her body in waves, like shudders of cold and fear.

This was my chance, she thought. *But I knew I might fail. It could have been worse, or better: I might have died.*

She slid her hand up her body, from her stomach to her ribs, across the adhesive tape and bandages and the tip of the new scar between her breasts, to her throat. Her fingers rested at the corner of her jaw, just above the carotid artery.

She could not feel a pulse.

Pushing herself up abruptly, Laenea ignored sharp twinges of pain. The vibration of a heartbeat continued beneath her palms, but now she could tell that it did not come from her own body.

The amplifier sat on the bedside table, sending out low-frequency thuddings in a steady pattern. Laenea felt laughter bubbling up; she knew it would hurt and she did not care. She lifted the speaker: such a small thing, to cause her so much worry. Its cord ripped from the wall as she flung it across the room, and it smashed in the corner with a satisfying clatter.

She threw aside the stiff starched sheets; she rose, staggered, caught herself. Her breathing was coarse from fluid in her lungs. She coughed, caught her breath, coughed again. Time was a mystery, measured only by weakness: she thought the doctors fools, to force sleep into her, risk her to pneumonia, and play recorded hearts, instead of letting her wake and move and adjust to her new condition.

The tile pressed cool against her bare feet. Laenea walked slowly to a warm patch of sunshine, yellow on the butter-cream floor, and gazed out the window. The day was variegated, gray and golden. Clouds moved from the west across the mountains and the Sound while sunlight still spilled over the city. The shadows moved along the water, turning it from shattered silver to slate.

White from the heavy winter snowfall, the Olympic Mountains lay between Laenea and the port. The approaching rain hid even the trails of spacecraft escaping the earth, and the bright glints of shuttles returning to their target in the sea. But she would see them soon. She laughed aloud, stretching against the soreness in her chest and the ache of her ribs, throwing back her tangled wavy hair. It tickled the back of her neck, her spine, in the gap between the hospital gown's ties.

Air moved past her as the door opened, as though the room were breathing. Laenea turned and faced the surgeon, a tiny frail-looking woman with strength like steel wires. The doctor glanced at the shattered amplifier and shook her head.

"Was that necessary?"

"Yes," Laenea said. "For my peace of mind."

"It was here for your peace of mind."

"It has the opposite effect."

"I'll mention that in my report," the surgeon said. "They did it for the first pilots."

"The administrators are known for continuing bad advice."

The doctor laughed. "Well, Pilot, soon you can design your own environment."

"When?"

"Soon. I don't mean to be obscure—I only decide if you can leave the hospital, not if you may. The scar tissue needs time to strengthen. Do you want to go already? I cracked your ribs rather thoroughly."

Laenea grinned. "I know." She was strapped up tight and straight, but she could feel each juncture of rib-end and cartilage.

"It will be a few days at least."

"How long has it been?"

"We kept you asleep almost three days."

"It seemed like weeks."

"Well . . . adjusting to all the changes at once could put you in shock."

"I'm an experiment," Laenea said. "All of us are. With experiments, you should experiment."

"Perhaps. But we would prefer to keep you with us." Her hair was short and iron gray, but when she smiled her face was that of a child. She had long, strong fingers, muscles and tendons sharply defined, nails pared short, good hands for doing any job. Laenea reached out, and they touched each other's wrists, quite gently.

"When I heard the heartbeat," Laenea said, "I thought you'd had to put me back to normal."

"It's meant to be a comforting sound."

"No one else ever complained?"

"Not quite so . . . strongly."

They would have been friends, if they had had time. But Laenea was impatient to progress, as she had been since her first transit, in which life passed without her awareness. "When can I leave?" The hospital was one more place of stasis that she was anxious to escape.

"For now go back to bed. The morning's soon enough to talk about the future."

Laenea turned away without answering. The windows, the walls, the filtered air cut her off from the gray clouds and the city. Rain slipped down the glass. She did not want to sleep any more.

"Pilot—"

Laenea did not answer.

The doctor sighed. "Do something for me, Pilot."

Laenea shrugged.

"I want you to test your control."

Laenea acquiesced with sullen silence.

"Speed your heart up slowly, and pay attention to the results."

Laenea intensified the firing of the nerve.

"What do you feel?"

"Nothing," Laenea said, though the blood rushed through what had been her pulse points: temples, throat, wrists.

Beside her the surgeon frowned. "Increase a little more, but very slowly."

Laenea obeyed, responding to the abundant supply of oxygen to her brain. Bright lights flashed just behind her vision. Her head hurt in a streak above her right eye to the back of her skull. She felt high and excited. She turned away from the window. "Can't I leave now?"

The surgeon touched her arm at the wrist; Laenea almost laughed aloud at the idea of feeling for *her* pulse. The doctor led her to a chair by the window. "Sit down, Pilot." But Laenea felt she could climb the helix of her dizziness: she felt no need for rest.

"Sit down." The voice was whispery, soft sand slipping across stone. Laenea obeyed.

"Remember the rest of your training, Pilot. Sit back. Relax. Slow the pump. Expand the capillaries. Relax."

Laenea called back her biocontrol. For the first time she was conscious of a presence rather than an absence. Her pulse was gone, but in its place she felt the constant quiet hum of a perfectly balanced rotary machine. It pushed her blood through her body so efficiently that the pressure would destroy her, if she let it. She relaxed and slowed the pump, expanded and contracted the tiny arterial muscles, once, twice, again. The headache, the light-flashes, the ringing in her ears faded and ceased.

She took a deep breath and let it out slowly.

"That's better," the surgeon said. "Don't forget how that feels. You can't go at high speed very long; you'll turn your brain to cheese. You can feel fine for quite a while, you can feel intoxicated. But the hangover is more than I'd care to reckon with." She patted Laenea's hand. "We want to keep you here till we're sure you can regulate the machine. I don't like doing kidney transplants."

Laenea smiled. "I can control it." She began to induce a slow arhythmic change in the speed of the new pump, in her blood pressure. She found she could do it without thinking, as was necessary to balance the flow. "Can I have the ashes of my heart?"

"Not just yet. Let's be sure first."

"I'm sure." Somewhere in the winding concrete labyrinth of the hospital, her heart still beat, bathed in warm saline and nutrient solution. As long as it existed, as long as it lived, Laenea would feel threatened in her ambitions. She could not be a pilot and remain a normal human being, with normal human rhythms. Her body still could reject the artificial heart; then she would be made normal again. If she could work at all she would have to remain a crew member, anesthetized and unaware from one end of every journey to the other. She did not think she could stand that any longer. "I'm sure. I won't be back."

Tests and questions and examinations devoured several days in chunks and nibbles. Though she felt strong enough to walk, Laenea was pushed through the halls in a wheelchair. The boredom grew more and more wearing. The pains had faded, and Laenea saw only doctors and attendants and machines: her friends would not come. This was a rite of passage she must survive alone and without guidance.

A day passed in which she did not even see the rain that passed, nor the sunset that was obscured by fog. She asked again when she could leave the hospital, but no one would answer. She allowed herself to become angry, but no one would respond.

Evening, back in her room: Laenea was wide awake. She lay in bed and slid her fingers across her collarbone to the sternum, along the shiny red line of the tremendous scar. It was still tender, covered with translucent synthetic skin, crossed once just below her breasts with a wide band of adhesive tape to ease her cracked ribs.

The efficient new heart intrigued her. She forced herself consciously to slow its pace, then went through the exercise of constricting and dilating arteries and capillaries. Her biocontrol was excellent. It had to be, or she would not have been passed for surgery.

Slowing the pump should have produced a pleasant lethargy and eventual sleep, but adrenaline from her anger lingered and she did not want to rest. Nor did she want a sleeping pill: she would take no more drugs. Dreamless drug-sleep was the worst kind of all. Fear built up, undischarged by fantasy, producing a great and formless tension.

The twilight was the texture of gray watered silk, opaque and irregular. The hospital's pastels turned cold and mysterious. Laenea threw off the sheet. She was strong again; she was healed. She had undergone months of training, major surgery, and these final capping days of boredom to free herself completely from biological rhythms. There was no reason in the world why she should sleep, like others, when darkness fell.

A civilized hospital: her clothes were in the closet, not squirreled away in some locked room. She put on black pants, soft leather boots, and a shiny leather vest that laced up the front, leaving her arms and neck bare. The sharp tip of the scar was revealed at her throat and between the laces.

To avoid arguments, she waited until the corridor was deserted. Green paint, meant to be soothing, had gone flat and ugly with age. Her boots were silent on the resilient tile, but in the hollow shaft of the fire stairs the heels clattered against concrete, echoing past her and back. Her legs were tired when she reached bottom. She speeded the flow of blood.

Outside, mist obscured the stars. The moon, just risen, was full and haloed. In the hospital's traffic eddy, streetlights spread Laenea's shadow out around her like the spokes of a wheel.

A rank of electric cars waited at the corner, tethered like horses in an old movie. She slid her credit key into a lock to release one painted like a turtle, an apt analogy. She got in and drove it toward the waterfront. The little beast rolled slowly along, its motor humming quietly on the flat, straining slightly in low gear on the steep downgrades. Laenea relaxed in the bucket seat and wished she were in a starship, but her imagination would not stretch quite that far. The control stick of a turtle could not become an information and control wall; and the city, while pleasant, was of unrelieved ordinariness compared to the places she had seen. She could not, of course, imagine transit, for it was beyond imagination. Language or mind was insufficient. Transit had never been described.

The waterfront was shabby, dirty, magnetic. Laenea knew she could find acquaintances nearby, but she did not want to stay in the city. She returned the turtle to a stanchion and retrieved her credit key to halt the tally against her account.

The night had grown cold; she noticed the change peripherally in the form of fog and condensation-slick cobblestones. The public market, ramshackle and shored up, littered here and there with wilted vegetables, was deserted. People passed as shadows.

A man moved up behind her while she was in the dim region between two streetlamps. "Hey," he said, "how about—" His tone was belligerent with inexperience or insecurity or fear. Looking down at him, surprised, Laenea laughed. "Poor fool—" He scuttled away like a crab. After a moment of vague pity and amusement, Laenea forgot him. She shivered. Her ears were ringing and her chest ached from the cold.

Small shops nestled between bars and cheap restaurants. Laenea entered one for the warmth. It was very dim, darker than the street, high-ceilinged and deep, so narrow she could have touched both side walls by stretching out her arms. She did not. She hunched her shoulders, and the ache receded slightly.

"May I help you?"

Like one of the indistinct masses in the back of the shop brought to life, a small ancient man appeared. He was dressed in shabby ill-matched clothes, part of his own wares: Laenea was in a pawnshop or secondhand clothing store. Hung up like trophies, feathers and wide hats and beads covered the walls. Laenea moved farther inside.

"Ah, Pilot," the old man said, "you honor me."

Laenea's delight was childish in its intensity. Only the surgeon had called her "pilot"; to the others in the hospital she had been merely another patient, more troublesome than most.

"It's cold by the water," she said. Some graciousness or apology was due, for she had no intention of buying anything.

"A coat? No, a cloak!" he exclaimed. "A cloak would be set off well by a person of your stature." He turned; his dark form disappeared among the piles and racks of clothes. Laenea saw bright beads and spangles, a quick flash of gold lamé, and wondered uncharitably what dreadful theater costume he would choose. But the garment the small man drew out was dark. He held it up: a long swath of black, lined with scarlet. Laenea had planned to thank him and demur; despite herself she reached out. Velvet-silk outside and smooth satin-silk within caressed her fingers. The cloak had one shoulder cape and a clasp of carved jet. Though heavy, it draped easily and gracefully. She slung it over her shoulders, and it flowed around her almost to her ankles.

"Exquisite," the shopkeeper said. He beckoned and she approached: a dim and pitted full-length mirror stood against the wall beyond him. Bronze patches marred its irregular silver face where the backing had peeled away. Laenea liked the way the cape looked. She folded its edges so the scarlet lining showed, so her throat and the upper curve of her breasts and the tip of the scar were exposed. She shook back her hair.

"Not quite exquisite," she said, smiling. She was too tall and big-boned for that kind of delicacy. She had a widow's peak and high cheekbones, but her jaw was strong and square. Her face laughed well but would not do for coyness.

"It does not please you." He sounded downcast. Laenea could not quite place his faint accent.

"It does," she said. "I'll take it."

He bowed her toward the front of the shop, and she took out her credit key.

"No, no, Pilot," he said. "Not that."

Laenea raised one eyebrow. A few shops on the waterfront accepted only cash, retaining an illicit flavor in a time when almost any activity was legal. But few even of those select establishments would refuse the credit of a crew member or a pilot. "I have no cash," Laenea said. She had not carried any for years, since once finding in various pockets three coins of metal, one of plastic, one of wood, a pleasingly atavistic animal claw (or excellent duplicate), and a boxed bit of organic matter that would have been forbidden on earth fifty years before. Laenea never expected to revisit at least three of the worlds the currency represented.

"Not cash," he said. "It is yours, Pilot. Only—" He glanced up; he looked her in the eyes for the first time. His eyes were very dark and deep, hopeful, expectant. "Only tell me, what is it like? What do you see?"

She pulled back, surprised. She knew people asked the question often. She had asked it herself, wordlessly after the first few times of silence and patient head-shakings. Pilots never answered. Machines could not answer, pilots could not answer. Or would not. The question was answerable only individually. Laenea felt sorry for the shopkeeper and started to say she had not yet been in transit awake, that she was new, that she had only traveled in the crew, drugged near death to stay alive. But, finally, she could not even say that. It was too easy; it would very nearly be a betrayal. It was an untrue truth. It implied she would tell him if she knew, while she did not know if she could or would. She shook her head; she smiled as gently as she could. "I'm sorry."

He nodded sadly. "I should not have asked."

"That's all right."

"I'm too old, you see. Too old for adventure. I came here so long ago . . . but the time, the time disappeared. I never knew what happened. I've dreamed about it. Bad dreams . . ."

"I understand. I was crew for ten years. We never knew what happened either."

"That would be worse, yes. Over and over again, no time between. But now you know."

"Pilots know," Laenea agreed. She handed him the credit key. Though he still tried to refuse it, she insisted on paying.

Hugging the cloak around her, Laenea stepped out into the fog. She fantasized that the shop would now disappear, like all legendary shops dispensing magic and cloaks of invisibility. But she did not look back, for everything a few paces away dissolved into grayness. In a small space around each low streetlamp, heat swirled the fog in wisps toward the sky.

The midnight ferry chuttered across the water, riding the waves on its loud cushion of air. Wrapped in her cloak, Laenea was anonymous. After the island stops, she was the only foot passenger left. With the food counters closed, the drivers on the vehicle deck remained in their trucks, napping or drinking coffee from thermoses. Laenea put her feet on the opposite bench, stretched, and gazed out the window into the darkness. Light from the ferry wavered across the tops of long low swells. Laenea could see both the water and her own reflection, very pale. After a while she dozed.

The spaceport was a huge floating artificial island, anchored far from shore. It gleamed in its own lights. The parabolic solar mirrors looked like the multiple compound eyes of a gigantic water insect. Except for the mirrors and the launching towers, the port's surface was nearly flat, few of its components rising more than a story or two. Tall structures would present saillike faces to the northwest storms.

Beneath the platform, under a vibration-deadening lower layer, under the sea, lay the tripartite city. The roar of shuttles taking off and the scream of their return would drive mad anyone who remained on the surface. Thus the northwest spaceport was far out to sea, away from cities, yet a city in itself, self-protected within the underwater stabilizing shafts.

The ferry climbed a low ramp out of the water and settled onto the loading platform. The hum of electric trucks replaced the growl of huge fans. Laenea moved stiffly down the stairs. She was too tall to sleep comfortably on two-seat benches. Stopping for a moment by the gangway, watching the trucks roll past, she concentrated for a moment and felt the increase in her blood pressure. She could well understand how dangerous it might be, and how easily addictive the higher speed could become, driving her high until like a machine her body was burned out. But for now her energy began returning and the stiffness in her legs and back slowly seeped away.

Except for the trucks, which purred off quickly around the island's perimeters and disappeared, the port was silent so late at night. The passenger shuttle waited empty on its central rail. When Laenea entered, it sensed her, slid its doors shut, and accelerated. A push-button command halted it above Stabilizer Three, which held quarantine, administration, and crew quarters. Laenea was feeling good, warm, and her vision was sparkling bright and clear. She let the velvet cloak flow back across her shoulders, no longer needing its protection. She was alight with the expectation of seeing her friends, in her new avatar.

The elevator led through the center of the stabilizer into the underwater city. Laenea rode it all the way to the bottom of the shaft, one of three that projected into the ocean far below the surface turbulence to hold the platform steady even through the most violent storms. The shafts maintained the island's flotation level as well, pumping sea water in or out of the ballast tanks when a shuttle took off or landed or a ferry crept on board.

The elevator doors opened into the foyer where a spiral staircase reached the lowest level, a bubble at the tip of the main shaft. The lounge was a comfortable cylindrical room, its walls all transparent, gazing out like a continuous eye into the deep sea. Floodlights cast a glow through the cold clear water, picking out the bright speedy forms of fish, large dark predators, scythe-mouthed sharks, the occasional graceful bow of a porpoise, the elegant black-and-white presence of a killer whale. As the radius of visibility increased, the light filtered through bluer and bluer, until finally, in violet, vague shapes eased back and forth with shy curiosity between dim illumination and complete darkness. The lounge, sculpted with plastic foam and carpeted, gave the illusion of being underwater, on the ocean floor itself, a part of the sea. It had not been built originally as a lounge for crew alone, but was taken over by unconscious agreement among the starship people. Outsiders were not rejected, but gently ignored. Feeling unwelcome, they soon departed. Journalists came infrequently, reacting to sensation or disaster. Human pilots had been a sensation, but Laenea was in the second pilot group; the novelty had worn away. She did not mind a bit.

Laenea took off her boots and left them by the stairwell. She

recognized one of the other pair: she would have been hard put
not to recognize those boots after seeing them once. The scarlet
leather was stupendously shined, embroidered with jewels, and
inlaid with tiny liquid crystal-filled discs that changed color with
the temperature. Laenea smiled. Crew members made up for the
dead-time of transit in many different ways; one was to overdo all
other aspects of their lives, and the most flamboyant of that group
was Minoru.

Walking barefoot in the deep carpet, between the hillocks and
hollows of conversation pits, was like walking on the sea floor
idealized. Laenea thought that the attraction of the lounge was its
relation to the mystery of the sea, for the sea still held mysteries
perhaps as deep as any she would encounter in space or in transit.
No one but the pilots could even guess at the truth of her assumption, but Laenea had often sat gazing through the shadowed
water, dreaming. Soon she too would know; she would not have
to imagine any longer.

She moved between small groups of people half hidden in the
recesses of the conversation pits. Near the transparent sea wall she
saw Minoru, his black hair braided with scarlet and silver to his
waist; tall Alannai hunched down to be closer to the others, the
light on her skin like dark opal, glinting in her close-cropped hair
like diamond dust; and pale, quiet Ruth, whose sparkling was rare
but nova bright. Holding goblets or mugs, they sat sleepily conversing, and Laenea felt the comfort of a familiar scene.

Minoru, facing her, glanced up. She smiled, expecting him to cry
out her name and fling out his arms, as he always did, with his
ebullient greeting, showing to advantage the fringe and beadwork
on his jacket. But he looked at her, straight on, silent, with an
expression so blank that only the unlined long-lived youthfulness
of his face could have held it. He whispered her name. Ruth
looked over her shoulder and smiled tentatively, as though she
were afraid. Alannai unbent, and, head and shoulders above the
others, raised her glass solemnly to Laenea. "Pilot," she said, and

drank, and hunched back down with her elbows on her sharp
knees. Laenea stood above them, outside their circle, looking
down on three people whom she had kissed goodbye. Crew always
said goodbye, for they slept through their voyages without any
certainty that they would wake again. They lived in the cruel
childhood prayer: "If I should die before I wake . . ."

Laenea climbed down to them. The circle opened, but she did
not enter it. She was as overwhelmed by uncertainty as her
friends.

"Sit with us," Ruth said finally. Alannai and Minoru looked uneasy but did not object. Laenea sat down. The triangle between
Ruth and Alannai and Minoru did not alter. Each of them was next
to the other; Laenea was beside none of them.

Ruth reached out, but her hand trembled. They all waited, and
Laenea tried to think of words to reassure them, to affirm that she
had not changed.

But she had changed. She realized the surgeon had cut more
than skin and muscle and bone.

"I came . . ." But nothing she felt seemed right to tell them. She
would not taunt them with her freedom. She took Ruth's outstretched hand. "I came to say goodbye." She embraced them and
kissed them and climbed back to the main level. They had all been
friends, but they could accept each other no longer.

The first pilots and crew did not mingle, for the responsibility
was great, the tensions greater. But Laenea already cared for Ruth
and Minoru and Alannai. Her concern would remain when she
watched them sleeping and ferried them from one island of light
to the next. She understood why she was perpetuating the separation even less than she understood her friends' reserve.

Conversations ebbed and flowed around her like the tides as she
moved through the lounge. Seeing people she knew, she avoided
them, and she did not try to join an unfamiliar group. Her pride
far exceeded her loneliness.

She put aside the pain of her rejection. She felt self-contained and self-assured. When she recognized two pilots, sitting together, isolated, she approached them straightforwardly. She had flown with both of them, but never talked at length with either. They would accept her, or they would not: for the moment, she did not care. She flung back the cloak so they would know her, and realized quite suddenly—with a shock of amused surprise at what she had never noticed consciously before—that all pilots dressed as she had dressed. Laced vest or deeply cut gowns, transparent´ shirts, halters, all in one way or another revealed the long scar that marked their changes.

Miikala and Ramona-Teresa sat facing each other, elbows on knees, talking together quietly, privately. Even the rhythms of their conversation seemed alien to Laenea, though she could not hear their words. Like other people they communicated as much with their bodies and hands as with speech, but the nods and gestures clashed.

Laenea wondered what pilots talked about. Certainly it could not be the ordinary concerns of ordinary people, the laundry, the shopping, a place to stay, a person, perhaps, to stay with. They would talk about . . . the experiences they alone had; they would talk about what they saw when all others must sleep near death or die.

Human pilots withstood transit better than machine intelligence, but human pilots too were sometimes lost. Miikala and Ramona-Teresa were ten percent of all the pilots who survived from the first generation, ten percent of their own unique, evolving, almost self-contained society. As Laenea stopped on the edge of the pit above them, they fell silent and gazed solemnly up at her.

Ramona-Teresa, a small, heavy-set woman with raven-black hair graying to roan, smiled and lifted her glass. "Pilot!" Miikala, whose eyes were shadowed by heavy brow ridges and an unruly shock of dark brown hair, matched the salute and drank with her.

This toast was a tribute and a welcome, not a farewell. Laenea was a part of the second wave of pilots, one who would follow the original experiment and make it work practically, now that Miikala and Ramona-Teresa and the others had proven time-independence successful by example. Laenea smiled and lowered herself into the pit. Miikala touched her left wrist, Ramona-Teresa her right. Laenea felt, welling up inside her, a bubbling, childish giggle. She could not stop it; it broke free as if filled with helium like a balloon. "Hello," she said, and even her voice was high. She might have been in an Environment on the sea floor, breathing oxy-helium and speaking donaldduck. She felt the blood rushing through the veins in her temples and her throat. Miikala was smiling, saying something in a language with as many liquid vowels as his name; she did not understand a word, yet she knew everything he was saying. Ramona-Teresa hugged her. "Welcome, child."

Laenea could not believe that these lofty, eerie people could accept her with such joy. She realized she had hoped, at best, for a cool and condescending greeting not too destructive of her pride. The embarrassing giggle slipped up and out again, but this time she did not try to stifle it. All three pilots laughed together. Laenea felt high, light, dizzy: excitement pumped adrenaline through her body. She was hot and she could feel tiny beads of perspiration gather on her forehead, just at the hairline.

Quite suddenly the constant dull ache in her chest became a wrenching pain, as though her new heart were being ripped from her, like the old. She could not breathe. She hunched forward, struggling for air, oblivious to the pilots and all the beautiful surroundings. Each time she tried to draw in a breath, the pain drove it out again.

Slowly Miikala's easy voice slipped beyond her panic, and Ramona-Teresa's hands steadied her.

"Relax, relax, remember your training . . ."

Yes: decrease the blood flow, open up the arteries, dilate all the

tiny capillaries, feel the involuntary muscles responding to voluntary control. Slow the pump. Someone bathed her forehead with
a cocktail napkin dipped in gin. Laenea welcomed the coolness
and even the odor's bitter tang. The pain dissolved gradually until
Ramona-Teresa could ease her back on the sitting shelf, onto the
cushioned carpet, out of a protective near-fetal position. The jet
fastening of the cloak fell away from her throat and the older pilot
loosened the laces of her vest.

"It's all right," Ramona-Teresa said. "The adrenaline works as
well as ever. We all have to learn more control of that than they
think they need to teach us."

Sitting on his heels beside Laenea, Miikala glanced at the exposed bright scar. "You're out early," he said. "Have they changed
the procedure?"

Laenea paled: she had forgotten that her leavetaking of hospitals was something less than official and approved.

"Don't tease her, Miikala," Ramona-Teresa said gruffly. "Or
don't you remember how it was when you woke up?"

His heavy eyebrows drew together in a scowl. "I remember."

"Will they make me go back?" Laenea asked. "I'm all right. I just
need to get used to it."

"They might try to," Ramona-Teresa said. "They worry so about
the money they spend on us. Perhaps they aren't quite so worried
any more. We do as well on our own as shut up in their ugly
hospitals listening to recorded hearts—do they still do that?"

Laenea shuddered. "It worked for you, they told me—but I
broke the speaker."

Miikala laughed with delight. "Causing all other machines to
make frantic noises like frightened little mice."

"I thought they hadn't done the operation. I wanted to be one
of you so long—" Feeling stronger, Laenea pushed herself up. She
left her vest open, glad of the cool air against her skin. "We
watched," Miikala said. "We watch you all, but a few are special.
We knew you'd come to us. Do you remember this one, Ramona?"

"Yes." She picked up one of the extra glasses, filled it from a shaker, and handed it to Laenea. "You always fought the sleep, my dear. Sometimes I thought you might wake."

"Ahh, Ramona, don't frighten the child."

"Frighten her, this tigress?"

Strangely enough, Laenea was not disturbed by the knowledge that she had been close to waking in transit. She had not, or she would be dead; she would have died quickly of old age, her body bound to normal time and normal space, to the relation between time dilation and velocity and distance by a billion years of evolution, rhythms planetary, lunar, solar, biological: sub-atomic, for all Laenea or anyone else knew. She was freed of all that now.

She downed half her drink in a single swallow. The air now felt cold against her bare arms and her breasts, so she wrapped her cloak around her shoulders and waited for the satin to warm against her body.

"When do you get your ship?"

"Not for a month." The time seemed a vast expanse of emptiness. She had finished the study and the training; now only her mortal body kept her earthbound.

"They want you completely healed."

"It's too long—how can they expect me to wait until then?"

"For the need."

"I want to know what happens; I have to find out. When's your next flight?"

"Soon," Ramona-Teresa said.

"Take me with you!"

"No, my dear. It would not be proper."

"Proper! We have to make our own rules, not follow theirs. They don't know what's right for us."

Miikala and Ramona-Teresa looked at each other for a long time. Perhaps they spoke to each other with eyes and expressions, but Laenea could not understand.

"No." Ramona's tone invited no argument.

"At least you can tell me—" She saw at once that she had said the wrong thing. The pilots' expressions closed down in silence. But Laenea did not feel guilt or contrition, only anger.

"It isn't because you can't! You talk about it to each other, I know that now at least. You can't tell me you don't."

"No," Miikala said. "We will not say we never speak of it."

"You're selfish and you're cruel." She stood up, momentarily afraid she might stagger again and have to accept their help. But as Ramona and Miikala nodded at each other, with faint infuriating smiles, Laenea felt the lightness and the silent bells overtaking her.

"She has the need," one of them said, Laenea did not even know which one. She turned her back on them, climbed out of the conversation pit, and stalked away.

The sitting-place she chose nestled her into a steep slope very close to the sea wall. She could feel the coolness of the glass, as though it, not heat, radiated. Grotesque creatures floated past in the spotlights. Laenea relaxed, letting her smooth pulse wax and wane. She wondered, if she sat in this pleasant place long enough, if she would be able to detect the real tides, if the same drifting plant-creatures passed again and again, swept back and forth before the window of the stabilizer by the forces of sun and moon.

Her privacy was marred only slightly, by one man sleeping or lying unconscious nearby. She did not recognize him, but he must be crew. His dark close-fitting clothes were unremarkably different enough, in design and fabric, that he might be from another world. He must be new. Earth was the hub of commerce; no ship flew long without orbiting it. New crew members always visited at least once. New crew usually visited every world their ships reached at first, if they had the time for quarantine. Laenea had done the same herself. But the quarantines were so severe and so necessary that she, like most other veterans, eventually remained acclimated to one world, stayed on the ship during other planetfalls, and arranged her pattern to intersect her home as frequently as possible.

The sleeping man was a few years younger than Laenea. She thought he must be as tall as she, but that estimation was difficult. He was one of those uncommon people so beautifully proportioned that from any distance at all their height can only be determined by comparison. Nothing about him was exaggerated or attenuated; he gave the impression of strength, but it was the strength of litheness and agility, not violence. Laenea decided he was neither drunk nor drugged but asleep. His face, though relaxed, showed no dissipation. His hair was dark blond and shaggy, a shade lighter than his heavy mustache. He was far from handsome: his features were regular, distinctive, but without beauty. Below the cheekbones his tanned skin was scarred and pitted, as though from some virulent childhood disease. Some of the outer worlds had not yet conquered their epidemics.

Laenea looked away from the new young man. She stared at the dark water-wall at light's-end, letting her vision double and unfocus. She touched her collarbone and slid her fingers to the tip of the smooth scar. Sensation seemed refined across the tissue, as though a wound there would hurt more sharply. Though Laenea was tired and getting hungry, she did not force herself to outrun the distractions. For a while her energy should return slowly and naturally. She had pushed herself far enough for one night.

A month would be an eternity; the wait would seem equivalent to all the years she had spent crewing. She was still angry at the other pilots. She felt she had acted like a little puppy, bounding up to them to be welcomed and patted, then, when they grew bored, they had kicked her away as though she had piddled on the floor. And she was angry at herself: she felt a fool and she felt the need to prove herself.

For the first time she appreciated the destruction of time during transit. To sleep for a month: convenient, impossible. She first must deal with her new existence, her new body; then she would deal with a new environment.

Perhaps she dozed. The deep sea admitted no time: the lights pierced the same indigo darkness day or night. Time was the least real of all dimensions to Laenea's people, and she was free of its dictates, isolated from its stabilities.

When she opened her eyes again she had no idea how long they had been closed, a second or an hour.

The time must have been a few minutes, at least, for the young man who had been sleeping was now sitting up watching her. His eyes were dark blue, black-flecked, a color like the sea. For a moment he did not notice she was awake, then their gazes met and he glanced quickly away, blushing, embarrassed to be caught staring.

"I stared, too," Laenea said.

Startled, he turned slowly back, not quite sure Laenea was speaking to him. "What?"

"When I was a grounder, I stared at crew, and when I was crew I stared at pilots."

"I *am* crew," he said defensively.

"From—?"

"Twilight."

Laenea knew she had been there, a long while before; images of Twilight drifted to her. It was a new world, a dark and mysterious place of high mountains and black, brooding forests, a young world, its peaks just formed. It was heavily wreathed in clouds that filtered out much of the visible light but admitted the ultraviolet. Twilight: dusk, on that world. Never dawn. No one who had ever visited Twilight would think its dimness heralded anything but night. The people who lived there were strong and solemn, even confronting disaster. On Twilight she had seen grief, death, loss, but never panic or despair.

Laenea introduced herself and offered the young man a place nearer her own. He moved closer, reticent. "I am Radu Dracul," he said.

The name touched a faint note in her memory. She followed it until it grew loud enough to identify. She glanced over Radu Dracul's shoulder, as though looking for someone. "Then—where's Vlad?"

Radu laughed, changing his somber expression for the first time. He had good teeth and deep smile lines that paralleled the drooping sides of his mustache. "Wherever he is, I hope he stays there."

They smiled together.

"This is your first tour?"

"Is it so obvious I'm a novice?"

"You're alone," she said. "And you were sleeping."

"I don't know anyone here. I was tired," he said, quite reasonably.

"After a while . . ." Laenea nodded toward a nearby group of people, hyper and shrill on sleep repressors, energizers. "You don't sleep when you're on the ground when there are people to talk to, when there are other things to do. You get sick of sleep, you're scared of it."

Radu stared toward the ribald group that stumbled its way toward the elevator. "Do all of us become like them?" He held his low voice emotionless.

"Most."

"The sleeping drugs are bad enough. They're necessary, everyone says. But that—" He shook his head slowly. His forehead was smooth except for two parallel vertical lines that appeared between his eyebrows when he frowned; it was below his cheekbones, to the square-angled corner of his jaw, that his skin was scarred.

"No one will force you," Laenea said. She was tempted to reach out and touch him; she would have liked to stroke his face from temple to chin, and smooth a lock of hair rumpled by sleep. But he was unlike other people she had met, whom she could touch and hug and go to bed with on short acquaintance and mutual whim. Radu had about him something withdrawn and protected, almost mysterious, an invisible wall that would only be strengthened by an attempt to broach it, however gentle. He carried himself, he spoke, defensively.

"But you think I'll choose it myself."

"It doesn't always happen," Laenea said, for she felt he needed reassurance; yet she also felt the need to defend herself and her former colleagues. "We sleep so much in transit, and it's such a dark time, it's so empty . . ."

"Empty? What about the dreams?"

"I never dreamt."

"I always do," he said. "Always."

"I wouldn't have minded transit time so much if I'd ever dreamed."

Understanding drew Radu from his reserve. "I can see how it might be."

Laenea thought of all the conversations she had had with all the other crew she had known. The silent emptiness of their sleep was the single constant of all their experiences. "I don't know anyone else like you. You're very lucky."

A tiny luminous fish nosed up against the sea wall. Laenea reached out and tapped the glass, leading the fish in a simple pattern drawn with her fingertip.

"I'm hungry," she said abruptly. "There's a good restaurant in the Point Stabilizer. Will you come?"

"A restaurant—where people . . . buy food?"

"Yes."

"I am not hungry."

He was a poor liar; he hesitated before the denial, and he did not meet Laenea's glance.

"What's the matter?"

"Nothing." He looked at her again, smiling slightly: that at least was true, that he was not worried.

"Are you going to stay here all night?"

"It isn't night, it's nearly morning."

"A room's more comfortable—you were asleep."

He shrugged; she could see she was making him uneasy. She realized he must not have any money. "Didn't your credit come through? That happens all the time. I think chimpanzees write the bookkeeping programs." She had gone through the red tape and annoyance of emergency credit several times when her transfers were misplaced or miscoded. "All you have to do—"

"The administration made no error in my case."

Laenea waited for him to explain or not, as he wished. Suddenly he grinned, amused at himself but not self-deprecating. He looked even younger than he must be, when he smiled like that. "I'm not used to using money for anything but . . . unnecessaries."

"Luxuries?"

"Yes, things we don't often use on Twilight, things I do not need. But food, a place to sleep—" He shrugged again. "They are always freely given on colonial worlds. When I got to Earth, I forgot to arrange a credit transfer." He was blushing faintly. "I won't forget again. I miss a meal and one night's sleep—I've missed more on Twilight, when I was doing real work. In a few hours I correct my error."

"There's no need to go hungry now," Laenea said. "You can—"

"I respect your customs," Radu said. "But my people never borrow and we never take what is unwillingly given."

Laenea stood up and held out her hand. "I never offer unwillingly. Come along."

His hand was warm and hard, like polished wood.

At the top of the elevator shaft, Laenea and Radu stepped out into the end of the night. It was foggy and luminous, sky and sea blending into uniform gray. No wind revealed the surface of the sea or the limits of the fog, but the air was cold. Laenea swung the cloak around them both. A light rain, almost invisible, drifted down, beading mistily in tiny brilliant drops on the black velvet and on Radu's hair. He was silver and gold in the artificial light.

"It's like Twilight now," he said. "It rains like this in the winter."

He stretched out his arm, with the black velvet draping down like quiescent wings, opened his palm to the rain, and watched the minuscule droplets touch his fingertips. Laenea could tell from the yearning in his voice, the wistfulness, that he was painfully and desperately homesick. She said nothing, for she knew from experience that nothing could be said to help. The pain faded only with time and fondness for other places. Earth as yet had given Radu no cause for fondness. But now he stood gazing into the fog, as though he could see continents, or stars. She slipped her arm around his shoulders in a gesture of comfort.

"We'll walk to the Point." Laenea had been enclosed in testing and training rooms and hospitals as he had been confined in ships and quarantine: she, too, felt the need for fresh air and rain and the ocean's silent words.

The sidewalk edged the port's shore; only a rail separated it from a drop of ten meters to the sea. Incipient waves caressed the metal cliff obliquely, sliding into darkness. Laenea and Radu walked slowly along, matching strides. Every few paces their hips brushed together. Laenea glanced at Radu occasionally and wondered how she could have thought him anything but beautiful. Her heart circled slowly in her breast, low-pitched, relaxing, and her perceptions faded from fever clarity to misty dark and soothing. A veil seemed to surround and protect her. She became aware that Radu was gazing at her, more than she watched him. The cold touched them through the cloak, and they moved closer together; it seemed only sensible for Radu to put his arm around her too, and so they walked, clasped together.

"Real work," Laenea said, musing.

"Yes . . . hard work with hands or minds." He picked up the second possible branch of their previous conversation as though it had never gone in any other direction. "We do the work ourselves. Twilight is too new for machines—they evolved here, and they aren't as adaptable as people."

Laenea, who had endured unpleasant situations in which machines did not perform as intended, understood what he meant. Older methods than automation were more economical on new worlds where the machines had to be designed from the beginning but people only had to learn. Evolution was as good an analogy as any.

"Crewing's work. Maybe it doesn't strain your muscles, but it is work."

"One never gets tired. Physically or mentally. The job has no challenges."

"Aren't the risks enough for you?"

"Not random risks," he said. "It's like gambling."

His background made him a harsh judge, harshest with himself. Laenea felt a tinge of self-contempt in his words, a gray shadow across his independence.

"It isn't slave labor, you know. You could quit and go home."

"I wanted to come—" He cut off the protest. "I thought it would be different."

"I know," Laenea said. "You think it will be exciting, but after a while all that's left is a dull kind of danger."

"I did want to visit other places. To be like—In that I was selfish."

"Ahh, stop. Selfish? No one would do it otherwise."

"Perhaps not. But I had a different vision. I remembered—" Again, he stopped himself in mid-sentence.

"What?"

He shook his head. "Nothing." Laenea had thought his reserve was dissolving, but all his edges hardened again. "We spend most of our time carrying trivial cargoes for trivial reasons to trivial people."

"The trivial cargoes pay for the emergencies."

Radu shook his head. "That isn't right."

"That's the way it's always been."

"On Twilight . . ." He went no further; the guarded tone had disappeared.

"You're drawn back," Laenea said. "More than anyone I've known before. It must be a comfort to love a place so much."

At first he tensed, as if he were afraid she would mock or chide him for weakness, or laugh at him. The tense muscles relaxed slowly. "I feel better after flights when I dream about home."

The fortunate dreamer: if Laenea had still been crew, she would have envied him. "Is it your family you miss?"

"I have no family—I still miss them sometimes, but they're gone."

"I'm sorry."

"You couldn't know," he said quickly, almost too quickly, as though he might have hurt her rather than the other way around. "They were good people, my clan. The epidemic killed them."

Laenea gently tightened her arm around his shoulder in silent comfort.

"I don't know what it is about Twilight that binds us all," Radu said. "I suppose it must be the combination—the challenge and the result. Everything is new. We try to touch the world gently. So many things could go wrong."

He glanced at her, his eyes deep as a mountain lake, his face solemn in its strength, asking without words a question Laenea did not understand.

The air was cold. It entered her lungs and spread through her chest, her belly, arms, legs . . . she imagined that the machine was cold metal, sucking the heat from her as it circled in its silent patterns. Laenea was tired.

"What's that?"

She glanced up. They were near the midpoint of the port's edge, nearing lights shining vaguely through the fog. The amorphous pink glow resolved itself into separate globes and torches. Laenea noticed a high metallic hum. Within two paces the air cleared.

The tall frames of fog catchers reared up, leading inward to the lights in concentric circles. The long wires, touched by the wind, vibrated musically. The fog, touched by the wires, condensed.

Water dripped from wires' tips to the platform. The intermittent sound of heavy drops on metal, like rain, provided irregular rhythm for the faint music.

"Just a party," Laenea said. The singing, glistening wires formed a multilayered curtain, each layer transparent but in combination translucent and shimmering. Laenea moved between them, but Radu, hanging back, slowed her.

"What's the matter?"

"I don't wish to go where I haven't been invited."

"You are invited. We're all invited. Would you stay away from a party at your own house?"

Radu frowned, not understanding. Laenea remembered her own days as a novice of the crew; becoming used to one's new status took time.

"They come here for us," Laenea said. "They come hoping we'll stop and talk to them and eat their food and drink their liquor. Why else come here?" She gestured—it was meant to be a sweeping movement, but she stopped her hand before the apex of its arc, flinching at the strain on her cracked ribs—toward the party, lights and tables, a tasselled pavilion, the fog catchers, the people in evening costume, servants and machines. "Why else bring all this here? They could be on a tropical island or under the Redwoods. They could be on a mountaintop or on a desert at dawn. But they're here, and I assure you they'll welcome us."

"You know the customs," Radu said, if a little doubtfully.

When they passed the last ring of fog catchers the temperature began to rise. The warmth was a great relief. Laenea let the damp velvet cape fall away from her shoulders and Radu did the same. A very young man, almost still a boy, smooth-cheeked and wide-eyed, appeared to take the cloak for them. He stared at them both, curious, speechless; he saw the tip of the scar between Laenea's breasts and looked at her in astonishment and admiration. "Pilot . . ." he said. "Welcome, Pilot."

"Thank you. Whose gathering is this?"

The boy, now speechless, glanced over his shoulder and gestured.

Kathell Stafford glided toward them, holding out her hands to Laenea. The white tiger followed.

Gray streaked Kathell's hair, like the silver thread woven into her blue silk gown, but her eyes were as dark and young as ever. Laenea had not seen her in several years, many voyages. They clasped hands, Laenea amazed as always by the delicacy of Kathell's bones. Veins glowed blue beneath her light brown skin. Laenea had no idea how old she was. Except for the streaks of gray, she was just the same. They embraced.

"My dear, I heard you were in training. You must be very pleased."

"Relieved," Laenea said. "They never know for sure if it will work till afterward."

"Come join us, you and your friend."

"This is Radu Dracul of Twilight."

Kathell greeted him, and Laenea saw Radu relax and grow comfortable in the presence of the tiny self-possessed woman. Even a party on the sidewalk of the world's largest port could be her home, where she made guests welcome.

The others, quick to sense novelty, began to drift nearer, most seeming to have no particular direction in mind. Laenea had seen all the ways of approaching crew or pilots: the shyness or bravado or undisguised awe of children; the unctuous familiarity of some adults; the sophisticated nonchalance of the rich. Then there were the people Laenea seldom met, who looked at her, saw her, across a street or across a room, whose expressions said aloud, *She has walked on other worlds, she has traveled through a place I shall never even approach.* Those people looked, and looked reluctantly away, and returned to their business, allowing Laenea and her kind to proceed unmolested. Some crew members never knew they existed. The most interesting people, the sensitive and intelligent and nonintrusive ones, were those one seldom met.

Kathell was one of the people Laenea would never have met, except that she had young cousins in the crew. Otherwise she was unclassifiable. She was rich, and used her wealth lavishly to entertain her friends, as now, and for her own comfort. But she had more purpose than that. The money she used for play was nothing compared to the totality of her resources. She was a student as well as a patron, and the energy she could give to work provided her with endurance and concentration beyond that of anyone else Laenea had ever met. There was no sycophancy in either direction about their fondness for each other.

Laenea recognized few of the people clustering behind Kathell. She stood looking out at them, down a bit on most, and she almost wished she had led Radu around the fog catchers instead of between them. She did not feel ready for the effusive greetings due a pilot; she did not feel she had earned them. The guests outshone her in every way, in beauty, in dress, in knowledge, yet they wanted her, they needed her, to touch what was denied them.

She could see the passage of time, one second after another, that quickly, in their faces. Quite suddenly she was overcome by pity.

Kathell introduced people to her. Laenea knew she would not remember one name in ten, but she nodded and smiled. Nearby Radu made polite and appropriate responses. Someone handed Laenea a glass of champagne. People clustered around her, waiting for her to talk. She found that she had no more to say to them than to those she left behind in the crew.

A man came closer, smiling, and shook her hand. "I've always wanted to meet an Aztec . . ."

His voice trailed off at Laenea's frown. She did not want to be churlish to a friend's guests, so she put aside her annoyance. "Just 'pilot,' please."

"But Aztecs—"

"The Aztecs sacrificed their captives' hearts," Laenea said. "We don't feel we've made a sacrifice."

She smiled and turned away, ending the conversation before he could press forward with a witty comment. The crowd was dense behind her, pressing in, all rich, free, trapped human beings. Laenea shivered and wished them away. She wanted quiet and solitude. Suddenly Kathell was near, stretching out her hand. Laenea grasped it. For Kathell, Kathell and her tiger, the guests parted like water. But Kathell was in front. Laenea grinned and followed in her friend's wake. She saw Radu and called to him. He nodded; in a moment he was beside her, and they moved through regions of fragrances: mint, carnation, pine, musk, orange blossom. The boundaries were sharp between the odors.

Inside the pavilion, the three of them were alone. Laenea immediately felt warmer, though she knew the temperature was probably the same outside in the open party. But the tent walls, though busily patterned and self-luminous, made her feel enclosed and protected from the cold vast currents of the sea.

She sat gratefully in a soft chair. The white tiger laid his chin on ` Laenea's knee and she stroked his huge head.

"You look exhausted, my dear," Kathell said. She put a glass in her hand. Laenea sipped from it: warm milk punch. A hint that she should be in bed.

"I just got out of the hospital," she said. "I guess I overdid it a little. I'm not used to—" She gestured with her free hand, meaning: everything. My new body, being outside and free again . . . this man beside me. She closed her eyes against blurring vision.

"Stay awhile," Kathell said, as always understanding much more than was spoken. Laenea did not try to answer; she was too comfortable, too sleepy.

"Have you eaten?" Kathell's voice sounded far away. The words, directed elsewhere, existed alone and separate, meaningless. Laenea slowed her heart and relaxed the arterial constricting muscles. Blood flowing through the dilated capillaries made her blush, and she felt warmer.

"She was going to take me to . . . a restaurant," Radu said.

"Have you never been to one?" Kathell's amusement was never

hurtful. It emerged too obviously from good humor and the ability to accept rather than fear differences.

"There is no such thing on Twilight."

Laenea thought they said more, but the words drowned in the murmur of guests' voices and wind and sea. She felt only the softness of the cushions beneath her, the warm fragrant air, and the fur of the white tiger.

Time passed, how much or at what rate Laenea had no idea. She slept gratefully and unafraid, deeply, dreaming, and hardly roused when she was moved. She muttered something and was reassured, but never remembered the words, only the tone. Wind and cold touched her and were shut out; she felt a slight acceleration. Then she slept again.

Laenea half woke, warm, warm to her center. A recent dream swam into her consciousness and out again, leaving no trace but the memory of its passing. She closed her eyes and relaxed, to remember it if it would come, but she could recall only that it was a dream of piloting a ship in transit. The details she could not perceive. Not yet. She was left with a comfortless excitement that upset her drowsiness. The machine in her chest purred fast and seemed to give off heat, though that was as impossible as that it might chill her blood.

The room around her was dim; she did not know where she was except that it was not the hospital. The smells were wrong; her first perceptions were neither astringent antiseptics nor cloying drugs but faint perfume. The sensation against her skin was not coarse synthetic but silky cotton. Between her eyelashes reflections glinted from the ceiling. She realized she was in Kathell's apartment in the Point Stabilizer.

She pushed herself up on her elbows. Her ribs creaked like old parquet floors, and deep muscle aches spread from the center of her body to her shoulders, her arms, her legs. She made a sharp

sound, more of surprise than of pain. She had driven herself too
hard: she needed rest, not activity. She let herself sink slowly back
into the big red bed, closing her eyes and drifting back toward
sleep. She heard the rustling and sliding of two different fabrics
rubbed one against the other, but did not react to the sound.

"Are you all right?"

The voice would have startled her if she had not been so nearly
asleep again. She opened her eyes and found Radu standing near,
his jacket unbuttoned, a faint sheen of sweat on his bare chest and
forehead. The concern on his face matched the worry in his voice.

Laenea smiled. "You're still here." She had assumed without
thinking that he had gone on his way, to see and do all the interesting things that attracted visitors on their first trip to Earth.

"Yes," he said. "Of course."

"You didn't need to stay . . ." But she did not want him to leave.

His hand on her forehead felt cool and soothing. "I think you
have a fever. Is there someone I should call?"

Laenea thought for a moment, or rather felt, lying still and
making herself receptive to her body's signals. Her heart was
spinning much too fast; she calmed and slowed it, wondering again
what adventure had occurred in her dream. Nothing else was
amiss; her lungs were clear, her hearing sharp. She slid her hand
between her breasts to touch the scar: smooth and body-tempera-
ture, no infection.

"I overtired myself," she said. "That's all. . . ." Sleep was overtaking her again, but curiosity disturbed her ease. "Why did you
stay?"

"Because," he said slowly, sounding very far away, "I wanted to
stay with you. I remember you . . ."

She wished she knew what he was talking about, but at last the
warmth and drowsiness were stronger lures than her curiosity.

When Laenea woke again, she woke completely. The aches and
pains had faded in the night—or in the day, for she had no idea

how long she had slept, or even how late at night or early in the morning she had visited Kathell's party.

She was in her favorite room in Kathell's apartment, one gaudier than the others. Though Laenea did not indulge in much personal adornment, she liked the scarlet and gold of the room, its intrusive energy, its Dionysian flavor. Even the aquaria set in the walls were inhabited by fish gilt with scales and jeweled with luminescence. Laenea felt the honest glee of compelling shapes and colors. She sat up and threw off the blankets, stretching and yawning in pure animal pleasure. Then, seeing Radu asleep, sprawled in the red velvet pillow chair, she fell silent, surprised, not wishing to wake him. She slipped quietly out of bed, pulled a robe from the closet, and padded into the bathroom.

Comfortable, bathed, and able to breathe properly for the first time since her operation, Laenea returned to the bedroom. She had removed the strapping in order to shower; as her cracked ribs hurt no more free than bandaged, she did not bother to replace the tape.

Radu was awake.

"Good morning."

"It's not quite midnight," he said, smiling.

"Of what day?"

"You slept what was left of last night and all today. The others left on the mainland zeppelin, but Kathell Stafford wished you well and said you were to use this place as long as you wanted."

Though Kathell was as fascinated with rare people as with rare animals, her curiosity was untainted by possessiveness. She had no need of pilots, or indeed of anyone, to enhance her status. She gave her patronage with affection and friendship, not as tacit purchase. Laenea reflected that she knew people who would have done almost anything for Kathell, yet she knew no one of whom Kathell had ever asked a favor.

"How in the world did you get me here? Did I walk?"

"We didn't want to wake you. One of the large serving carts was empty so we lifted you onto it and pushed you here."

Laenea laughed. "You should have folded a flower in my hands and pretended you were at a wake."

"Someone did make that suggestion."

"I wish I hadn't been asleep—I would have liked to see the expressions of the grounders when we passed."

"Your being awake would have spoiled the illusion," Radu said.

Laenea laughed again, and this time he joined her.

As usual, clothes of all styles and sizes hung in the large closets. Laenea ran her hand across a row of garments, stopping when she touched a pleasurable texture. The first shirt she found near her size was deep green velvet with bloused sleeves. She slipped it on and buttoned it up to her breastbone, no farther.

"I still owe you a restaurant meal," she said to Radu.

"You owe me nothing at all," he said, much too seriously.

She buckled her belt with a jerk and shoved her feet into her boots, annoyed. "You don't even know me, but you stayed with me and took care of me for the whole first day of your first trip to Earth. Don't you think I should—don't you think it would be friendly for me to give you a meal?" She glared at him. "Willingly?"

He hesitated, startled by her anger. "I would find great pleasure," he said slowly, "in accepting that gift." He met Laenea's gaze, and when it softened he smiled again, tentatively. Laenea's exasperation melted and flowed away.

"Come along, then," she said to him for the second time. He rose from the pillow chair, quickly and awkwardly. None of Kathell's furniture was designed for a person his height or Laenea's. She reached to help him; they joined hands.

The Point Stabilizer was itself a complete city in two parts, one, a blatant tourist world, the second a discrete and interesting permanent supporting society. Laenea often experimented with restaurants here, but this time she went to one she knew well. Experiments in the Point were not always successful. Quality spanned as wide a spectrum as culture.

Marc's had been fashionable a few years before, and now was not, but its proprietor seemed unperturbed by cycles of fashion. Pilots or princes, crew members or diplomats could come and go; Marc did not care. Laenea led Radu into the dim foyer of the restaurant and touched the signal button. In a few moments a screen before them brightened into a pattern like oil paint on water. "Hello, Marc," Laenea said. "I didn't have a chance to make a reservation, I'm afraid."

The responding voice was mechanical and harsh, initially unpleasant, difficult to understand without experience. Laenea no longer found it ugly or indecipherable. The screen brightened into yellow with the pleasure Marc could not express vocally. "I can't think of any punishment terrible enough for such a sin, so I'll have to pretend you called."

"Thank you, Marc."

"It's good to see you back after so long. And a pilot now."

"It's good to be back." She drew Radu forward a step, farther into the range of the small camera. "This is Radu Dracul, of Twilight, on his first Earth landing."

"Hello, Radu Dracul. I hope you find us neither too depraved nor too dull."

"Neither one at all," Radu said.

The headwaiter appeared to take them to their table.

"Welcome," Marc said, instead of goodbye, and from drifting blues and greens the screen faded to darkness.

Their table was lit by the blue reflected glow of light diffusing into the sea, and the fish watched them like curious urchins.

"Who is Marc?"

"I don't know," Laenea said. "He never comes out, no one ever goes in. Some say he was disfigured, some that he has an incurable disease and can never be with anyone again. There are always new rumors. But he never talks about himself and no one would invade his privacy by asking."

"People must have a higher regard for privacy on Earth than elsewhere," Radu said dryly, as though he had had considerable experience with prying questions.

Laenea knew boorish people too, but had never thought about their possible effect on Marc. She realized that the least consider-ate of her acquaintances seldom came here, and that she had never met Marc until the third or fourth time she had come. "It's nothing about the people. He protects himself," she said, knowing it was true.

She handed him a menu and opened her own. "What would you like to eat?"

"I'm to choose from this list?"

"Yes."

"And then?"

"And then someone cooks it, then someone else brings it to you."

Radu glanced down at the menu, shaking his head slightly, but he made no comment.

"Do you wish to order, Pilot?" At Laenea's elbow, Andrew bowed slightly.

Laenea ordered for them both, for Radu was unfamiliar with the dishes offered.

Laenea tasted the wine. It was excellent; she put down her glass and allowed Andrew to fill it. Radu watched scarlet liquid rise in crystal, staring deep.

"I should have asked if you drink wine," Laenea said. "But do at least try it."

He looked up quickly, his eyes focusing; he had not, perhaps, been staring at the wine, but at nothing, absently. He picked up the glass, held it, sniffed it, sipped from it.

"I see now why we use wine so infrequently at home."

Laenea drank again, and again could find no fault. "Never mind, if you don't like it—"

But he was smiling. "It's what we have on Twilight that I never cared to drink. It's sea water compared to this."

Laenea was so hungry that half a glass of wine made her feel lightheaded; she was grateful when Andrew brought bowls of thick, spicy soup. Radu, too, was very hungry, or sensitive to alcohol, for his defenses began to ease. He relaxed; no longer did he seem ready to leap up, take Andrew by the arm, and ask the quiet old man why he stayed here, performing trivial services for trivial reasons and trivial people. And though he still glanced frequently at Laenea—watched her, almost—he no longer looked away when their gazes met.

She did not find his attention annoying; only inexplicable. She had been attracted to men and men to her many times, and often the attractions coincided. Radu was extremely attractive. But what he felt toward her was obviously something much stronger; whatever he wanted went far beyond sex. Laenea ate in silence for some time, finding nothing, no answers, in the depths of her own wine. The tension rose until she noticed it, peripherally at first, then clearly, sharply, almost as a discrete point separating her from Radu. He sat feigning ease, one arm resting on the table, but his soup was untouched and his hand was clenched into a fist.

"You—" she said finally.

"I—" he began simultaneously.

They both stopped. Radu looked relieved. After a moment Laenea continued.

"You came to see Earth. But you haven't even left the port. Surely you had more interesting plans than to watch someone sleep."

He glanced away, glanced back, slowly opened his fist, touched the edge of the glass with a fingertip.

"It's a prying question but I think I have the right to ask it of you."

"I wanted to stay with you," he said slowly, and Laenea remembered those words, in his voice, from her half-dream awakening.

" 'I remember you,' you said."

He blushed, spots of high color on his cheekbones. "I hoped you wouldn't remember that."

"Tell me what you meant."

"It all sounds foolish and childish and romantic."

She raised one eyebrow, questioning.

"For the last day I've felt I've been living in some kind of unbelievable dream. . . ."

"Dream rather than nightmare, I hope."

"You gave me a gift I wished for for years."

"A gift? What?"

"Your hand. Your smile. Your time. . . ." His voice had grown very soft and hesitant again. He took a deep breath. "When the plagues came, on Twilight, all my clan died, eight adults and the four other children. I almost died, too. . . ." His fingers brushed his scarred cheek. Laenea thought he was unaware of the habit. "But the serum came, and the vaccines. I recovered. The crew of the mercy mission—"

"We stayed several weeks," Laenea said. More details of her single visit to Twilight returned: the settlement in near collapse, the desperately ill trying to attend the dying.

"You were the first crew member I ever saw, the first off-worlder. You saved my people, my life—"

"Radu, it wasn't only me."

"I know. I even knew then. It didn't matter. I was sick for so long, and when I came to and knew I would live, it hardly mattered. I was frightened and full of grief and lost and alone. I needed . . . someone . . . to admire. And you were there. You were the only stability in our chaos, a hero . . ." his voice trailed off in uncertainty at Laenea's smile, though she was not laughing at him. "This isn't easy for me to say."

Reaching across the table, Laenea grasped his wrist. The beat of his pulse was as alien as flame. She could think of nothing to tell him that would not sound patronizing or parental, and she did not care to speak to him in either guise. He raised his head and looked at her, searching her face. "When I joined the crew I don't think I ever believed I would meet you. I joined because it was what I always wanted to do, after . . . I never considered that I might really meet you. But I saw you, and I realized I wanted . . . to be something in your life. A friend, at best, I hoped. A shipmate, if nothing else. But—you'd become a pilot, and everyone knows pilots and crew stay apart."

"The first ones take pride in their solitude," Laenea said, for Ramona-Teresa's rejection still stung. Then she relented, for she might never have met Radu Dracul if they had accepted her completely. "Maybe they needed it."

"I saw a few pilots, before I met you. You're the only one who ever spoke to me or even glanced at me. I think . . ." He looked at her hand on his, and touched his scarred cheek again, as if he could brush the marks away. "I think I've loved you since the day you came to Twilight." He stood abruptly, but withdrew his hand gently. "I should never—"

She rose too. "Why not?"

"I have no right to . . ."

"To what?"

"To ask anything of you. To expect—" Flinching, he cut off the word. "To burden you with my hopes."

"What about my hopes?"

He was silent with incomprehension. Laenea stroked his rough cheek, once when he winced like a nervous colt, and again: the lines of strain across his forehead eased almost imperceptibly. She brushed back the errant lock of dark blond hair. "I've had less time to think of you than you of me," she said, "but I think you're beautiful, and an admirable man."

Radu smiled with little humor. "I'm not thought beautiful on Twilight."

"Then Twilight has as many fools as any other human world."

"You . . . want me to stay?"

"Yes."

He sat down again like a man in a dream. Neither spoke. Andrew appeared, to remove the soup plates and serve the main course. He was diplomatically unruffled, but not quite oblivious to Laenea and Radu's near departure. "Is everything satisfactory?"

"Very much so, Andrew. Thank you."

He bowed and smiled and pushed away the serving cart.

"Have you contracted for transit again?"

"Not yet," Radu said.

"I have a month before my proving flights." She thought of places she could take him, sights she could show him. "I thought I'd just have to endure the time—" She fell silent, for Ramona-Teresa was standing in the entrance of the restaurant, scanning the room. She saw Laenea and came toward her. Laenea waited, frowning; Radu turned, froze, struck by Ramona's compelling presence: serenity, power, determination. Laenea wondered if the older pilot had relented, but she was no longer so eager to be presented with mysteries, rather than to discover them herself.

Ramona-Teresa stopped at their table, ignoring Radu, or, rather, glancing at him, dismissing him in the same instant, and speaking to Laenea. "They want you to go back."

Laenea had almost forgotten the doctors and administrators, who could hardly take her departure as calmly as did the other pilots. "Did you tell them where I was?" She knew immediately that she had asked an unworthy question. "I'm sorry."

"They always want to teach us that they're in control. Sometimes it's easiest to let them believe they are."

"Thanks," Laenea said, "but I've had enough tests and plastic tubes." She felt very free, for whatever she did she would not be grounded: she was worth too much. No one would even censure her for irresponsibility, for everyone knew pilots were quite perfectly mad.

"Don't use your credit key."

"All right . . ." She saw how easily she could be traced, and wished she had not got out of the habit of carrying cash. "Ramona, lend me some money."

Now Ramona did look at Radu, critically. "It would be better if you came with the rest of us." Radu flushed. She was, all too obviously, not speaking to him.

"No, it wouldn't." Laenea's tone was chill. The dim blue light glinted silver from the gray in Ramona's hair as she turned back to Laenea and reached into an inner pocket. She handed her a folded sheaf of bills. "You young ones never plan." Laenea could not be sure what she meant, and she had no chance to ask. Ramona-Teresa turned away and left.

Laenea shoved the money into her pants pocket, annoyed not so much because she had had to ask for it as because Ramona-Teresa had been so sure she would need it.

"She may be right," Radu said slowly. "Pilots, and crew—"

She touched his hand again, rubbing its back, following the ridges of strong fine bones to his wrist. "She shouldn't have been so snobbish. We're none of her business."

"She was . . . I never met anyone like her before. I felt like I was in the presence of someone so different from me—so far beyond —that we couldn't speak together." He grinned, quick flash of strong white teeth behind his shaggy mustache, deep smile lines in his cheeks. "If she'd cared to." With his free hand he stroked her green velvet sleeve. She could feel the beat of his pulse, rapid and upset. As if he had closed an electrical circuit, a pleasurable chill spread up Laenea's arm.

"Radu, did you ever meet a pilot or a crew member who wasn't different from anyone you had ever met before? I haven't. We all start out that way. Transit didn't change Ramona."

He acquiesced with silence only, no more certain of the validity of her assurance than she was.

"For now it doesn't make any difference anyway," Laenea said.

The unhappiness slipped from Radu's expression, the joy came back, but uncertainty remained.

They finished their dinner quietly, in expectation, anticipation, paying insufficient attention to the excellent food. Though annoyed that she had to worry about the subject at all, Laenea considered available ways of preserving her freedom. She wished Kathell Stafford were still on the island, for she of all people could have helped. She had already helped, as usual, without even meaning to.

But the situation was hardly serious; evading the administrators as long as possible was a matter of pride and personal pleasure. "Fools . . ." she muttered.

"They may have a special reason for wanting you to go back," Radu said. Anticipation of the next month flowed through both their minds. "Some problem—some danger."

"They'd've said so."

"Then what do they want?"

"Ramona said it—they want to prove they control us." She drank the last few drops of her brandy; Radu followed suit. They rose and walked together toward the foyer. "They want to keep me packed in styrofoam padding like an expensive machine until I can take my ship."

Andrew awaited them, but as Laenea reached for Ramona-Teresa's money Marc's screen glowed into brilliance. "Your dinner's my gift," he said. "In celebration."

She wondered if Ramona had told him of her problem. He could as easily know from his own sources; or the free meal might be an example of his frequent generosity. "I wonder how you ever make a profit, my friend," she said. "But thank you."

"I overcharge tourists," he said, the mechanical voice so flat that it was impossible to know if he spoke cynically or sardonically or if he were simply joking.

"I don't know where I'm going next," Laenea told him, "but are you looking for anything?"

"Nothing in particular," he said. "Pretty things—" Silver swirled across the screen.

"I know."

The corridors were dazzling after the dim restaurant; Laenea wished for gentle evenings and moonlight. Between cold metal walls, she and Radu walked close together, warm, arms around each other. "Marc collects," Laenea said. "We all bring him things."

"Pretty things."

"Yes . . . I think he tries to bring the nicest bits of all the worlds inside with him. I think he creates his own reality."

"One that has nothing to do with ours."

"Exactly."

"That's what they'd do at the hospital," Radu said. "Isolate you from what you'll have to deal with, and you disagree that that would be valuable."

"Not for me. For Marc, perhaps."

He nodded. "And . . . now?"

"Back to Kathell's for a while at least." She reached up and rubbed the back of his neck. His hair tickled her hand. "The rule I disagreed with most while I was in training was the one that forbade me any sex at all."

The smile lines appeared again, bracketing his mouth parallel to his drooping mustache, crinkling the skin around his eyes. "I understand entirely," he said, "why you aren't anxious to go back."

Entering her room in Kathell's suite, Laenea turned on the lights. Mirrors reflected the glow, bright niches among red plush and gold trim. She and Radu stood together on the silver surfaces, hands clasped, for a moment as hesitant as children. Then Laenea turned to Radu, and he to her; they ignored the actions of the mirrored figures. Laenea's hands on the sides of Radu's face touched his scarred cheeks; she kissed him lightly, again, harder. His mustache was soft and bristly against her lips, against her tongue. His hands tightened over her shoulder blades, moved down. He held her gently. She slipped one hand between their bodies, beneath his jacket, stroking his bare skin, tracing the taut muscles of his back, his waist, his hip. His breathing quickened.

At the beginning nothing was different—but nothing was the same. The change was more important than motions, positions, endearments; Laenea had experienced those in all their combinations, content with involvement for a few moments' pleasure. That had always been satisfying and sufficient; she had never suspected the potential for evolution that depended on the partners. Leaning over Radu, with her hair curling down around their faces, looking into his smiling blue eyes, she felt close enough to him to absorb his thoughts and sense his soul. They caressed each other leisurely, concentrating on the sensations between them. Laenea's nipples hardened, but instead of throbbing they tingled. Radu moved against her, and her excitement heightened suddenly, irrationally, grasping her, shaking her. She gasped but could not force the breath back out. Radu kissed her shoulder, the base of her throat, stroked her stomach, drew his hand up her side, cupped her breast.

"Radu—"

Her climax was sudden and violent, a clasping wave contracting all through her as her single thrust pushed Radu's hips down against the mattress. He was startled into a climax of his own as Laenea shuddered involuntarily, straining against him, clasping him to her, unable to catch his rhythm. But neither of them cared.

They lay together, panting and sweaty.

"Is that part of it?" His voice was unsteady.

"I guess so." Her voice, too, showed the effects of surprise. "No wonder they're so quiet about it."

"Does it—is your pleasure decreased?" He was ready to be angry for her.

"No, that's not it, it's—" She started to say that the pleasure was tenfold greater, but remembered the start of their loveplay, be-

fore she had been made aware of just how many of her rhythms
were rearranged. The beginning had nothing to do with the fact
that she was a pilot. "It was fine." A lame adjective. "Just unexpected. And you?"

He smiled. "As you say—unexpected. Surprising. A little . . .
frightening."

"Frightening?"

"All new experiences are a little frightening. Even the very
enjoyable ones. Or maybe those most of all."

Laenea laughed softly.

They lay wrapped in each other's arms. Laenea's hair curled
around to touch the corner of Radu's jaw, and her heel was hooked
over his calf. She was content for the moment with silence, stillness, touch. The plague had not scarred his body.

In the aquaria, the fish flitted back and forth before dim lights,
spreading blue shadows across the bed. Laenea breathed deeply,
counting to make the breaths even. Breathing is a response, not
a rhythm, a reaction to levels of carbon dioxide in blood and brain;
Laenea's breathing had to be altered only during transit itself. For
now she used it as an artificial rhythm of concentration. Her heart
raced with excitement and adrenaline, so she began to slow it, to
relax. But something disturbed her control: the rate and blood
pressure slid down slightly, then slowly slid back up. She could
hear nothing but a dull ringing in her inner ears. Perspiration
formed on her forehead, in her armpits, along her spine. Her heart
had never before failed to respond to conscious control.

Angry, startled, she pushed herself up, flinging her hair back
from her face. Radu raised his head, tightening his hand around
the point of her shoulder. "What—?"

He might as well have been speaking underwater. Laenea lifted
her hand to silence him.

One deep inhalation, hold; exhale, hold. She repeated the sequence, calming herself, relaxing voluntary muscles. Her hand fell

to the bed. She lay back. Repeat the sequence, again. Again. In the hospital and since, her control over involuntary muscles had been quick and sure. She began to be afraid, and had to imagine the fear evaporating, dissipating. Finally the arterial muscles began to respond. They lengthened, loosened, expanded. Last the pump answered her commands as she recaptured and reproduced the indefinable states of self-control.

When she knew her blood pressure was no longer likely to crush her kidneys or mash her brain, she opened her eyes. Above, Radu watched, deep lines of worry across his forehead. "Are you—?" He was whispering.

She lifted her heavy hand and stroked his face, his eyebrows, his hair. "I don't know what happened, I couldn't get control for a minute. But I have it back now." She drew his hand across her body, pulling him down beside her, and they relaxed again and dozed.

Later, Laenea took time to consider her situation. Returning to the hospital would be easiest; it was also the least attractive alternative. Remaining free, adjusting without interference to the changes, meeting the other pilots, showing Radu what was to be seen: outwitting the administrators would be more fun. Kathell had done them a great favor, for without her apartment Laenea would have rented a hotel suite. The records would have been available, a polite messenger would have appeared to ask her respectfully to come along. Should she overpower an innocent hireling and disappear laughing? More likely she would have shrugged and gone. Fights had never given her either excitement or pleasure. She knew what things she would not do, ever, though she did not know what she would do now. She pondered.

"Damn them," she said.

His hair as damp as hers, after their shower, Radu sat down facing her. The couches, of course, were both too low. Radu and Laenea looked at each other across two sets of knees draped in caftans that clashed violently. Radu lay back on the cushions, chuckling. "You look much too undignified for anger."

She leaned toward him and tickled a sensitive place she had discovered. "I'll show you undignified—" He twisted away and batted at her hand but missed, laughing helplessly. When Laenea relented, she was lying on top of him on the wide soft couch. Radu unwound from a defensive curl, watching her warily, laugh lines deep around his eyes and mouth.

"Peace," she said, and held up her hands. He relaxed. Laenea picked up a fold of the material of her caftan with one of his. "Is anything more undignified than the two of us in colors no hallucination would have—and giggling as well?"

"Nothing at all." He touched her hair, her face. "But what made you so angry?"

"The administrators—their red tape. Their infernal tests." She laughed again, this time bitterly. " 'Undignified'—some of those tests would win on that."

"Are they necessary? For your health?"

She told him about the hypnotics, the sedatives, the sleep, the time she had spent being obedient. "Their redundancies have redundancies. If I weren't healthy I'd be back out on the street wearing my old heart. I'd be . . . nothing."

"Never that."

But she knew of people who had failed as pilots, who were reimplanted with their own saved hearts, and none of them had ever flown again, as pilots, as crew, as passengers. *"Nothing."*

He was shaken by her vehemence. "But you're all right. You're who you want to be and what you want to be."

"I'm angry at inconvenience," she admitted. "I want to be the one who shows you Earth. They want me to spend the next month shuttling between cinderblock cubicles. And I'll have to if they find me. My freedom's limited." She felt very strongly that she needed to spend the next month in the real world, neither hampered by experts who knew, truly, nothing, nor misdirected by controlled environments. She did not know how to explain the feeling; she thought it must be one of the things pilots tried to talk about during their hesitant, unsyncopated conversations with their insufficient vocabularies. "Yours isn't, though, you know."

"What do you mean?"

"Sometimes I come back to Earth and never leave the port. It's like my home. It has everything I want or need. I can easily stay a month and never see an administrator or have to admit receiving a message I don't want." Her fingertips moved back and forth across the ridge of new tissue over her breastbone. Somehow it was a comfort, though the scar was the symbol of what had cut her off from her old friends. She needed new friends now, but she felt it would be stupid and unfair to ask Radu to spend his first trip to Earth on an artificial island. "I'm going to stay here. But you don't have to. Earth has a lot of sights worth seeing."

He did not answer. Laenea raised her head to look at him. He was intent and disturbed. "Would you be offended," he said, "if I told you I am not very interested in historical sights?"

"Is this what you really want? To stay with me?"

"Yes. Very much."

Laenea led Radu through the vast apartment to the swimming pool. Flagstones surrounded a pool with sides and bottom of intricate mosaic that shimmered in the dim light. This was a grotto more than a place for athletic events or children's noisy beach ball games.

Radu sighed; Laenea brushed her hand across the top of his shoulder, questioning.

"Someone spent a great deal of time and care here," he said.

"That's true." Laenea had never thought of it as the work of someone's hands, individual and painstaking, though of course it was exactly that. But the economic structure of her world was based on service, not production, and she had always taken the results for granted.

They took off their caftans and waded down the steps into body-warm water. It rose smooth and soothing around the persistent soreness of Laenea's ribs.

"I'm going to soak for a while." She lay back and floated, her hair drifting out, a strand occasionally drifting back to brush her shoulder, the top of her spine. Radu's voice rumbled through the water, incomprehensible, but she glanced over and saw him waving toward the dim far end of the pool. He flopped down in the water and thrashed energetically away, retreating to a constant background noise. All sounds faded, gaining the same faraway quality, like audio slow motion. Something was strange, wrong . . . Laenea began to tense up again. She turned her attention to the warmth and comfort of the water, to urging the tension out of her body through her shoulders, down her outstretched arms, out the tips of spread fingers. But when she paid attention again, something still was wrong. Tracing unease, slowly and deliberately, going back so far in memory that she was no longer a pilot (it seemed a long time), she realized that though she had become well and easily accustomed to the silence of her new heart, to the lack of a pulse, she had been listening unconsciously for the echo of the beat, the double or triple reverberation from throat and wrists, from femoral artery, all related by the same heartbeat, each perceived at a slightly different time during moments of silence.

She thought she might miss that, just a little, for a little while.

Radu finished his circumnavigation of the pool; he swam under her and the faint turbulence stroked her back. Laenea let her feet sink to the pool's bottom and stood up as Radu burst out of the water, a very amateur dolphin, hair dripping in his eyes, laughing. They waded toward each other through the retarding chest-deep water and embraced. Radu kissed Laenea's throat just at the corner of her jaw; she threw her head back like a cat stretching to prolong the pleasure, moving her hands up and down his sides.

"We're lucky to be here so early," he said softly, "alone before anyone else comes."

"I don't think anyone else is staying at Kathell's right now," Laenea said. "We have the pool to ourselves all the time."

"This is . . . this belongs to her?"

"The whole apartment does."

He said nothing, embarrassed by his error.

"Never mind," Laenea said. "It's a natural mistake to make." But it was not, of course, on Earth.

Laenea had visited enough new worlds to understand how Radu could be uncomfortable in the midst of the private possessions and personal services available on Earth. What impressed him was expenditure of time, for time was the valuable commodity in his frame of reference. On Twilight everyone would have two or three necessary jobs, and none would consist of piecing together intricate mosaics. Everything was different on Earth.

They paddled in the shallow end of the pool, reclined on the steps, flicked shining spray at each other. Laenea wanted Radu again. She was completely free of pain for the first time since the operation. That fact began to overcome a certain reluctance she felt, an ambivalence toward her new reactions. The violent change in her sexual responses disturbed her more than she wanted to admit.

And she wondered if Radu felt the same way; she discovered she was afraid he might.

In the shallow water beside him, she moved closer and kissed him. As he put his arm around her she slipped her hand across his stomach and down to his genitals, somehow less afraid of a physical indication of reluctance than a verbal one. But he responded to her, hardening, drawing circles on her breast with his fingertips, caressing her lips with his tongue. Laenea stroked him from the back of his knee to his shoulder. His body had a thousand textures, muted and blended by the warm water and the steamy air. She pulled him closer, across the mosaic step, grasping him with her legs. They slid together easily. Radu entered her with little friction

between them. This time Laenea anticipated a long, slow increase
of excitement.

"What do you like?" Radu whispered.

"I—I like—I—" Her words changed abruptly to a gasp. Imagination exaggerated nothing: the climax again came all at once in a
powerful solitary wave. Radu's fingers dug into her shoulders, and
though Laenea knew her short nails were cutting his back, she
could not ease the wire-taut muscles of her hands. Radu must have
expected the intensity and force of Laenea's orgasm, but the body
is slower to learn than the mind. He followed her to climax almost
instantly, in solitary rhythm that continued, slowed, finally ceased.
Trembling against him, Laenea exhaled in a long shudder. She
could feel Radu's stomach muscles quiver. The water around
them, that had seemed warmer than their bodies, now seemed
cool.

Laenea liked to take more time with sex, and she suspected that
Radu did as well. Yet she felt exhilarated. Her thoughts about
Radu were bright in her mind, but she could put no words to them.
Instead of speaking she laid her hand on the side of his face,
fingertips at the temple, the palm of her hand against deep scars.
He no longer flinched when she touched him there, but covered
her hand with his.

He had about him a quality of constancy, of dependability and
calm, that Laenea had never before encountered. His admiration
for her was of a different sort entirely than what she was used to:
grounders' lusting after status and vicarious excitement. Radu had
seen her and stayed with her when she was as helpless and ordinary and undignified as a human being can be; that had not
changed his feelings. Laenea did not understand him yet.

They toweled each other dry. Radu's hip was scraped from the
pool steps, and he had long scratches down his back.

"I wouldn't have thought I could do that," Laenea said. She
glanced at her hands, nails shorter than fingertips, cut just above
the quick. "I'm sorry."

Radu reached around to dry her back. "I did the same to you."

"Really?" She looked over her shoulder. The angle was wrong to see anything, but she could feel places stinging. "We're even, then." She grinned. "I never drew blood before."

"Nor I."

They dressed in clean clothes from Kathell's wardrobes and went walking through the multileveled city. It was, as Radu had said, very early. Above on the sea it would be nearing dawn. Below only street cleaners and the drivers of delivery carts moved here and there across a mall. Laenea was more accustomed to the twenty-four-hour crew city in the second stabilizer.

She was getting hungry enough to suggest a shuttle trip across to #2, where everything would be open, when ahead they saw waiters arranging the chairs of a sidewalk café, preparing for business.

"Seven o'clock," Radu said. "That's early to open around here, it seems."

"How do you know what time it is?"

He shrugged. "I don't know how, but I always know."

"Twilight's day isn't even standard."

"I had to convert for a while, but now I have both times."

A waiter bowed and ushered them to a table. They breakfasted and talked, telling each other about their home worlds and about places they had visited. Radu had been to three other planets before Earth. Laenea knew two of them, from several years before. They were colonial worlds, which had grown and changed since her visits.

Laenea and Radu compared impressions of crewing, she still fascinated by the fact that he dreamed.

She found herself reaching out to touch his hand, to emphasize a point or for the sheer simple pleasure of contact. And he did the same, but they were both right-handed and a floral centerpiece occupied the center of their table. Finally Laenea picked up the vase and moved it to one side, and she and Radu held left hands across the table.

"Where do you want to go next?"

"I don't know. I haven't thought about it. I still have to go where they tell me to, when there's a need."

"I just . . ." Laenea's voice trailed off. Radu glanced at her quizzically, and she shook her head. "It sounds ridiculous to talk about tomorrow or next week or next month . . . but it feels so right."

"I feel . . . the same."

They sat in silence, drinking coffee. Radu's hand tightened on hers. "What are we going to do?" For a moment he looked young and lost. "I haven't earned the right to make my own schedules."

"I have," Laenea said. "Except for the emergencies. That will help."

He was no more satisfied than she.

"We have a month," Laenea said. "A month not to worry."

Laenea yawned as they entered the front room of Kathell's apartment. "I don't know why I'm so sleepy." She yawned again, trying to stifle it, failing. "I slept the clock around, and now I want to sleep again—after what? Half a day?" She kicked off her boots.

"Eight and a half hours," Radu said. "Somewhat busy hours, though."

She smiled. "True." She yawned a third time, jaw-hinges cracking. "I've got to take a nap."

Radu followed as she padded through the hallways, down the stairs to her room. The bed was made, turned down on both sides. The clothes Laenea and Radu had arrived in were clean and pressed. They hung in the dressing room along with the cloak, which no longer smelled musty. Laenea brushed her fingers across the velvet. Radu looked around. "Who did this?"

"What? The room? The people Kathell hires. They look after whoever stays here."

"Do they hide?"

Laenea laughed. "No—they'll come if we call. Do you need something?"

"No," he said sharply. "No," more gently. "Nothing."

Still yawning, Laenea undressed. "What about you, are you wide awake?"

He was staring into a mirror; he started when she spoke, and looked not at her but at her reflection. "I can't usually sleep during the day," he said. "But I am rather tired."

His reflection turned its back; he, smiling, turned toward her.

They were both too sleepy to make love a third time. The amount of energy Laenea had expended astonished her; she thought perhaps she still needed time to recover from the hospital. She and Radu curled together in darkness and scarlet sheets.

"I do feel very depraved now," Radu said.

"Depraved? Why?"

"Sleeping at nine o'clock in the morning? That's unheard of on Twilight." He shook his head; his mustache brushed her shoulder. Laenea drew his arm closer around her, holding his hand in both of hers.

"I'll have to think of some other awful depraved Earth customs to tempt you with," she said sleepily, chuckling, but thought of none just then.

Later (with no way of knowing how much later) something startled her awake. She was a sound sleeper and could not think what noise or movement would awaken her when she still felt so tired. Lying very still she listened, reaching out for stimuli with all her senses. The lights in the aquaria were out, the room was dark except for the heating coils' bright orange spirals. Bubbles from the aerator, highlighted by the amber glow, rose like tiny half moons through the water.

The beat of a heart pounded through her.

In sleep, Radu still lay with his arm around her. His hand, fingers half curled in relaxation, brushed her left breast. She stroked the back of his hand but moved quietly away from him, away from the sound of his pulse, for it formed the links of a chain she had worked hard and wished long to break.

The second time she woke she was frightened out of sleep, confused, displaced. For a moment she thought she was escaping a nightmare. Her head ached violently from the ringing in her ears, but through the clash and clang she heard Radu gasp for breath, struggling as if to free himself from restraints. Laenea reached for him, ignoring her racing heart. Her fingers slipped on his sweat. Thrashing, he flung her back. Each breath was agony just to hear. Laenea grabbed his arm when he twisted again, held one wrist down, seized his flailing hand, partially immobilized him, straddled his hips, held him.

"Radu!"

He did not respond. Laenea called his name again. She could feel his pulse through both wrists, feel his heart as it pounded, too fast, too hard, irregular and violent.

"Radu!"

He cried out, a piercing and wordless scream.

She whispered his name, no longer even hoping for a response, in helplessness, hopelessness. He shuddered beneath her hands. He opened his eyes. "What . . . ?"

Laenea remained where she was, leaning over him. He tried to lift his hand, and she realized she was still forcing his arms to the bed. She released him and sat back on her heels beside him. She, too, was short of breath, and hypertensive to a dangerous degree.

Someone knocked softly on the bedroom door.

"Come in!"

One of the aides entered hesitantly. "Pilot? I thought— Pardon me." She bowed and backed out.

"Wait—you did right. Call a doctor immediately."

Radu pushed himself up on his elbows. "No, don't, there's nothing wrong."

The young aide glanced from Laenea to Radu and back to the pilot.

"Are you sure?" Laenea asked.

"Yes." He sat up. Sweat ran in heavy drops down his temples to the edge of his jaw. Laenea shivered from the coolness of her own evaporating sweat.

"Never mind, then," Laenea said. "But thank you."

The aide departed.

"Gods, I thought you were having a heart attack." Her own heart was beginning to slow in rhythmically varying rotation. She could feel the blood slow and quicken at her temples, in her throat. She clenched her fists reflexively and felt her nails against her palms.

Radu shook his head. "It was a nightmare." His somber expression suddenly changed to a quick but shaky grin. "Not illness. As you said—we're never allowed this job if we're not healthy." He lay back, hands behind his head, eyes closed. "I was climbing, I don't remember, a cliff or a tree. It collapsed or broke and I fell —a long way. I knew I was dreaming and I thought I'd wake up before I hit, but I fell into a river." She heard him and remembered what he said, but knew she would have to make sense of the words later. She remained kneeling and slowly unclenched her hands. Blood rushed through her like a funneled tide, high, then low, and back again.

"It had a very strong current that swept me along and pulled me under. I couldn't see banks on either side—not even where I fell from. Logs and trash rushed along beside me and past me, but every time I tried to hold on to something I'd almost be crushed. I got tireder and tireder and the water pulled me under—I needed a breath, but I couldn't take one.... Have you felt the way the body tries to breathe when you can't let it?"

She did not answer, but her lungs burned, her muscles contracted convulsively, trying to clear a way for the air to push its way in.

"Laenea—" She felt him grasp her shoulders: she wanted to pull him closer, she wanted to push him away. Then the change broke the compulsion of his words and she drew deep, searing breath.

"What—?"

"A . . . moment . . ." She managed, finally, to damp the sine-curve velocity of the pump within her. She was shivering. Radu pulled a blanket around her. Laenea's control returned slowly, more slowly than any other time she had lost it. She pulled the blanket closer, seeking stability more than warmth. She should not slip like that: her biocontrol, to now, had always been as close to perfect as anything associated with a biological system could be. But now she felt dizzy and high, hyperventilated, from the need-less rush of blood through her brain. She wondered how many millions of nerve cells had been destroyed.

She and Radu looked at each other in silence.

"Laenea . . ." He still spoke her name as if he were not sure he had the right to use it. "What's happening to us?"

"Excitement—" she said, and stopped. "An ordinary night-mare—" She had never tried to deceive herself before, and found she could not start now.

"It wasn't an ordinary nightmare. You always know you're going to be all right, no matter how frightened you are. This time—until I heard you calling me and felt you pulling me to the surface, I knew I was going to die."

Tension grew: he was as afraid to reach toward her as she was to him. She threw off the blanket and grasped his hand. He was startled, but he returned the pressure. They sat crosslegged, fac-ing each other, hands entwined.

"It's possible . . ." Laenea said, searching for a way to say this that was gentle for them both, "it's possible . . . that there is a reason, a real reason, pilots and crew don't mix."

By Radu's expression Laenea knew he had thought of that explanation too, and only hoped she could think of a different one.

"It could be temporary—we may only need acclimatization."

"Do you really think so?"

She rubbed the ball of her thumb across his knuckles. His pulse throbbed through her fingers. "No," she said, almost whispering. Her system and that of any normal human being would no longer mesh. The change in her was too disturbing, on psychological and subliminal levels, while normal biorhythms were so compelling that they interfered with and would eventually destroy her new biological integrity. She would not have believed those facts before now. "I don't. Dammit, I don't."

Exhausted, they could no longer sleep. They rose in miserable silence and dressed, navigating around each other like sailboats in a high wind. Laenea wanted to touch Radu, to hug him, slide her hand up his arm, kiss him and be tickled by his mustache. Denied any of those, not quite by fear but by reluctance, unwilling either to risk her own stability or to put Radu through another nightmare, she understood for the first time the importance of simple, incidental touch, directed at nothing more important than momentary contact, momentary reassurance.

"Are you hungry?" Isolation, with silence as well, was too much to bear.

"Yes . . . I guess so."

But over breakfast (it was, Radu said, midafternoon), the silence fell again. Laenea could not make small talk; if small talk existed for this situation she could not imagine what it might consist of. Radu pushed his food around on his plate and did not look at her: his gaze jerked from the sea wall to the table, to some detail of carving on the furniture, and back again.

Laenea ate fruit sections with her fingers. All the previous worries, how to arrange schedules for time together, how to defuse the disapproval of their acquaintances, seemed trivial and frivolous. The only solution now was a drastic one, which she did not feel she could suggest herself. Radu must have thought of it; that he had said nothing might mean that volunteering to become a pilot was as much an impossibility for him as returning to normal was for Laenea. Piloting was a lifetime decision, not a job one took for a few years' travel and adventure. The way Radu talked about his home world, Laenea believed he wanted to return to a permanent home, not a rest stop.

Radu stood up. His chair scraped against the floor and fell over. Laenea looked up, startled. Flushing, Radu turned, picked up the chair, and set it quietly on its legs again. "I can't think down here," he said. "It never changes." He glanced at the sea wall, perpetual blue fading to blackness. "I'm going on deck. I need to be outside." He turned toward her. "Would you—?"

"I think . . ." Wind, salt spray on her face: tempting. "I think we'd each better be alone for a while."

"Yes," he said, with gratitude. "I suppose . . ." His voice grew heavy with disappointment. "You're right." His footsteps were soundless on the thick carpet.

"Radu—"

He turned again, without speaking, as though his barriers were forming around him again, still so fragile that a word would shatter them.

"Never mind . . . just . . . oh—take my cape if you want, it's cold on deck in the afternoons."

He nodded once, still silent, and went away.

In the pool Laenea swam hard, even when her ribs began to hurt. She felt trapped and angry, with nowhere to run, knowing no one deserved her anger. Certainly not Radu; not the other pilots, who had warned her. Not even the administrators, who in their own misguided way had tried to make her transition as protected as possible. The anger could go toward herself, toward her strong-willed stubborn character. But that, too, was pointless. All her life she had made her own mistakes and her own successes, both usually by trying what others said she could not do.

She climbed out of the pool without having tired herself in the least. The warmth had soothed away whatever aches and pains were left, and her energy was returning, leaving her restless and snappish. She put on her clothes and left the apartment to walk off her tension until she could consider the problem calmly. But she could not see even an approach to a solution; at least, not to a solution that would be a happy one.

Hours later, when the grounder city had quieted to night again, Laenea let herself into Kathell's apartment. Inside, too, was dark and silent. She could hardly wonder where Radu was: she remembered little enough of what she herself had done since afternoon. She remembered being vaguely civil to people who stopped her, greeted her, invited her to parties, asked for her autograph. She remembered being less than civil to someone who asked how it felt to be an Aztec. But she did not remember which incident preceded the other or when either had occurred or what she had actually said. She was no closer to an answer than before. Hands jammed in her pockets, she went into the main room, just to sit and stare into the ocean and try to think. She was halfway to the sea wall before she saw Radu standing silhouetted against the window, dark and mysterious in her cloak, the blue light glinting ghostly off his hair.

"Radu—"

He did not turn. Her eyes more accustomed to the dimness, Laenea saw his breath clouding the glass.

"I applied to pilot training," he said softly, his tone utterly neutral.

Laenea felt a quick flash of joy, then uncertainty, then fear for him. She had been ecstatic when the administrators accepted her for training. Radu did not even smile. Making a mistake in this choice would hurt him more, much more, than even parting forever could hurt both of them. "What about Twilight?"

"It doesn't matter," he said, his voice unsteady. "They refused—" He choked on the words and forced them out. "They refused me."

Laenea went to him, put her arms around him, turned him toward her. The fine lines around his blue eyes were deeper, etched by distress and failure. She touched his cheek. Embracing her, he rested his forehead on her shoulder. "They said . . . I'm bound to our own four dimensions. I'm too dependent . . . on night, day, time . . . my circadian rhythms are too strong. They said . . ." His muffled words became more and more unsure, balanced on a shaky edge. Laenea stroked his hair, the back of his neck, over and over. That was the only thing left to do. There was nothing at all left to say. "If I survived the operation . . . I'd die in transit."

Laenea's vision blurred, and the warm tears slipped down her face. She could not remember the last time she had cried. A convulsive sob shook Radu and his tears fell cool on her shoulder, soaking through her shirt. "I love you," Radu whispered. "Laenea, I love you."

"Dear Radu, I love you too." She could not, would not, say what she thought: *That won't be enough for us. Even that won't help us.*

She guided him to a wide low cushion that faced the ocean; she drew him down beside her, neither of them really paying attention to what they were doing, to the cushions too low for them, to anything but each other. Laenea held Radu close. He said something she could not hear.

"What?"

He pulled back and looked at her, his gaze passing rapidly back and forth over her face. "How can you love me? We could only stay together one way, but I failed—" He broke the last word off, unwilling and almost unable to say it.

Laenea slid her hands from his shoulders down his arms and grasped his hands. "You can't fail at this, Radu. The word doesn't

mean anything. You can tolerate what they do to you, or you can't.
But there's no dishonor."

He shook his head and looked away: he had never, Laenea
thought, failed at anything important in his life, at anything real
that he desperately wanted. He was so young ... too young to have
learned not to blame himself for what was out of his control.
Laenea drew him toward her again and kissed the outer curve of
his eyebrow, his high cheekbone. Salt stung her lips.

"We can't—" He pulled back, but she held him.

"I'll risk it if you will." She slipped her hand inside the collar
of his shirt, rubbing the tension-knotted muscles at the back of
his neck, her thumb on the pulse-point in his throat, feeling it
beat through her. He spoke her name so softly it was hardly a
sound.

Knowing what to expect, and what to fear, they made love a
third, final, desperate time, exhausting themselves against each
other beside the cold blue sea.

Radu was nearly asleep when Laenea kissed him and left him,
forcibly feigning calm. In her scarlet and gold room she lay on the
bed and pushed away every concern but fighting her spinning
heart, slowing her breathing. She had not wanted to frighten Radu
again, and he could not help her. Her struggle required peace and
concentration. What little of either remained in her kept escaping
before she could grasp and fix them. They flowed away on the
channels of pain, shallow and quick in her head, deep and slow in
the small of her back, above the kidneys, spreading all through her
lungs. Near panic, she pressed the heels of her hands against her
eyes until blood-red lights flashed; she stimulated adrenaline until
excitement pushed her beyond pain, above it.

Instantly she forced an artificial, fragile calmness that glim-
mered through her like sparks.

Her heart slowed, sped up, slowed, sped (not quite so much this
time), slowed, slowed, slowed.

Afraid to sleep, unable to stay awake, she let her hands fall from her eyes, and drifted away from the world.

In the morning she staggered out of bed, aching as if she had been in a brawl against a better fighter. In the bathroom she splashed ice water on her face; it did not help. Her urine was tinged but not thick with blood; she ignored it.

Radu was gone. He had told the aide he could not sleep, but he had left no message for Laenea. Nor had he left anything behind, as if wiping out the traces of himself could wipe out the loss and pain of their parting. Laenea knew nothing could do that. She wanted to talk to him, touch him—just one more time—and try to show him, insist he understand, that he could not label himself with the title failure. He could not demand of himself what he could break himself—break his heart—attempting.

She called the crew lounge, but he did not answer the page. He had left no message. The operator cross-checked, and told Laenea that Radu Dracul was in the crew hold of A-28493, already prepared for transit.

An automated ship, on a dull run, the first assignment Radu could get: nothing he could have said or done would have told Laenea more clearly that he did not want to see or touch or talk to her again.

She could not stay in Kathell's apartment any longer. She threw on the clothes she had come in; she left the vest open, defiantly, to well below her breastbone, not caring if she were recognized, returned to the hospital, anything.

At the top of the elevator shaft the wind whipped through her hair and snapped the cape behind her. Laenea pulled the black velvet close and waited. When the shuttle came she boarded it, to return to her own city and her own people, the pilots, to live apart with them and never tell their secrets.

The Nebula Winners, 1965-1977

1965

Best Novel: DUNE *by Frank Herbert*
Best Novella: "The Saliva Tree" *by Brian W. Aldiss* "He Who Shapes" *by Roger Zelazny* (tie)
Best Novelette: "The Doors of His Face, the Lamps of His Mouth" *by Roger Zelazny*
Best Short Story: " 'Repent, Harlequin!' Said the Ticktockman" *by Harlan Ellison*

1966

Best Novel: FLOWERS FOR ALGERNON *by Daniel Keyes* BABEL-17 *by Samuel R. Delany* (tie)
Best Novella: "The Last Castle" *by Jack Vance*
Best Novelette: "Call Him Lord" *by Gordon R. Dickson*
Best Short Story: "The Secret Place" *by Richard McKenna*

1967

Best Novel: THE EINSTEIN INTERSECTION *by Samuel R. Delany*
Best Novella: "Behold the Man" *by Michael Moorcock*
Best Novelette: "Gonna Roll the Bones" *by Fritz Leiber*
Best Short Story: "Aye, and Gomorrah" *by Samuel R. Delany*

1968

Best Novel: RITE OF PASSAGE *by Alexei Panshin*
Best Novella: "Dragonrider" *by Anne McCaffrey*
Best Novelette: "Mother to the World" *by Richard Wilson*
Best Short Story: "The Planners" *by Kate Wilhelm*

1969

Best Novel: THE LEFT HAND OF DARKNESS *by Ursula K. Le Guin*
Best Novella: "A Boy and His Dog" *by Harlan Ellison*
Best Novelette: "Time Considered as a Helix of Semi-Precious
    Stones" *by Samuel R. Delany*
Best Short Story: "Passengers" *by Robert Silverberg*

1970

Best Novel: RINGWORLD *by Larry Niven*
Best Novella: "Ill Met in Lankhmar" *by Fritz Leiber*
Best Novelette: "Slow Sculpture" *by Theodore Sturgeon*
Best Short Story: No award

1971

Best Novel: A TIME OF CHANGES *by Robert Silverberg*
Best Novella: "The Missing Man" *by Katherine MacLean*
Best Novelette: "The Queen of Air and Darkness" *by Poul Ander-
    son*
Best Short Story: "Good News from the Vatican" *by Robert Silver-
    berg*

1972

Best Novel: THE GODS THEMSELVES *by Isaac Asimov*
Best Novella: "A Meeting with Medusa" *by Arthur C. Clarke*
Best Novelette: "Goat Song" *by Poul Anderson*
Best Short Story: "When It Changed" *by Joanna Russ*

1973

Best Novel: RENDEZVOUS WITH RAMA *by Arthur C. Clarke*
Best Novella: "The Death of Doctor Island" *by Gene Wolfe*
Best Novelette: "Of Mist, and Grass, and Sand" *by Vonda N. McIntyre*
Best Short Story: "Love Is the Plan the Plan Is Death" *by James Tiptree, Jr.*

1974

Best Novel: THE DISPOSSESSED *by Ursula K. Le Guin*
Best Novella: "Born with the Dead" *by Robert Silverberg*
Best Novelette: "If the Stars Are Gods" *by Gordon Eklund and Gregory Benford*
Best Short Story: "The Day Before the Revolution" *by Ursula K. Le Guin*
Grand Master: *Robert A. Heinlein*

1975

Best Novel: THE FOREVER WAR *by Joe Haldeman*
Best Novella: "Home Is the Hangman" *by Roger Zelazny*
Best Novelette: "San Diego Lightfoot Sue" *by Tom Reamy*
Best Short Story: "Catch That Zeppelin!" *by Fritz Leiber*
Grand Master: *Jack Williamson*

1976

Best Novel: MAN PLUS *by Frederik Pohl*
Best Novella: "Houston, Houston, Do You Read?" *by James Tiptree, Jr.*
Best Novelette: "The Bicentennial Man" *by Isaac Asimov*
Best Short Story: "A Crowd of Shadows" *by Charles L. Grant*
Grand Master: *Clifford Simak*

1977

Best Novel: GATEWAY *by Frederik Pohl*
Best Novella: "Stardance" *by Spider and Jeanne Robinson*
Best Novelette: "The Screwfly Solution" *by Raccoona Sheldon*
Best Short Story: "Jeffty Is Five" *by Harlan Ellison*